THE ULTIMATE BIKER ANTHOLOGY

An Introduction To Books About Motorcycle Clubs & Outlaw Bikers

Edited by

Edward Winterhalder & Iain Parke

BLOCKHEAD CITY INC
Grand Rapids, Michigan

Published by Blockhead City, PO Box 145, Jenison MI 49429.

Copyright © 2013 by Edward Winterhalder and Iain Parke. All rights reserved. No part of this book may be reproduced or transmitted in any form or by any means, electronic or mechanical, including photocopying, recording or by any information storage and retrieval system, without prior permission in writing from the publisher, except in the case of brief quotations embodied in reviews.

LIBRARY OF CONGRESS CATALOGING-IN-PUBLICATION DATA

Winterhalder, Edward, 1955 -
   The ultimate biker anthology: An introduction to books about motorcycle clubs & outlaw bikers

Parke, Iain, 1960 -
   The ultimate biker anthology: An introduction to books about motorcycle clubs & outlaw bikers

   p. cm.

   1: Motorcycle Clubs—Fiction. 2. Motorcycle Clubs—Non-Fiction. 3. Motorcycle Clubs—Anthology 4. Outlaw Bikers—Fiction. 5. Outlaw Bikers— Non-Fiction. 6. Outlaw Bikers—Anthology. 7. Motorcycles—Fiction. 8. Motorcycles—Non-Fiction. 9. Motorcycles—Anthology 10. Biography. 11. History—Motorcycles. 12. Winterhalder, Edward. 13. Parke, Iain

   I. Title: The ultimate biker anthology: An introduction to books about motorcycle clubs & outlaw bikers.

ISBN: 979-8-4531602-4-2

Paperback edition: August 2021

BOOKS BY EDWARD WINTERHALDER:

BIKER CHICKS
THE ATTRACTION OF WOMEN TO MOTORCYCLES AND OUTLAW BIKERS
(with Wil De Clercq)

THE BLUE AND SILVER SHARK
A BIKER'S STORY - Book 5 of the Series
(with Marc Teatum)

THE ULTIMATE BIKER ANTHOLOGY
AN INTRODUCTION TO BOOKS ABOUT MOTORCYCE RIDERS AND OUTLAW BIKERS
(with Iain Parke)

THE MOON UPSTAIRS
A BIKER'S STORY - Book 4 of the Series
(with Marc Teatum)

ONE LIGHT COMING
A BIKER'S STORY - Book 3 of the Series
(with Marc Teatum)

BIKER CHICZ OF NORTH AMERICA
(with Wil De Clercq)

THE MIRROR
A BIKER'S STORY - Book 2 of the Series
(with James Richard Larson)

BIKER CHICKS
THE MAGNETIC ATTRACTION OF WOMEN TO BAD BOYS AND MOTORBIKES
(with Arthur Veno & Wil De Clercq)

ALL ROADS LEAD TO STURGIS
A BIKER'S STORY - Book 1 of the Series
(with James Richard Larson)

THE ASSIMILATION
ROCK MACHINE BECOME BANDIDOS - BIKERS UNITED AGAINST THE HELLS ANGELS
(with Wil De Clercq)

OUT IN BAD STANDINGS
INSIDE THE BANDIDOS MOTORCYCLE CLUB – THE MAKING OF A WORLDWIDE DYNASTY

MUSIC BY EDWARD WINTERHALDER:

AT LONG LAST
Warren Winters Band
(Vinyl LP Record - 1980)

AS I WAS
Warren Winters Band
(Vinyl LP Record - 1984)

CROSSBAR HOTEL
Warren Winters Band
(Vinyl LP Record/Cassette - 1988)

THE BEST OF WARREN WINTERS
Warren Winters Band
(CD - 1995)

THEN & NOW
Warren Winters Band
(Digital Album - 2020)

THE NAME OF THE GAME
Warren Winters Band
(Music Video/Digital Song - 2020)

FOR MORE INFORMATION:

Wikipedia dot org/wiki/Edward_Winterhalder

BlockheadCity dot com

Amazon dot com/v/blockheadcity

YouTube dot com/BlockheadCity

OTHER BOOKS BY IAIN PARKE:

OPERATION BOURBON – THE FIRST CHAPTER
(coming in 2014)

THE BRETHREN TRILOGY - HEAVY DUTY TROUBLE

THE BRETHREN TRILOGY - HEAVY DUTY ATTITUDE

THE BRETHREN TRILOGY - HEAVY DUTY PEOPLE

THE LIQUIDATOR

For more information about Iain Parke:

bad-press dot co dot uk

Table of Contents

Introduction   iv

Part One
Non-Fiction

Big House Crew by Peter Edwards	1
Sturgis 1990 by David Charles Spurgeon	17
Sturgis High…Montreal Low by Edward Winterhalder & Wil De Clercq	30
Houston, September 1977 by Ralph "Teach" Elrod	50
Mayhem In The Midlands by Tony Thompson	59
Church by Peter Edwards	70

Part Two
Fiction

The Offer by Iain Parke	80
Meeting Up With Old Friends by Edward Winterhalder & Marc Teatum	99
The Garage by Vic Shurtz	110
Meeting Bill by Max Billington	120
The Run by Iain Parke	130
Brothers Of War—Forever United by Edward Winterhalder & James Richard Larson	166
On The Road by Troy Mason	179

Too Many Questions By Vic Shurtz	185
A Night Out With The Boys by Edward Winterhalder & Marc Teatum	192
The Big House Crew by Iain Parke	209
Duke The Barbarian by Gene Lewis	232
Kung-Fu by Max Billington	242
Time For Revenge by Vic Shurtz	253
Nowhere To Run by Edward Winterhalder & James Richard Larson	266
I Know A Man Who Can by Iain Parke	278

Acknowledgments

As an anthology of writing about motorcycle clubs and outlaw bikers, this book could not exist without the kind permission of each of the authors and their publishers for use of the extracts included in this compilation.

To all who were involved, your contributions are much appreciated.

Edward Winterhalder and Iain Parke

November 2013

Introduction

Are outlaw bikers heroes, villains, or something more complex? A lot of things have been written and said about 1%er motorcycle clubs and outlaw bikers since 1947, when they first came to the attention of the media during the AMA Gypsy Tour rally in Hollister, California, where the image of persistent troublemaker and social deviant was born.

Whether in the press, pulp novels, or on television and film, a lot of what has been depicted has been highly sensationalized and overwhelmingly negative, just playing on caricature images of crime and violence. As a result, the outlaw biker has become a stock fictional character, appearing as cameo villains in everything from Clint Eastwood comedies to *ride-on* parts in popular sagas from Steig Larson's highly successful *Millennium Trilogy* to *The Sopranos*.

Law enforcement agencies from many countries, aided by the ability to point to a few well-known violent episodes between motorcycle clubs, have sweepingly sought to label all outlaw bikers as criminals, and all clubs as criminal enterprises. This has in turn given birth to a range of books painting the clubs as a new two-wheeled international mafia.

But what lies behind this public perception? In the past both the sensationalist approach and the sweeping characterization of clubs simply being criminal gangs has had a pretty free hand in setting the agenda.

The outlaw biker's own policy of carefully guarded privacy, under which club business is club business, as well as a general, and probably understandable, distrust of the press, have by contrast meant that the motorcycle clubs, and their members' sides of the story, have had relatively little exposure.

However, over the past few years, an increasing number of groundbreaking literary works have begun to give a more balanced view of the biker lifestyle, with some current, and some ex-club members, publishing books that speak about the realities of life within a club from the insiders' point of view—from what led them to join, what being a patch holder and outlaw biker is really like, to why they left the culture.

At the same time, a number of *Biker Lit* novelists have begun exploring the themes that come naturally to the world of outlaw bikers—the culture of brotherhood, the commitment it involves, and the old-fashioned concepts of trust, honor, and loyalty to oneself and others.

For the outsider, the outlaw biker world can look paradoxical. Although it is an environment that stresses ideas of individuality and freedom, where members dedicate themselves to living within a tight knit band of brothers who can act as one, it has rules governing what you can and can't wear, and a strict and absolute code of conduct.

From the inside it can look like a clear and simple question of attitude and commitment, and this contrast with the ordinary world of compromise and hypocrisy is a gift for writers.

Whatever else you think about them for good or bad, the outlaw biker is someone who is different, someone who has chosen to stand apart from ordinary society to live by the rules of his club. As such, they demand respect, inspire those who secretly aspire to be one of them, and stir a wide range of reactions, from suspicion to fascination, from those who hate them and those who love them.

So for anyone interested in seeing past the popular public image of persistent troublemaker and social deviant to the reality of the outlaw biker lifestyle, warts and all, this book will introduce you to some of the key books about the culture that have been published over the past few years, both factual and fiction, through a series of chapter-length extracts.

We hope you enjoy this anthology, and that it provides you with the inspiration to further educate yourself about the outlaw biker lifestyle and motorcycle clubs.

Edward Winterhalder and Iain Parke
November 2013

PART ONE
Non-Fiction

Big House Crew

By Peter Edwards

"Guys that don't have anybody are preyed upon a lot."
Lorne Campbell on prison life

It's not unusual for prisoners to shake or even break down and blubber like babies by the time they're fingerprinted at Millhaven super-maximum-security penitentiary. By this time, a prisoner has likely ridden for hours on a bus, with his hands cuffed together and his legs shackled to the floor. He has already passed along treeless lawns, through two nine-metre chain-link fences, each topped and linked in razor and barbed wire, and a metre-high "warning fence" that marks the outer limit of how far prisoners can walk from the exercise yard before deadly force can be used to stop them. He has also passed under guard towers, and if he looked up, he may have seen guards staring down at him, gripping machine guns.

Once he has been escorted into the mesh-lined holding cell where he's fingerprinted, the prisoner has become an unwilling member of a community comprising 525 of Canada's meanest, most dysfunctional men. Odds are, even if he was once the toughest kid in the class, he's not even close to the most feared convict on his new range. Millhaven, also known as "Thrill Haven," was Canada's highest-security prison, and a third of the inmates were serving life terms when Campbell arrived.

Some locals and inmates believed it was built on a Native burial ground, making it forever cursed. The prison itself certainly had a nasty birth. It opened prematurely in 1971 to accommodate prisoners from nearby Kingston Penitentiary, which required an extensive cleanup after a bloody four-day riot that year.

When he was there in 1972, Satan's Choice president Bernie Guindon saw a prisoner lead another inmate across the weight room, stop, and pull out a hidden shank (an improvised knife). It was so smooth and seemingly effortless that it looked somehow choreographed, and it took just seconds for the shank to be thrust into the inmate's chest a dozen times. "I went, 'Wow, quick.' It's just like watching television." Guindon saw another inmate get shanked in the exercise yard after demanding pharmaceuticals from fellow prisoners. That attacker also led his prey to a spot where he had hidden a shank.

"Are you going to help?" an inmate asked. "No, he can die," Guindon replied. "He was stealing pills."

Like all new arrivals, Campbell first went to the assessment centre in E-Unit. He was slated for psychological and IQ testing and an audience with Dr. George Ducolon Scott. A jaunty, charismatic, terrier-like little man, Scott had the all-knowing air of someone who had borne witness at least once to almost every form of human depravity. He once told the Ottawa Citizen that he was fascinated as a boy growing up in Kingston by what he imagined lay inside the stone walls of the Kingston Prison for Women, which loomed within eyeshot of his childhood home. Somehow, the sight of the prison stirred "a deeper part of my soul," and tantalized him with a sense of mystery—"like running into the sun; you can't quite see what's there."

The doctor was in his early seventies when Campbell walked into his office, and by that time Scott had peered inside the minds of tens of thousands of prisoners. He hadn't just asked them questions from across a desk, either. He had overseen LSD experimentation on prisoners funded by the Canadian Department of National Defence, as well as testing on the effects of shock therapy, sensory deprivation and pain tolerance. When the press caught wind of this in the 1990s, he dismissed suggestions that such experimentation reduced patients to the status of mere guinea pigs. "It's a lot of bullshit," Scott told the Ottawa Citizen. "It was good research back then. It was good research with good motivation, with good supervision, and the government sup- plied the bucks for the whole thing." Pressed another time by the newspaper, he was even more to the point: "I am happy with myself. I don't give a shit."

Unfortunately for the doctor, some people in power did give a shit. A dozen years after he met Campbell, Scott was stripped of his licence to practise medicine for testing of a profoundly lurid sort: using Sodium Pentothal and electroshock to drop female patients into an almost comatose state. Then he would implant sexual suggestions and revive them with Ritalin.

But when Campbell met Scott that day in his office, the doctor still displayed the easy confidence of a man who enjoyed a secure, fascinating job for life, since there was little chance of prisons shutting down due to an outbreak of lawfulness. Every day, he could take a close-up view of varying degrees of deviance, and then stroll out again to have a quiet supper with his family in the comfort of his century-old hobby farm. "He took things in stride, like he was a movie star," Campbell says.

Given his decades of experience, perhaps it wasn't surprising that Dr. Scott seemed a little blasé as he scanned Campbell's lengthy rap sheet of assaults and other bikerish misdeeds.

"What are you here for?" the doctor asked. Campbell was sure he must already know, but he answered anyway. "Do you have any remorse for beating a man with a hammer?" "Actually, no. He deserved what he got." Campbell's reply didn't seem to faze Scott even a bit. Finally, the doctor looked up and said, "You're all right." "I'll never forget him saying, 'You're all right,' after I was telling him about beating a guy with a hammer and selling dynamite," Campbell says. Dr. Scott dropped his head again, the cue for Campbell to leave. With that, Campbell was dispatched to A-Unit, where he would spend half of each day in a cell measuring 3 metres by 2.1 metres. The other half of his new life was to be spent outside his cell, alongside inmates who were often happy, or at least indifferent, at the thought of slitting his throat.

The only other biker in A-Unit was Ken Logan of the Lobos Motorcycle Club in Windsor. Logan ran a sports betting enterprise in which the payoff was money and cigarettes. The rest of the penitentiary's bikers, including Rick Sauvé and Gary (Nutty) Comeau, were in J-Unit, Millhaven's other general population wing. They were all classified as part of the "Big House Crew" by their clubs, the biker term for members behind prison bars. None of the bikers in the prison were from the hated Outlaws.

Less than twelve hours after he arrived on the range, Campbell stood in the gymnasium with John Dunbar, also of the Lobos. Dunbar was a smallish, trim man whose appearance belied the enormity of his crime. He and fellow Lobo Ken Logan had gone into a house to kill a former Lobos president over a drug beef, and ended up also murdering another man and a woman when they showed up unexpectedly. Campbell and Dunbar had never met before, but as outlaw bikers they naturally gravitated to each other.

It was a little after nine in the morning, and Campbell and Dunbar watched as an inmate picked up a baseball bat and walked briskly towards them.

"Stand here, Lorne," Dunbar said, and Campbell obeyed.

Seconds later, the man with the bat clubbed Michel Lafleur, a member of the Front de Libération du Québec, to death. Lafleur was thirty-three and he had been behind bars for fourteen years, sentenced to a term of more than forty-one years for an assortment of crimes relating to the Quebec separatist group, including armed robbery and discharging a firearm with intent to kill. His role with the FLQ was to raise money through robbery, and he was already an inmate when fellow terrorists kidnapped Quebec labour minister Pierre Laporte and British diplomat James Cross, eventually murdering Laporte.

Lafleur's murder was never solved, as no one in the gymnasium spoke with investigators, but it's doubtful there were any great political under- tones to his death that morning in the exercise yard. Killings at Millhaven often happened for reasons that would seem petty to outsiders but which had a peculiar logic to someone inside the prison. "I was amazed that it happened so fast," Campbell says. "I heard he was a good guy. I never talked to him. I saw him a few minutes and then he was dead." "Within six months, you'll have a sixth sense," Dunbar told him, describing a heightened awareness akin to how birds know to hightail it before a storm. "You'll know when something's going to go down,"

Dunbar continued. "It's a feeling. So you just clear out." As Campbell settled in, he thought about something Mike Everett had said when he'd dropped by to see Campbell, alluding to a potential threat. Everett had said something cryptic to the effect of: "If you're classified for Millhaven, you have a problem with somebody there." He declined to expand, leaving the impression it was an inter-club problem in which he couldn't take sides. There was a barbecue at the prison during Campbell's first week there, one of four held each year. It gave him a chance to look into Everett's warning, and so he walked up to Sauvé. "I saw him and

Nutty for the first time in five years. They had been in jail for five years." Campbell had always confronted beefs head-on and that's what he planned to do right now. "I asked Rick and Nutty in the first half-hour, 'Who in this prison has a beef with me?' They didn't know. If anybody had a beef with me in Millhaven, they would have known about it."

Sauvé and Nutty talked about it between themselves later in the day. The next day, Sauvé told Campbell that they still didn't know of any real beef against him. Perhaps Everett was mistakenly referring to an old and false story that had circulated during the trial. There had been an unfounded rumour, started by one of the Port Hope Eight's lawyers, that Campbell had balked at the prospect of pleading guilty to the Bill Matiyek shooting. It wasn't true, but it was as dangerous as a shank to the ribs. Perhaps that's why Everett was so cryptic: he felt he was caught in a beef between brothers. Whatever the case, things were fine now. "That was the rumour," Campbell says. "They had found out the truth long before I got there, but it was never discussed again. There wasn't a beef."

Over time, Campbell learned there were shanks hidden throughout Millhaven. They were made out of anything that could be sharpened enough to cut into a human body, with pieces of metal from the machine shop, toothbrushes and hobby craft tools all fashioned into instruments of death and protection. "The nicest and largest shank I ever seen belonged to my close friend John Dunbar," Campbell recalls. "He had it machined to be part of his window frame so it was not detected during the frequent cell searches." Dunbar called it Excalibur, and he sometimes smuggled it from his cell by dropping it into his pant leg. "It was a beautiful piece of craftsmanship," Campbell says. "After work hours the odd day, John would retrieve it from his cell and before the doors closed for the count he would come to my cell and start swinging it within inches of my face while I was lying on my bed. As calmly as I could, I would ask, 'Is this John or the other guy?' This was insinuating that he had a split personality."

Both men found this a fine example of jailhouse humour. Even for a tough and relatively grounded inmate, Millhaven was a hard place to endure day in and day out, twenty-four hours a day. Inmates sometimes took a break by going "fishing" for seagulls. They'd put little bits of food on safety pins so a gull might swoop down and grab it. The payoff came when the gull reached the end of the line and its guts were suddenly ripped out. "That's the most humane thing that happened in Millhaven," Campbell says. He once watched as two inmates were shot by guards as they tried to scale the inner fence. It was like live theatre, as the shotgun pellets hit them and they went tumbling downwards, seemingly in slow motion. "It was like spiders falling," Campbell recalls.

A voice came over the loudspeakers: "Clear the yard!" One of the inmates who'd been hit wasn't about to give himself up and face charges for attempting to escape, so he ran back inside with the crowd. "He threw his coat down," Campbell says. "Somebody else gave him another coat." Once back in his cell, another prisoner treated his buckshot wounds. It was simple enough for guards to figure out what had happened, but they didn't press the matter. "They asked if he wanted to be treated. He said no. He didn't admit to it and was never charged. That was Millhaven."

Campbell didn't play hockey as a kid, but he was recruited as an assistant coach of a Millhaven inmates team anyway. He was replacing Nutty Comeau, who seemed on the verge of getting maimed or murdered by the Green Team's other coach, Gary Barnes, who was also a player. "This guy would eat Nutty," Campbell says. "I was asked to be coach in case he tried something."

As expected, things got ugly in a hurry. Behind the Green Team's bench, Campbell turned to Barnes and said, "I'm not Nutty, so go for it." What might have happened next could have taken hockey violence to a new low. "I had a skate in my hands. I was going to cut his throat. He still had his skates on. He could just kick me. He just wouldn't go."

Finally, Barnes eased up, saying, "Fuck it, I'll go to the Red Team."

The Green Team was a formidable bunch in the corners, and none of its players was more feared than its clean-cut defenceman John Drummond. He only weighed about 170 pounds and looked like a schoolteacher, but folks who knew him considered him a truly dangerous man, even for Millhaven.

Some one hundred inmates routinely gathered around the boards to watch games, and during one shift when Drummond was on the ice, a voice from the spectator section screamed out, "Kill the sonofabitch!" It may surprise habitués of mainstream hockey games, but there were unwritten rules about what you just didn't do at a Millhaven shinny game, where a large percentage of the players were convicted killers. Hollering "Kill the sonofabitch" was one of those things. "You don't scream that to a rink full of lifers, of killers," Campbell says. "You don't yell 'Kill 'em' in Millhaven."

The words hit Drummond like a hard slash across his back. Everyone went silent as he immediately skated to the boards and surveyed the spectators with cold eyes.

"Who the fuck said that?"

The moment couldn't have been more serious. The prisoners watching the game couldn't have gone more silent. It was a long-time inmate who finally dared to reply.

"It's a guy who don't know better. I'll talk with him later. It's a fish. A new guy."

Drummond was still fuming as he skated away.

When the game was over, Drummond's mood wasn't any better. "Me and so-and-so and so-and-so are coming out tomorrow and we're bringing steel. The first guy that says anything is getting it."

Assistant coach Campbell found himself in the unaccustomed role of peacekeeper. "It's an expression," Campbell said to Drummond. "There ain't nobody going to die."

People who weren't familiar with prison hockey might have been surprised by the scarcity of fighting in the games. Things in Millhaven were too hard-core for the kind of brawling typical of how the game is often played in the free world. If violence anywhere in the prison were allowed to gradually escalate, people were killed. "In Millhaven, you don't often see a fight," Campbell says. "If there's a beef, somebody's died."

There were no disputes amongst Green Team members or coaches that resulted in murders—which was a victory of sorts. On the ice, success was more modest. In the three-team league, the Greens settled for bronze.

Christmas in Millhaven saw three drag queens in Campbell's unit slash themselves. These weren't superficial slashes, intended only to gain attention. They were deep, dangerous, potentially fatal cuts, which meant the three queens were carried from the unit on stretchers.

Campbell and Sauvé found themselves speculating about how it had happened. Did the drag queens decide on a particular order of who would be slashed first, second and third? Did one do it and the others thought it was a good idea and joined in? Campbell couldn't help but smile as he ran over his alternate theories with Sauvé, surprised that he could be so glib about something so grim, involving people who had never done anything to hurt him. Was it possible that prison was making him an even harder man? "We're not that fucking cruel, me and Rick."

Campbell had been behind bars plenty of times, but this was super maximum security and he was still a newcomer; there were plenty of things to absorb. He learned that he needed to be constantly on guard, especially in the mornings. The craziest, angriest inmates often stew about grievances all night, and by daybreak they're in a murderous rage, ready to bolt out of their cells to avenge some perceived slight that others have often forgotten. "You're on point as soon as your cell doors open," Campbell says. "Almost all murders there happen when the doors open. Even if you had only two hours' sleep, you're on point when the door opens, if you had any sense about you."

Campbell learned it was a dangerous thing to say hello to someone for ten consecutive mornings and then forget to do so on the eleventh. This could well be taken as a slight that must be avenged with violence. He learned that a 120-pound man can kill you just as dead as a 300-pounder, with a shank to your heart. Sometimes that 120-pound man will be more prone to using that shank than a bigger man, since he can't handle him- self with his fists.

Campbell learned to walk with his eyes straight ahead and look slightly downwards and never peer into an open cell. Peeking into a prisoner's cell and catching him choking the chicken potentially invites a death sentence. Campbell recalls how one inmate warned another to control his wandering eyes. "Don't look in my cell," he ordered. The lesson didn't sink in. The next time the offending inmate looked into the cell, he witnessed a shank being rammed into his own heart.

Campbell learned that you do your time without complaining. Whining about a five-year term to someone serving life with no eligibility for parole for twenty-five years comes across as taunting, and taunting invites a violent response. You also don't ask anyone why they're in prison. They can tell you if they want, but there's a good chance you don't want to hear anyway. "It's doing your own time," Campbell says. "It's just none of your business." Once, he did venture to ask an inmate if he had any regrets about stabbing his wife seventeen times.

"Would you change anything?" Campbell asked.

"No, she was a fucking stool pigeon. I would do it all over again. She deserved every stab."

With that, the conversation ended. Campbell didn't want to hear another word about it.

Rather than pepper a prisoner with questions or random observations, Campbell understood that it was generally best simply to shut up. Prisoners were often one sharp glance or one clumsy word away from exploding. Campbell often felt like blowing up too, especially when he got the sense that someone figured his prison time was somehow easy because he didn't whine. "They'd think this was rolling off my back," Campbell says. "That it was not affecting me. Listen, I was doing every fucking minute. Think this doesn't bother me? That I don't have a life? That you're the only one that doesn't deserve to be in here? Go fuck yourself."

In prison, crazy was normal. A convict from the United States one day volunteered to Campbell why he was behind bars. Until that time Campbell had known him primarily as a guy who was good at making wooden flowerpots, a pleasant-enough way to pass the hours. Deciding to unburden himself, the flowerpot man told Campbell how he came home one day and caught his wife with another man.

"Oh yeah?" Campbell replied, not really wanting to know the details. "She came after me with a pistol." "Oh yeah?" "I tried to get it from her and then it went off and then the trigger guard got stuck on my hand." He gesticulated wildly, trying to demonstrate how easy it was for a hand to get stuck in a pistol and how the stream of bullets that filled the air and ended the life of his cheating wife was a horrible—but totally understandable—accident that could have happened to anyone.

At this point, Campbell couldn't control his laughter. At first, he had thought the flowerpot man just had a dry sense of humour. When he realized he was deadly serious, somehow it got even funnier.

"Tell me that, but don't tell a judge," Campbell advised, leaving with- out a flowerpot.

Campbell was on the incline bench in the gym not long after his arrival at Millhaven when he got chatting with a prisoner from the Kitchener area. The prisoner, whom Campbell calls Bow, began explaining how his partner in the drug world was ratting on him, so he tricked his partner into believing he had a deal for them. They drove out into a wooded area and he directed his partner to walk ahead of him as he took his hunting bow out of his car's trunk. Campbell recalls, "As he was telling me all of this, he was getting angrier by the minute, calling his partner a stool pigeon."

Bow was soon totally lost in the moment of the murder. "I shot him in the back with the arrow and the fucker didn't die, so I had to run over with my knife and stab him till he died. That motherfucker, that cock-sucking rat. He deserved to die."

Campbell feigned outrage too and looked for the next possible exit point from the conversation.

Then Bow abruptly halted his rant. "Do you know how they got me?" "No." "So he proceeded to tell me," Campbell says. "He cut off his partner's head and buried it. His reasoning was that the bugs would eat away the flesh and he would be able to take the skull home and use it for an ashtray. I'm thinking, 'Of course, why didn't I think of that?' He kept going back to check on the skull, and—wouldn't you know it?— the police had him under their radar and the bastards followed him one day. Ain't life a bitch?"

"I gotta go back to my cell," Campbell told Bow.

"I had to tell the guy to get the fuck away from me a few times after that before he got the hint," says Campbell.

Campbell learned that inmates are safer with the right friends. "Guys that don't have anybody are preyed upon a lot." That said, it's often better to stick to yourself rather than get involved with just anyone, since you'll inherit all of your new friend's enemies. Anyone suspected of being an informant or a sexual offender, or someone who'd been convicted of crimes against children, was a prime target for a shank in the exercise room. So was anyone who looked like a friend to a diddler or a rat. There is a theory that convicts are so tough on sex criminals because they feel powerless to protect their own families on the outside from people like that. Whatever the reasons, rats and diddlers were for- ever targeted. Campbell's advice to a newbie inmate was simple: "Just stay to yourself and do your own time. Don't get involved with groups. If you do, see what they're up to."

Some inmates, such as a bodybuilder named Nick Nero, grated on Campbell's nerves because they acted somehow surprised and offended to be behind bars. "He was a wimpy motherfucker," Campbell says. "I liked Robert Blake's line [from the 1970s TV show Baretta], 'If you can't do the time, don't do the crime.' . . . You're a fucking drug dealer. Suck it up. Shut up and do your fucking time."

Sometimes there's just something about a prisoner that creeps others out. It's hard to define why they give off this vibe, but the creepiness is palpable. Any association with someone like that can be dangerous. Nutty Comeau couldn't abide the sight of a glue sniffer who sat down next to Campbell at an inmates baseball game. Prisoners could easily get glue to sniff from woodwork or leather craft hobby work, and when they did, they became a menace, or at best annoying. "Lorne, don't be fucking talking to that guy," Nutty cautioned.

At first, Campbell had no problems chatting with the man. Then Campbell saw what Nutty meant, when the man began babbling in verbal circles one day, making no sense to anyone but himself. That's when Campbell decided that Nutty, for all his own issues, was right: "The guy's nuts. A glue sniffer. Anybody that's on downers, glue sniffers, too fucked up when they do something, we'd stay away from in jail. He was too screwed up to hang around with. If you're sniffing glue, it's gluing your brain cells or something."

Keeping the company of glue sniffers was hardly on the same level as being friendly with a diddler, but Campbell quickly learned that seemingly little things in Millhaven could bring major and irreversible penal- ties. Bad personal hygiene was often enough for an attack. So was a sloppy cell. Potentially capital crimes behind bars also included stiffing someone on a gambling debt, failing to deliver drugs as promised, and theft. For the weaker inmates, it could be dangerous to snub sexual advances. And sometimes prisoners saw their time behind bars as an opportunity to avenge grudges from the outside.

Campbell was repeatedly reminded that it was often best just to keep his thoughts to himself. Prison drag queens weren't preyed upon or goaded, as they fashioned halter tops from boxer shorts and makeup from ash and food colouring. There was just nothing to gain in hassling them and provoking confrontations. One drag queen who was given a particularly wide berth by the other inmates was a solidly built, six-foot-five former army sergeant. Underneath the makeup and woman's clothing, he still had a soldier's strength and skills. He also had a chilling reputation, having landed in prison for stabbing his mother to death. Her crime was to call him a faggot.

His wife Charmaine dropped by for visits religiously, reminding Campbell of the life that awaited him once his time was served. "She visited every week, rain or shine," Campbell says. "Bad weather or good, she was there."

Campbell had been running his stripper agency with Joe Napolitano when he was sent to prison, and Charmaine continued working as a dancer. Campbell was alarmed one day to hear that she was working at a bar in Windsor run by the Outlaws. It was easy to imagine them doing something terrible to her, just to punish him. "I said, 'Just go to the owner and get your pay. Don't work there. I just don't like the idea of some fucking wacko finding out you're my wife and doing harm on you.' I worried. Worried."

*Excerpted from *Unrepentant: The Strange and Sometimes Terrible Life of Lorne Campbell, Satan's Choice and Hells Angels Biker* aka *Satan's Choice: My Life As A Hardcore Biker With Satan's Choice And Hells Angels* by Peter Edwards, published by Random House and Sidgwick & Jackson (2013), ISBN 9780307362568.

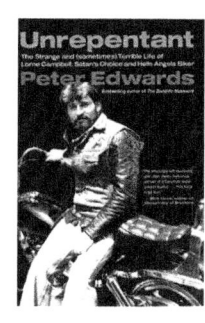

Peter Edwards is the author of eleven non-fiction books, most of which have been national bestsellers. He has also written for *The Toronto Star* for twenty-seven years, specializing in organized crime and justice issues. His most recent book is *Unrepentant: The Strange and (sometimes) Terrible Life of Lorne Campbell, Satan's Choice and Hells Angels Biker*, (Random House) which was published in the United Kingdom as *Satan's Choice: My Life as a Hard Core Biker with Satan's Choice and Hells Angels* (Sidgwick & Jackson).

The Bandido Massacre was reprinted in German by Statt Verlag and won the Hamilton Literary Award for non-fiction. Other books include *One Dead Indian: The Premier, the Police and the Ipperwash Crisis* (McClelland & Stewart), which became a Gemini-award-winning movie on CTV and won Edwards an eagle feather from the Union of Ontario Indians. *The Encyclopedia of Canadian Organized Crime* (McClelland & Stewart, with Michel Auger), has been in print for almost a decade. A historical work, *Delusion: The True Story of Victorian Superspy Henri Le Caron* (Key-Porter Books) was published in Britain under the title *The Infiltrator: Henri Le Caron, the British Spy Inside the Fenian Movement* (Maverick House). Excerpts from *A Mother's Story: the fight to free my son David* (Doubleday, with Joyce Milgaard) were reprinted in *Reader's Digest* and *Reader's Digest Crime Files*.

Edwards has lectured on organized crime at several universities, including the Nathanson Centre for the Study of Organized Crime and McGill University, and has been interviewed about organized crime for the BBC, CBC, CTV and the *Mob Stories* Parts 1 and 2 and *Outlaw Bikers* series for History Television. He is currently writing his twelfth book with Italian journalist Antonio Nicaso on the Mafia wars of mobster Vito Rizzuto.

Sturgis 1990

By David Charles Spurgeon

Although Daytona was our biggest run of the year, it was decided in the fall of 1989 that we needed to go back to the "Black Hills Classic" in South Dakota the following year. The event was attracting hundreds of thousands of bikers every year, as well as getting an immense amount of exposure in all the biker magazines. The other big clubs had been cashing in on it, so we determined we needed to as well.

In January of 1990, a scouting party was sent to Sturgis to make arrangements to accommodate several hundred of us. Taco (Detroit), Dan (Milwaukee), and I flew into Rapid City, rented a car, and headed west to the obscure, yet famous, town of Sturgis. I had never been there before, though the club had made an appearance there in 1978. Several members wore a "Cattle Rustler" patch on their colors after getting busted shooting a couple of cows in order to help feed the massive gathering of Outlaws. Shooting a cow was no problem; however, dragging its dead carcass up into a U-haul trailer was. My suggestion after the fact was, "Wouldn't it have been easier to have the cow walk into the trailer and then shoot it?" Hindsight is always 20/20, isn't it? That incident, as well as some other issues, worked together to do anything but endear the rural Western community to us. It was decided that the Outlaws would concentrate their energy and resources closer to home. Sturgis was in Bandido territory anyway.

The tiny town was anything but impressive to me when the three of us rolled in incognito. It was a dreary, overcast, and cold January day. The town consisted of about two blocks of Main Street, complete with what you'd expect in a Western community this size: a general store with groceries, a livestock feed store, and a clothing store or two. It was hard to picture this place hosting two hundred thousand bikers or to imagine why anyone would even want to come here.

We located the local distributors we were going to need for beer, ice, and meat. We decided to buy it this time, rather than forage for it. That stuff was easy. What we really needed to have nailed down by the end of this recon trip was a place to stay. We needed a place large enough for a national run, affordable, but most importantly, securable. We inquired at some motels and found out where the Hells Angels had made reservations. We checked out several campgrounds and were enlightened as to where some other large and unfriendly clubs were going to be staying. I'll never forget proprietors of two campgrounds opening their reservation books to us, showing us what sections other clubs had reserved, oblivious to the fact that they might be revealing important confidential information.

We finally found a large hill on the South side of town with only one access road and about five acres of usable area on top. We determined it would be perfect for us and rented it for the August Bike Week, as well as the week prior. With the logistical tasks complete, Taco, Dan, and I headed down to Deadwood, which had recently legalized gambling. The once-quiet town was now teeming with activity as tour buses brought people to try their luck. These weren't Vegas-style casinos by any means, but a black jack table is a black jack table. Taco and I both did pretty well, leaving with more money than we had when we went in. We, of course, were attracted to Saloon No. 10, where Wild Bill Hickok had been shot in the back and killed. They even had the chair he was sitting in at the time he was bushwhacked mounted over the door.

In the preparations to take the American Outlaw Association to the Black Hills, there were still a few important details that needed attention.

South Dakota was technically a Bandido state. In fact, they had a chapter in Rapid City, which was only thirty miles southwest of Sturgis. Since they were also a one percenter club, the respectful thing to do was to notify them of our intention to bring a large number of Outlaws through their territory. This presented no problem at all. Taco had known their national president, Ronnie Hodges, for years.

The next challenge was going to be much more interesting. It had to do with the fact that the Hells Angels would also be there. There had been tension, to put it mildly, between the Outlaws and the Angels dating back to before most members of either organization could remember. We both knew the law-enforcement community loved the fact that we didn't get along and looked forward to picking up the pieces after any confrontation. We resented the fact that the Feds often instigated problems between the clubs. They would be the real winners if anything got out of hand in Sturgis. The problem was neither of us trusted the other enough to be able to agree on a meeting place to discuss keeping our personal differences personal.

The solution to the meeting location problem was solved through the Terre Haute Federal Penitentiary Jaycee Chapter. It was made up predominantly of members of the Outlaws and the Angels; there at least, the two clubs got along. They began to petition the warden for permission to have a prison bike show that would allow visitors into the yard for the event. It had been done before in other prisons and proved to be a good public relations move, as well as a morale booster to the inmates involved.

It was determined that if the Outlaws and the Hells Angels could each get a high-ranking representative behind the ominous walls of this federal pen, perhaps groundwork could begin for a truce at the upcoming Sturgis Rally. Sonny Barger was currently serving time over the Louisville deal. The highest ranking Angel at the time of the May 1990 bike show was George Christy, president of the Ventura, California Hells Angels chapter. He got cleared to go in and meet with the Outlaws spokesman, which was me.

George flew in to Indianapolis while I led a small pack west to Terre Haute from Dayton, Ohio. A half dozen of us were cleared to take our bikes in for entry in the show. Upon arrival, we were escorted into a sally port for careful inspection. We had already drained all but enough fuel to get us back to a gas station, so all that needed to be addressed was making sure the scooters wouldn't start. Taking the spark plugs out took care of that. Once inside the walls, we pushed the bikes into the yard where the judging would take place. Some other bikers showed up as well, and they had to go through the same process. Eventually, we had about fourteen bikes lined up, waiting for the prisoners to be released for participation in the event.

When the incarcerated brothers first appeared, I recognized several from before they went to prison. It was good to see them again. They were accompanied by some men I didn't know. One of them was an infamous Outlaw who'd been locked up since before I'd come around. His name was "Big Jim." He had been the Florida boss before getting into big trouble for numerous reasons. "Free Big Jim" tee shirts were frequently seen at Outlaw events back in the 70s, implying he'd been the target of some unfair effort to eliminate the club. If everyone behind bars who claimed to be innocent actually was, there would be an awful lot of very dangerous criminals on the loose. On second thought, there are.

I was introduced as the AOA officer-in-charge not only to the Outlaws, but also to the Hells Angels members of the prison Jaycee organization. We were all on the same page. Whatever different ideologies we had on the street, behind the walls of a penitentiary, we had more in common than not. If for no other reason, we were both white. That alone put us in a minority, and minorities stick together. Actually, we had much more in common than that. We were one percenters, and our lives were dedicated to the principles of bikin' and brotherhood. That's no small thing.

It wasn't long before another Hells Angel made his way to the area designated for this bike show. He wasn't an inmate, though. George Christy and I introduced ourselves to each other, shook hands for all to see (especially the prison officials), and commenced to talk with our individual members for a while. As the prisoners gathered around to look at the bikes and the Jaycee's assessed the motorcycles with their clipboards, George and I stepped back to discuss the subject that had brought us to this place. We both knew there would be a multitude of law-enforcement personnel from every conceivable agency at Sturgis.

They'd be there with their expensive cameras and zoom lenses, recording the faces of as many members as possible. They'd be there looking for fugitives, like they did at all our events, including funerals. We knew we were going to make their job really easy for them by gathering together in one public place. In some ways, they would be looking forward to Sturgis more than we would. The Feds knew it would be all but impossible for us to avoid some kind of conflict. It was in our very nature. They didn't really care who did what to whom; they hated us all. They shouldn't have. We provided the means for their very handsome federal budget. Let's face it. Who's going to be easier to do surveillance on? A highly organized and secretive Mafioso or a bunch of bearded, high-profile, colors-wearing bikers? Go figure. Without us, they would have had to work much harder for their salaries.

This historic meeting, built on the foundation of the one in Louisville, was for much the same purpose, only this time the subject was a national motorcycle event instead of a trial. The common desire between George, me, and the organizations we represented was the fact that we wanted the privilege of settling any differences we had, whatever they may be at any given point in time, in private. The idea of the government coming in to pick up the pieces and then claim credit for what we did to ourselves was unacceptable, if it could at all be avoided.

At the end of the day, we agreed that great effort be made to maintain a semblance of civility pertaining to this upcoming Sturgis Run, including on the roads to and from the event. We agreed to do our best to behave ourselves in public. He gave me contact numbers of the Cleveland Hells Angels, so I could further coordinate details with them. We then shook hands again before joining the others. It was a good meeting for a good purpose. The icing on the cake for me was that I was awarded the first place plaque in the bike show. That came as no surprise, really. I knew I had the best-looking scooter in the show. Besides, several of the judges were Outlaws!

I met several times with members of the Cleveland Angels during the months of June and July. It was an uncomfortable situation for both of us, especially at first. I must say, everything proceeded remarkably on track as far as cooperation goes. We all had the safety of our brothers as our foremost agenda. Many of my own brothers were very leery of having any dealing with the Hells Angels at all, but I was convinced this endeavor was valid. If it could save one brother's life it was worth it to me, regardless of what anyone thought.

As the end of July rolled around, I volunteered to head up the early crew. We'd made all sorts of arrangements, from land rental to ice and beer deliveries which needed to be solidified prior to the arrival of the Outlaw Nation en masse. I had no problem getting four volunteers to go with me, so I bought a motor home, loaded our bikes in an enclosed trailer, and headed west. We, of course, traveled incognito due to the number of guns we felt we needed to take everywhere we went. Many of us were veterans, and we just liked them, I guess. Imagine five tattooed, bearded men traveling cross-country in a recreational vehicle trying to look inconspicuous. We probably had Feds following us from the first campground at which we stopped.

My crew and I arrived a good week and a half before Bike Week actually began and took possession of the property we'd rented back in January. The plateau on the high hill south of town had a single, winding road leading up to it and would be easy to secure and to defend, if necessary. After doing some routine surveillance, we settled in and began to reconnect with the different vendors with whom Taco, Dan, and I had contracted. Things were falling into place nicely and, slowly but surely, the little town began to fill up. Groups of bikers began to roll in constantly in anticipation of the fiftieth anniversary of the annual Black Hills Motorcycle Classic. Most were no more interested in the races than we were. They came to Sturgis to ride and to party. The sound of two-wheeled thunder permeated the atmosphere. At times, it seemed the very earth shook. I loved it.

Three days before the official kick-off date, Taco showed up with twenty more brothers. Our reconnaissance revealed the Hells Angels had rented a motel, also on the South side of town. As a matter of fact, our elevated knoll overlooked it. We liked that. In our favorite training film of the 80s, *The Outlaw Josey Wales*, the importance of having the high ground with the sun at your back was the utmost priority in any gunfight.

Of course, we weren't here for a gunfight, especially in such a public setting so closely observed by law enforcement.

It was time to make contact with the Angels. Since I had been the chief liaison officer with them throughout this operation, Taco sent me down into the midst of a hundred or so "Red and White" to make sure we were still on the same page. I guess if I had been killed, it would have confirmed that we were not. I remember hoping Kenny from Cleveland would be there, or at least someone that was aware of our clubs' attempts to formulate this truce. If not, it wouldn't have been a very smart move to ride in there.

A faithful brother named Ed, from our Warren, Ohio chapter, volunteered to go with me. He was a former U.S. Army paratrooper as I was, and he didn't have enough sense to be afraid of anything. Ed loved the club and had no ulterior motive whatsoever for his loyalty. Bikin' and brotherhood was what he was about, and I can't think of a greater compliment to pay the man. As he and I rode into the Angel camp, I'll never forget the looks of disbelief on their faces. They could not believe a couple of Outlaws would ride right into their midst unprotected. Many of them had never seen an Outlaw before, just as many of our guys had never seen a real Hells Angel. We had been rivals for so long, many on either side didn't even remember why. Of course, Ed and I were not without backup. I'm not talking about the Colt .45's we both carried. They wouldn't have helped very much had this situation gone wrong. Our backs were covered by twenty-plus Outlaws up on the ridge behind us with high-powered rifles, visibly and obviously capable of covering us. I remember thinking, "I hope none of these Angels have a good pair of binoculars." The truth of the matter was the truck with our high-powered rifles hadn't arrived yet, so Taco had the brothers find branches that resembled long guns in an effort to bluff them. I don't attribute that to our safety. I was counting on the word of George and Kenny to keep us safe. It did.

In the days to come, Sturgis transformed itself into the largest city in the state of South Dakota. Literally hundreds of thousands of bikers converged on this normally quiet, even boring, little town. Main Street was closed to all but motorcycle traffic. Bikes lined the several blocks of "downtown" area, and a constant flow of scooters would be going up one side of the street and down the other. The citizen biker groups would ride by, see-sawing back and forth, gunning their engines, trying to attract attention.

When a procession of one percenters, whether they were Outlaws, Hells Angels, or Bandidos, descended onto Main Street, everyone took notice. These clubs rode uniformly side by side, carefully maintaining their military-style formation. It was an ominous and intimidating sight that caused everyone on the street to stop what he was doing and watch. Many observed with curiosity, others with fear, and some even with envy, because we were what they didn't have the guts to be. We were what they pretended to be back home the rest of the year, reading their *Easyriders* magazines, memorizing the lingo, and imagining themselves to be hardcore bikers. Don't get me wrong. Many who came to Sturgis were the real deal. I never believed you had to ride with a club to be a true biker. I was one before I ever joined a club. The truth is there was something intriguing about those of us who were *totally* sold out to the lifestyle of bikin' and brotherhood.

During the course of the next week, I spent more time with the Angels than with my own club. This peacemaker position was certainly different from what I was accustomed. At major functions like this, my responsibility usually consisted of policing our own guys. In this situation,

I diligently watched my own back because the most sincere agreements sometimes get violated when drugs and liquor work their way into the equation. As I observed these Angels, I was reminded of something George Christy told me behind the walls of the Terre Haute Federal Correctional Facility. He said, "Cowboy, the biggest difference between you and me is logistical. If I lived where you do, I'd be what you are. If you lived where I do, you'd be what I am." As hard as every club tries to convince itself that it's totally superior to every other, the truth of the matter was we weren't so different after all. That was a sobering reality after all those years of thinking the other way.

My motor home was parked up on the hill, at the edge of our perimeter. If there was any problem with security or if anyone needed an executive decision, they'd wake me up instead of Taco. If I deemed it necessary, I would go to Taco myself. Such was the case the fourth night of Bike Week. One of the brothers was riding through the campsite, not paying attention, and ran into Big Moe, who was on foot. (Big Moe from Dayton was well named, for he was a huge man, strong as a bull and twice as mean if you got on the wrong side of him.) A foot peg gashed Moe's leg deeply, and it was decided he should go to the hospital. Of course, Sturgis didn't have one. The nearest medical facility was in Rapid City. Several brothers took him there for treatment where the doctor advised he spend the night for observation. Amazingly, Big Moe agreed. He was sore from the collision anyway and knew he'd have a better chance to rest there than at the campsite with two hundred Outlaws asking him how he was feeling.

About three in the morning I was awakened by one of the front gate guards, informing me the Sheriff's Department wanted to speak to whoever was in charge. I made my way over to them, unhappy about having been woken up, demanding to know what was going on. I knew it couldn't have been due to any trouble our people had caused. Everyone was accounted for. The sheriff's deputy informed me that Gary Elmore, a.k.a. Big Moe, had died in the Rapid City Hospital due to a blood clot to his heart. I couldn't believe my ears! I thought of all the effort that had gone into trying to prevent anyone from being hurt, and now they're telling me this beloved brother was dead. I immediately suspected foul play. I don't know whom I suspected specifically, but I knew one thing--I sure wasn't just going to take some cop's word for it.

The first thing that had to be done was inform Taco. When I headed to his campsite, I didn't know whether he would be awake or not, but it didn't matter. He had to be told right away. I hated to bear that kind of news. He took it about the same way I did. He told me to get to the hospital and verify the information personally. I immediately grabbed two Dayton brothers, and we headed to Rapid City. We got there a little after four in the morning and the place was pretty quiet. I told the information desk clerk we were there to see Big Moe, but I was informed visiting hours were long since over. Obviously, that didn't go over too well. When security showed up, they told us Mr. Elmore had died, and we would need to come back in the morning. That didn't go over too well either.

I told the guard I was next of kin and "convinced" him to let me see the body. We were escorted to the room where he lay there on a gurney, deader than a doornail. Cause of death? A blood clot in his leg broke loose, traveling to his heart. I'd known Moe since before I'd become an Outlaw. This was an unexpected, and very sad, turn of events. For me and for the Dayton chapter of the Outlaws, the party was over. Upon arrival back at camp and confirming to Taco that Big Moe was indeed dead, my crew and the rest of the Dayton brothers began to load up. We were heading home to prepare for another funeral. Taco would be bringing the rest of the club with him in a few days.

Hundreds of brothers came, as well as many locals. Even Big Moe's son, who was serving time in prison, was there to pay his final respects. Of course, he was in shackles, escorted by correctional officers, but we were glad he was able to make it. Big Moe's funeral was a classic: the long procession of motorcycles, the traditional gun salute at the gravesite, the ritual of taking turns at the shovel, filling in the grave. "God forgives, Outlaws don't," echoed around the cemetery. Life in the fast lane had claimed another one percenter.

*Excerpted from *Bikin' and Brotherhood: My Journey* by David Charles Spurgeon (2011), ISBN 9781449728052

For more information, please go to: bikinandbrotherhood dot com

Spurgeon saw his first Harley-Davidson roll out of a driveway across the street from his junior high school in 1966. Impressed by the rumble of that stripped-down Panhead dresser, a curiosity took root in him that was only encouraged by the 1969 film "Easy Rider." Something about the wind in your hair, and the freedom of the road, fascinated him. Upon his discharge from the 509th Airborne Infantry in 1974, Spurgeon's dream of owning his own Harley finally became a reality.

On the country roads of Northwest Ohio, he learned to ride. Hanging out in the local bike shops, he learned to wrench. In the bars of rural Lucas County, he earned a reputation for sticking up for the underdog. Life was simple. Life was good. He became a patch member of a local motorcycle club called the Mongols and soon after met some Detroit members of the infamous 1%er club, the Outlaws. Impressed by their beautiful machines, their love of the road, and their relentless dedication to one another, he knew he had found the Brotherhood for which he had been longing.

In October of 1979, Spurgeon, a.k.a. "Cowboy", became the charter president of the Toledo chapter of the American Outlaw Association. He served the club faithfully as an officer at every level for the next eleven years, until drugs and alcohol abuse finally got the best of him. It a miracle he survived. This is his story.

Sturgis High…Montreal Low

By Edward Winterhalder & Wil De Clercq

"If you attend only one rally in your life Sturgis is the one to attend," I told Alain. "You won't believe it. It makes most other rallies look like a backyard picnic."

Sturgis, South Dakota is home to the largest biker event in the United States if not the world. It takes place the first full week of August and hot, dry weather is practically guaranteed. Actually, the event, simply known as the Sturgis Motorcycle Rally, gets underway on the Friday before the first full week and ends on the following Sunday, running some ten days in total. It has been estimated that in the past few years more than 750,000 people, and a staggering 500,000 motorcycles, gathered in Sturgis for this rally to end all rallies.

The Bandidos Motorcycle Club has a chapter and clubhouse near Sturgis at Rapid City and every year Sturgis has been a major event for the entire Bandidos club. For me the 2001 Sturgis Rally was going to be exceptional, for I had convinced Bandido Alain to come to Tulsa and ride with me all the way to South Dakota and back.

When Alain mentioned that he wouldn't have a bike to ride, I assured him I'd stick a set of wheels beneath him.

"Well, okay then. I guess I'm going to Sturgis with you," he said in his charming French-Canadian English.

Sturgis has always been one of my favorite destinations. Located in the Black Hills of South Dakota, the region's scenery and solitude are second to none. Its roads are ideal for cruising on a motorcycle.

Within a few hours of Sturgis are such western American landmarks as the sweeping Badlands and the imposing Devil's Tower, featured in the movie Close Encounters of the Third Kind, among others. Also nearby is Sylvan Lake, known as the "crown jewel" of Custer State Park. These majestic places are a feast for the eyes and nature at its best.

Like many events that have attained legendary status the Sturgis Motorcycle Rally began simply enough as a low-key affair. The first rally, which wasn't even a true rally, saw the light of day in 1938 when Clarence "Pappy" Hoel and some of his friends from the Jackpine Gypsies Motorcycle Club – a club Hoel had founded in 1936 – decided to hold a motorcycle race and stunt competition.

Hoel, a motorcycle shop owner in Sturgis, persuaded local business owners to put up a five hundred dollar purse, a small fortune at that time. Only a handful of racers entered the inaugural event to bang handlebars on the town's half-mile oval and participate in hair raising stunts, which included boardwall crashes and ramp jumps.

Although few spectators showed up to watch the action the event quickly took on a life of its own, especially after World War II when motorcycling gained in popularity.

In addition to half-mile flat track racing, the program evolved to include motocross, short track racing, drag racing, and hill climbs. Touring, which originally was not included in the festivities, was incorporated within a few years of the rally's launch; today it makes up the lion's hare of the Sturgis Motorcycle Rally.

Motorcyclists from all walks of life ranging from factory workers to teachers, doctors, nurses, engineers, and numerous other professions are represented at the Sturgis Rally. And there is always sizeable presence of 1%ers, representing many clubs from across the United States, mingling with the crowd.

Bandido Alain arrived in Tulsa a few days before our planned departure for Sturgis. Looking like a regular citizen and his tattoos concealed, he had taken a Greyhound bus from Toronto hoping to blend in with the rest of the passengers so as not to draw attention to himself at the U.S./Canada border. The plan worked well, but he paid the price having to endure an uncomfortable 1,180 miles, twenty-hours plus bus journey to Tulsa.

For someone of Bandido Alain's size a ride in the cramped seats of a bus approximates sheer hell. When he finally got to my home outside of Tulsa, he spent two days recuperating from the long trip. It was great to have a Canadian brother around and Caroline, Taylor and I truly enjoyed his company. Alain had a way of making us all laugh and after a while we even became quite adept at understanding his French-Canadian English.

To make the trip to Sturgis, I borrowed a 1999 Harley FXDX Superglide for Alain from my attorney friend Jonathan Sutton. I was going to ride my own 1999 Harley FXDL Superglide, very similar to Jonathan's machine. On Saturday, August 4th Alain, Caroline, and I set out for Sturgis. Ahead of us was a nine hundred and fifty mile odyssey that would take us through Missouri, Nebraska, and South Dakota. It was trip I had made on numerous occasions and one I never tired of. Although I was an east coast boy by birth, I had long ago become a Midwesterner at heart and considered the plains my stomping grounds.

Accompanied by the distinctive rumble of two hotrod Harley engines, Alain and I rode side by side like the consummate bikers we were, every once in a while exchanging a thumbs up out of sheer joy. I'm sure that for much of the time we had contented grins on our faces mirroring the passion we felt for our bikes, the open road…and being Bandidos. There is no better feeling than blasting down the highway with another guy on a motorcycle, especially a club brother. Well, actually, there might be: blasting down the highway with dozens if not hundreds of other club brothers – a deafening convoy of modern day cowboys slicing through the countryside on their iron horses.

Caroline, an avid motorcyclist in her own right who owned a Sportster when I met her, had her arms wrapped around me. She was enjoying being a carefree passenger and letting her eyes wander over the passing scenery. We left Oklahoma behind and traveled northeast up Interstate 44 into Missouri, the only state in addition to Tennessee that is bordered by eight other states.

As we cruised along past Joplin heading towards Springfield, I couldn't help but think again about the first time I had met Alain and my subsequent involvement with the patched over Rock Machine. I was proud that I had done my part to get Bandidos Canada to where they were and knew I would have a long association with them. I was prouder still to be riding next to Alain, a brave soul who had gone from a rank and file Rock Machine to the enviable position of Bandidos Canada Presidente.

"This is the first time in a long time I have been able to ride a motorcycle without worrying that somebody might shoot me off it," Alain mentioned while fueling up at a gas station along the way. "I'm sure glad you talked me into coming."

In early August southwest Missouri is especially beautiful country to be traveling through, with many treed areas that provide quite a bit of shade and pockets of cooler air. In the stifling heat we were extremely thankful for the trees. One of the stops on our itinerary was Springfield, where we were scheduled to rendezvous with two Arkansas members of the Ozark Riders Motorcycle Club – a Bandidos support club – who were going to ride with us to Sturgis.

I also made arrangements to see a childhood friend of mine, Kurt Newman, who had lived in Springfield for some ten years. After lunch, and reminiscing with Kurt, we met up with Andy and Nick, the two Ozark Riders. By mid afternoon Bandido Alain, Ozark Rider Andy, Ozark Rider Nick and his girlfriend, and Caroline and I rode out of Springfield and traveled another sixty miles northeast, close to Ozark Lake, where we were scheduled to visit a group of guys who had expressed interest in joining the Ozark Riders.

This was a good opportunity to combine a little business with pleasure. Considering that club business usually is pleasure, the meeting was bonus. We arrived at our destination near Ozark Lake early in the evening with a blazing sunset coloring the darkening sky. After dinner and a short meeting we retired for the night. We had been well received at the meeting and the group of guys we spoke with would eventually become Ozark Riders.

Early the next day we set out for Kansas City, Missouri where we had planned to stop and pay our respects to the local chapter of the Boozefighters Motorcycle Club, popularly known in American folklore as "The Original Wild Ones" because they were part of the inspiration behind the first biker movie, The Wild One. It was our intention to get to Kansas City before the heat became unbearable, but unfortunately that was not the case. By the time we got to the north side of Kansas City it was very hot and probably close to one hundred degrees Fahrenheit. Most of us southerners could tolerate the heat fairly well, but Bandido Alain – a denizen of the land of ice and snow – was having some difficulty coping with the broiler like conditions. He was beginning to look like an overripe tomato so stopping for the afternoon was a welcome relief.

We spent a few hours in Kansas City, situated at the junction of the Missouri and Kansas Rivers, and considered to be one of the most beautiful cities in the United States. It is renowned for having more boulevards than any other city in the world except Paris and more fountains than any other city except Rome. Although nothing beats the grandeur of nature in my eyes, Kansas City is a visual delight, a perfect example of diligent city planning.

After relaxing a bit and enjoying a good meal, we left Kansas City around 6:00PM, hoping to make Omaha just after dark. This time we were on schedule, rolling into Omaha according to plan. We found a decent motel and spent a restful night recharging our batteries for the next leg of the journey. It had been a good day with no major breakdowns, just plenty of water breaks, food, and gas stops. The following day would be another story. We were now far away from all the bountiful shade trees and rolling hills of Missouri and would be heading into the hot, dry plains of South Dakota.

The next morning, Monday, August 6th, we got up early and headed for Sioux Falls, South Dakota. We knew that we needed to be there by late morning if we wanted to avoid the stifling heat predicted for that day. By high noon temperatures of one hundred degrees were called for. Under a blazing plains sun that was just too hot for comfort: it wasn't good for the bikes, it surely wasn't good for us. And I was very worried about Bandido Alain; the heat was literally kicking his ass!

Despite the sun block he and the rest of us had been generously slapping on any exposed skin, Alain's face and neck were an alarming bright red. Fortunately the ride went well and men, women, and machines held up. Just after twelve noon we arrived in Sioux Falls, known as the "Gateway to the Plains". I was scheduled to meet another 1%er friend of mine, Mike, who rode with the Sons of Silence Motorcycle Club in Minnesota. Mike was going to join our group, which now included five riders and two passengers, for the rest of the ride to Sturgis.

Sons of Silence Mike and I had previously agreed to meet at a local Sioux Falls tattoo shop where we both had a mutual friend. Mike and I knew the shop's "piercing girl", who was the widow of a Bandido from Louisiana. We spent most of the early afternoon just hanging out, relaxing, catching up on things and watching TV in the air-conditioned shop.

Later that day, after the temperature had dropped and much of the heat dissipated, we all headed west on Interstate 90 for Chamberlain, South Dakota, our final stop of the day. By now I-90 was crammed full of Harleys, hundreds and hundreds of them, heading west towards Sturgis. It was a sight to behold, the thundering sound of the many motorcycle engines music to my ears.

Our traveling entourage now consisted of me, Caroline, Bandido Alain, Ozark Rider Andy, Ozark Rider Nick, Ozark Rider Nick's girlfriend, and Sons of Silence Mike. We were hoping to reach Chamberlain, some 210 miles east of Sturgis, just before nightfall and meet up with about fifty other members of the Sons of Silence. While at the tattoo shop in Sioux Falls we had made reservations at a motel in Chamberlain. Fortunately we had been able to find one with some vacant rooms. I had been this way many times before and knew it was very easy to get stranded in these environs without gasoline, water, food, or lodging.

We made good time and cruised into Chamberlain just around dusk. We had no trouble finding our motel in the small town whose population at that time was around two thousand three hundred and thirty-eight residents. This number probably included the cats and dogs, for there was hardly a soul to be seen anywhere. I was surprised by how much the heat had affected everyone. Even with the layover in Sioux Falls during the worst part of the day everyone was drained and looking forward to a good meal and kicking back for the night. Although only in my early forties, I was starting to realize I was no longer twenty-one years old anymore. It seemed the older I got the harder the ride got.

Alain, although more wrecked than the rest of us, still behaved like a kid in a candy store. Despite his discomfort Tulsa to Sturgis was a ride of discovery for him. He was thrilled by seeing new places on the vast expanse of the American Midwest and meeting all kinds of new people. By now Alain was quite sunburned, especially his face; thinking of a new name for him I asked him what "head" and "tomato" were called in French.

"Head is 'tête' and tomato is 'tomate', which is pronounced in English as 'tight toe mat'," he explained.

From that time on we all affectionately called him "Tomato Head", or should I say correctly in French "Tête Tomate".

After settling into my room with Caroline, I took a quick shower and then headed to the local bar to visit with some of the Sons of Silence; and there were plenty of them there to visit with – some forty in total. But I didn't last long at the bar and was barely able to keep my eyes open. After only a few ginger ales – I had given up drinking alcoholic beverages in 1986 – I was toast. It seemed like it was way past my bedtime, and after bidding everyone a "good night", I went back to the motel around 10:00PM. I wanted to get a good night's sleep, for once again we were going to try and get an early start to stay ahead of the blast furnace heat the weatherman had predicted.

We figured if all went well we could make it into Rapid City around noon. Had it not been for the "Probationary" bottom rocker

Bandido Alain was wearing we probably would have. In the world of 1%ers, when the Bandidos accept a patchholder who has been in another club, it is a rule that he becomes a probationary member for at least one year. This is based upon the fact that a probationary member already has some motorcycle club experience, and that this previous experience will give him a good foundation to build upon while learning what it is like to be a member of the Bandidos.

Probationary members are easily identified by their bottom rocker which says exactly that, "Probationary". After making it through the probationary period, a new member receives the 1% patch and a "chapter" bottom rocker, which replaces the "Probationary" bottom rocker. Usually the "chapter" bottom rocker designates the geographical area the member resides in. In Bandido Alain's case his bottom rocker would eventually read "Canada".

In the early days of outlaw motorcycle clubs, the bottom rocker indicated the name of the city the chapter was located in. This practice has largely been replaced by listing the state, province, or country on the bottom rocker. The reason for this is twofold: to confuse law enforcement, other clubs, and the public so as not be able to pinpoint the exact location the member resides and to create the illusion that there are a lot more members than there actually are.

*   *   *

We managed to get everybody out of bed by seven o'clock the following morning. Chamberlain wasn't much active at this time of day than it had been when we rode into town. We enjoyed breakfast of bacon, eggs, sausage, pancakes and toast, washed down with orange juice, milk, and coffee. Keeping to our plan we were back on the road before 8:30AM. This was a good thing, because the weather forecast had been right on the money. Another scorcher was unfolding.

On a motorcycle, the heat emitted from the engine easily increases the temperature by fifteen to twenty degrees; at times like this the prospect of an air-conditioned car is very attractive. But we were bikers and dealing with sauna like riding conditions comes with the territory during the hot summer months. We continued our journey down I-90 towards Sturgis, happily zooming along at the speed limit and minding our own business.

About mid morning, without any warning, a South Dakota Highway Patrol car nosed right into the middle of our entourage, effectively cutting us into two groups. We were very fortunate that he didn't cause an accident. It was obvious he pulled this reckless maneuver with full intent, not caring about the consequences. The officer behind the wheel looked like he was pointing at Bandido Alain and signaling him to pull over to the side of the road.

Although it seemed pretty obvious that Alain was being singled out, Ozark Rider Andy, who was riding next to Alain at the rear of the pack, pulled over with him just in case. When someone in a biker convoy gets signaled by law enforcement to pull over, everyone behind him will follow suit; all those ahead of him keep going to the next exit.

It became pretty clear Alain was the main man of interest because the first thing the cop did was order Andy to get lost. When it looked like Andy wasn't going to desert Alain, Alain nodded that he better follow the cop's advice. Taking the cue from Alain, Andy did the smart thing and hightailed it. At the time we had no idea why Alain got the short end of the straw, but we learned later that the state trooper wanted to know who the new probationary Bandido riding a bike from Oklahoma was. It has always been the task of law enforcement officers in South Dakota to determine who we are, but this one wanted to know so badly he didn't seem to mind if some of us got killed in the process.

The frontrunners of the group, which included me and Caroline, continued riding farther down the road for about four miles until coming to the next exit. We got off at the exit and parked under the highway overpass to shield ourselves from the blazing sun. It didn't take long for Ozark Rider Andy to catch up with us. By now we knew that the cop's sole interest was in Bandido Alain, and we wondered what was going to happen to him. We were quite concerned that he would be arrested for some kind of immigration violation. I can only imagine the look of surprise on the cop's face when he discovered Alain spoke English with a heavy French accent; that he was a Canadian Bandido riding a motorcycle he had borrowed in Oklahoma; and that he had a driver's license from Quebec.

It took the lawman quite a while to check out our French-Canadian brother. Fortunately he came up empty; he didn't even discover that Alain Brunette was the president of Bandidos Canada. To ensure his effort wasn't a complete waste of time, the Highway Patrol officer wrote Alain a one hundred dollar traffic citation for having too loud an exhaust system. This was interesting because the bike was brand new and still had the stock factory exhaust installed on it. Actually, the cop didn't even bother to test the exhaust system; no doubt he knew if he did the monitor would indicate the exhaust system met the required noise level standards.

This scenario reminded me somewhat of the incident on the Autobahn in Germany, when we were ticketed for supposedly speeding in a construction zone. When you're a biker on the road and get pulled over by the authorities you can bet your bottom dollar it's going to cost you money, especially if you fail to satisfy their suspicions that there must be some kind of warrant floating around for your arrest.

As per biker protocol, when someone in a group gets pulled over, the rest of the convoy waits at the next exit for at least an hour. If he's not coming down the road within that period of time you know he was taken into custody. That's why we were all overjoyed when we finally saw Bandido Alain barreling down the highway in our direction. He joined us underneath the bridge and gave us a thumbs up as he coasted to a stop.

"Well, that was really interesting for sure. I thought I was gonna be in deep shit, but all I got was a ticket for a noisy muffler. Go figure," Alain said.

"Yeah, go figure," I said. "But at least you're still going to Sturgis and that has to be considered a good thing."

We all let out a war whoop, fired up our bikes and got back on the highway. In the back of my mind I was hoping we weren't going to be pulled over again a few miles down the road. This had happened to me many times before; you get stopped once chances are you'll get stopped twice. Alain had been lucky, because he could just as easily have ended up in the same predicament I had in his country, dealing with immigration officials who got their jollies messing with people's lives, all in the name of doing their duty, of course. The last thing I wanted was for Alain to be a guest of Uncle Sam. In total the encounter with the Highway Patrol cop cost us more than an hour and it was getting very, very, hot!

The final stretch of our journey was pleasantly uneventful, but we did have to stop more often for water. We seemed to be dehydrating as quickly as we were hydrating. We got into Rapid City about 1:00PM and headed straight to the Bandidos clubhouse property on the east side of town. Everyone at the clubhouse was very happy to see us, and quite surprised to see Bandido Alain. Alain was just happy to be there, period, still in one piece but very sunburned. For him this had been the longest ride on a bike in his entire life – it was, as he called it, his "grand adventure".

*   *   *

We spent almost four days in the Sturgis/Rapid City area. We had actually arrived on the morning of Tuesday, August 7th and would eventually leave around 4:00PM on the 11th. When we got to the chaotic downtown core of Sturgis Bandido Alain, still behaving like the kid in the proverbial candy store, couldn't believe his eyes. The town's historic Main Street and central five blocks – open to motorcycle traffic only for the duration of Rally Week – were an ocean of multicolored bikes and equally colorful people of all shapes and sizes.

Add into the mix close to one thousand 1%ers, four hundred of which were Bandidos at the 2001 Rally, and you had soap operas, reality shows, and circuses to appease even the most jaded visitor. During Rally Week Sturgis is a place to "see" and be "seen". The streets are also lined with vendors selling a wide selection of goods ranging from leathers to the ever present souvenir t-shirts, jewelry, and of course, motorcycle parts of every description. And there's plenty of food to be had ranging from old standbys like hamburgers and fries to the exotic like alligator, ostrich, and jambalaya.

In addition to hanging out and taking in the madness I made sure that Bandido Alain got to see some of the more popular tourist attractions in the surrounding area. The highlight of our out-of-town tour was Mount Rushmore, the famous site of the humongous head sculptures of the of former U.S. Presidents George Washington, Thomas Jefferson, Theodore Roosevelt, and Abraham Lincoln. Like good tourists we took the usual requisite photos to show the folks back home.

When not sightseeing or carousing in Sturgis, we spent our nights at a house we rented in Rapid City. The entire Oklahoma Bandidos chapter stayed there plus Andy and Nick from the Ozark Riders as well as all of the Canadian Bandidos who made it across the border. It was a decent, completely furnished four-bedroom house in a nice neighborhood; it had a very handy kitchen, which kind of became grand central during our stay. The ladies cooked huge meals every day; we just made sure there was always plenty of food in the fridge.

In the basement was a huge open room where different groups congregated at all hours of the day. We had bought a stack of inflatable mattresses at Wal-Mart, which we used for everyone to sleep on, and then shipped them home through the post office the day we left. By the end of the week, the house had been a hotel for more than twenty people and we left it just like we found it…immaculate! For anyone buying into the stereotype biker image, expecting the place to be trashed, seeing the vacated house in such condition would have come as a big shock.

Late in the week a carload of Bandidos from Canada showed up at the house. In the group was Bandido Vice Presidente Peppi from Toronto – the ex-Loners Motorcycle Club member who had become a Bandido a few months earlier – and another Bandido named Luis Manny "Porkchop" Raposo. Bandido Peppi and Bandido Porkchop drove all the way to Rapid City from Toronto non-stop, spent two days there, and drove all the way back non-stop. I felt bad for them because all they ever saw while they were there was the clubhouse property and the house we rented. They never had a chance to really experience what Sturgis is all about during Rally Week or see the sights like Bandido Alain did.

I had really hoped that Bandido El Secretario Robert "Tout" Leger was going to be with Peppi and Porkchop but unfortunately he was not. I had spoken with Bandido Tout nearly every day since I had left Canada. From the time Bandido Alain arrived in Oklahoma, we had both been on the phone with him whenever the opportunity presented itself. We both tried unsuccessfully to talk Tout into coming to Sturgis; on one occasion we actually thought he was going to join us.

"Hey guys, you know I would really like to come, but if I get busted in the States for any reason whatsoever, I'll really be screwed. I don't know what to do." Tout said. "My heart says go but my mind say no. You know what I mean?"

Despite wanting him with us we did indeed know what he meant. Bandido Tout was very hesitant about leaving Canada, as at the time he was subject to bond stipulations that prevented him from leaving the Montreal area. In the end he decided it was too risky to take the chance. I spoke with him two or three more times while I was in Sturgis, and I had to agree with him he had made the right decision.

"Don't feel bad for me, okay? I'll be cool. I'm going to my house in the country and spend the weekend there with my family. We can use a break," he told me during our last conversation. "I'm sure we'll all get together sometime soon."

After four days of revelry and fun in the sun, and getting together with Bandidos from all over the world Alain, Caroline, and I hit the road for the long ride back to Oklahoma. We left late on Saturday afternoon, August 11th and rode all the way to the railroad town of North Platte, Nebraska, a distance of about three hundred and twenty-five miles. In

North Platte we grabbed a motel room for the night where we fell asleep shortly after arriving. We had planned on making the trip in just two day. Bandido Alain was scheduled to fly back to Canada on Tuesday morning and he wanted a day to relax before the flight.

We got up early the next morning to tackle the remaining six hundred miles to Tulsa. It was a cloudy day and rain had been predicted. On our way out of town we rode past the Union Pacific Railroad Bailey Yard, the largest railroad classification yard in the world. This humongous yard covers a staggering two thousand eight hundred and fifty acres and reaches a total length of eight miles. As we rode eastbound on Interstate 80 across Nebraska it started to look like we were definitely going to get rained on. When we finally encountered the rain we turned south, then east, to get around it. Dealing with hot weather when traveling on a bike is one thing, rain is quite another and I'll do just about anything to avoid it. Detouring around the rain took us way off the beaten path, but soon we were into clear, sunny skies. We traveled down an array of county roads, which except for some local vehicles, was devoid of traffic.

Although we were losing valuable time we got to see a slice of Nebraska no tourist ever sees: quaint little country towns and miles upon miles of cornfields. Baking under the hot plains sun a sweet smell wafts into the air from those cornfields; it's no wonder they call Nebraska the "Cornhusker State".

At one desolate point on our journey I thought I was going to run out of gas. Because I was packing Caroline with me, I burned more fuel per mile than Alain even though we were on nearly identical bikes. That day I discovered the Superglide FXDL would go nearly twenty-five miles on reserve, which turned out to be just enough to find a gas station. After refueling, we crossed into Kansas, running south on State Highway 81, heading through the wheat fields for Salina and Wichita.

We finally crossed the Oklahoma border in the very late afternoon and stopped just north of Blackwell on Interstate 35 at a Conoco Service Station for more fuel. While at the station I took the opportunity to check my cellphone for messages and noticed there were quite a few. They weren't for me, however, but for Alain. All of the messages, coming from voices that sounded rather urgent, basically relayed the same thing, call home "immediately". I had checked for messages two hours earlier at the last gas stop and there had been none – obviously something was up. I handed Alain my cell and watched him nervously punch in some numbers.

"I do not think this is good," Alain said. "I hate messages that say to call home immediately. It is never good news."

I knew it was really bad when I saw a tear slide down Alain's face before he even got off the phone. I had no idea what was going on, because he was talking in French; the only word I recognized was "Tout". If it had just been bad news, I would have been relieved, but it was worse than bad news: it was the worst possible news I had heard for many years. When he got off the phone, Bandido Alain sadly explained to me and Caroline that Bandido El Secretario Robert "Tout" Leger had been murdered by the Hells Angels.

"The bastards shot him right in front of his wife and kids at their country house. He had seen them coming and got in between them and his family," Alain said in a faltering voice. "You won't believe this but Tout was a Rock Machine prospect for almost seven years, not because he was a screw-up or anything. I don't think he really cared if he ever made it into the club. Tout was his own man. He was one hell of a biker. We all looked up to him and respected him."

Alain went on to explain that one assassin had fired a machine gun and the other a pistol, riddling Bandido Tout with bullets. I couldn't believe my ears. I had only known Tout for a short period of time but I felt like I lost a lifelong friend. We sat in stone silence at the gas station for what seemed like an eternity. It was a sad day for all of us – for all Bandidos. Tout was the first national chapter officer in the history of the Bandidos to be killed by another motorcycle club.

"You know, Tout died as he had lived. He was a man of courage and action, always thinking of others before himself," Alain mumbled after a long silence.

I knew it was best to give Alain some quiet time and I retreated into my own jumbled thoughts. Caroline, always with her emotions in check, just stared into her own space thinking about who knows what. I reflected on some of the Rock Machine history Bandido Tout had told me about during the brief eight months I had known him. Back in the mid 1990s Tout had been the first Rock Machine to ever venture into the United States. He had a clearly defined mission ahead of him: make contact with the Bandidos and talk to them about the Rock Machine wanting to patch over. Because Tout spoke excellent English, he had been sent to Houston to search out members of the Bandidos. As there had been no advance communication, any members of the Bandidos he could track down would have to do.

"I didn't know a soul in Texas. Nobody! But we figured I would have nothing to lose so I went," Tout had told me. "We really hated the Angels because they figured they could tell us and everybody else what to do."

Somehow a self-assured and resourceful Tout managed to locate a group of Bandidos at a bar in Houston. When he mentioned he was a member of the Rock Machine from Canada, and that he had been sent there to make contact because they wanted to become Bandidos, they told him in no uncertain terms to get lost.

"When I think about it now, that was a pretty crazy thing to do. I was fortunate not to have my ass kicked all the way back to Canada," Tout said, laughing. "We were pretty naïve to think that we were going to be received with open arms by the American Bandidos."

I was drawn back into the moment when I suddenly felt Caroline's hand on my shoulder, giving me a little nudge. Alain was already sitting on his bike.

"I think we should go now," Caroline said. "Alain looks like he's ready to hit the road."

With a heavy heart I got back on my Harley and we set out to complete the last hundred miles or so to Tulsa. We rode east and about stopped halfway, just south of a town called Pawhuska. This was the site of Biker Days, a huge annual biker party that was Oklahoma's version of Sturgis, albeit on a much smaller scale. I had promised Alain we would stop and take his picture at the actual location of the site. He had always wanted to attend the event, but had never been able to. At least now he could say he was at the place where the party was held every year.

The picture Caroline took of us will always trigger the memory of that fateful day: a red faced Bandido Alain and me, trying in vain to look like we were happy when we were clearly not. Our final hours on the road had turned out to be a horrible end to a wonderful week. But such is life: a complex tapestry of ups and downs, joys and sorrows – you simply have to take the good with the bad. We resumed our journey and got to my house just after dark on Sunday night.

Everyone took a hot shower, had a bite to eat, and went straight to bed. I fell asleep thinking about Tout and the senselessness of his death. I knew that violence, death, and tragedy sometimes were unpleasant side effects of the outlaw biker lifestyle but the brutality of what had been going on in Canada – and previously to that in Scandinavia – numbed my mind. In the United States, which has a high concentration of 1%ers, unbridled slaughter was relatively rare. As I drifted off to sleep my last waking thoughts were on the fragility of life…and my childhood. I was happy to be still among the living…

*Excerpted from *The Assimilation: Rock Machine Become Bandidos – Bikers United Against The Hells Angels* by Edward Winterhalder & Wil De Clercq, published by ECW Press (2008), ISBN 9781550228243.

Edward Winterhalder is one of the world's leading authorities on motorcycle clubs and the Harley-Davidson biker lifestyle; his books are published in multiple languages and sold all over the world. He was a member, and/or an associate, of outlaw motorcycle clubs for almost thirty years. The creator and executive producer of the *PHASS MOB*, *Biker Chicz* and *Living On The Edge* television series, Winterhalder has appeared worldwide on television networks such as Bravo, Prime, CBC, Fox, National Geographic, History Channel, Global, AB Groupe and History Television. In addition to his literary endeavors, he is a consultant to the entertainment industry for TV, feature film and DVD projects that focus on the Harley-Davidson biker lifestyle.

Wil De Clercq has worked as a freelance writer & editor, a visual artist, and in such diverse fields as demolition, the merchant marines, faux finish painting, advertising copywriting, and film and television production; he is and has been a dynamic force in the world of motorcycle journalism for more than twenty-five years.

Houston, September 1977

By Ralph "Teach" Elrod

Captain, President of the Reapers MC assisted in setting up a meeting with Ronnie Hodges, President of the Bandidos. After what had happened at Sturgis with Wheelz and the two Bandidos, I wanted to get this over with. I was nervous. Savage and I headed for Texas, I took Kate along with me. Our new chapter in Farmington, New Mexico was our first stop where we picked up one of our newer members, Little John and a prospect named Teepee.

Carlsbad, New Mexico was our next stop but only because we met some outriders and were invited to an impromptu party at which I did some acid. I'm sure that Kate did not partake but the rest of us probably did because right after mid-night, we all loaded up, including the locals, and rode out to Carlsbad Caverns National Park, to the entrance of the cavern. We left town all jacked up and sped out of town at ninety to a hundred miles an hour. Before we reached White City, the entrance to the park, a distance of about twenty miles, the locals dropped off and returned to Carlsbad. I think we frightened them. Nothing was open at White City so after a short stop, the five of us raced up the steep twisted road to the cavern itself. None of us had a speedometer so we don't know how fast we rode up the little two-lane but it was too fast. Stopping in the parking lot at the cavern entrance, Kate and I waited for a second for Savage and a minute or two for Little John and Teepee. Little John said, "Didn't you see those deer?" I hadn't really noticed them except for a couple at the bottom of the canyon. According to Little John and Teepee there was more than that. Kate said that she could have reached out and touched several of them as we raced past.

We had come to the entrance so we would be able to see the bats enter the cave at dawn. I had seen the bats leave the caverns at dusk on several occasions, and it was cool to see them spread out like smoke across the desert. I had always heard that the returning of the bats was really special, so I had convinced everyone we should see it, few people ever got up early enough to witness a million bats return to their sleeping quarters. The bats fold their wings and drop from out of the sky only opening their wings about a foot above the asphalt walkway. The wings operated like a parachute and the sound of the wings popping as they caught air was happening all around us. It was almost impossible to see the bats as they fell at a high speed, once the wings popped full of air, the bats shot forward at a ninety degree angle into the cave's darkness.

Laying and sitting on the concrete benches, we were watching as the last of the little black dots popped and shot into the darkness, it was relaxing and our buzz was gone when a Ranger, whom I'm sure was an ex-drill sergeant before he joined the Park Service, came marching down the trail and when he spotted us, he spat out orders, "Up, Up, Up! We all hopped right up and started talking to our new, personal guide. After three hours of underworld wonders we exited by way of the elevator.

Walking out of the Visitors Center into the bright New Mexico sun was almost blinding, but we still could see a crowd gathered around our motorcycles! That could be good or bad. Getting a few yards closer we could see that the six admirers of our bikes were all Bandidos. I'm sure our outrider friends of the night before had alerted the Bandidos. That's known as home turf advantage, we all have it to one degree or another. We were on their turf, and we expected this from time to time on the long trip into the heart of the Bandidos nation. As we approached, they turned to face us, one of the Bandidos yelled as he turned, "Where's Harpo?"

Knucklehead Joe was a friend who had spent time in Salt Lake City with some other Bandidos. Harpo and Knucklehead Joe had become close friends, it was good to see friends so far from anywhere. We smoked a bowl or two and then they went back home. It showed class that they had ridden from El Paso to say hello. They also were keeping a close eye on their turf. All good. We turned east toward Monahan's, Texas, my home town. It's not far from the caverns, only about a hundred and twenty miles, over between Odessa and Pecos. A desolate part of the country, oil country.

We stayed at my aunt and uncle's place, we didn't cause quite the same stir as the first time the club was there. My aunt really enjoyed taking a ride behind me on my motorcycle so much so that she bought herself a 175cc Honda after we left. She loved that little Honda and rode it all over Monahan's for about a year. Next her plans were for a Honda 350cc. Her family found out that she was thinking about stepping up to a bigger bike so they called a family meeting to ask her to stop riding altogether, and of course she did. That woman worked herself into an early grave for her husband and children but when she found something just for her enjoyment they all joined together to stop her from her personal fun. I have always found it strange how Americans are often really against anything that is different. Different does not translate to bad or wrong.

The next stop was San Angelo, cool town at the time. We went to a real Texas honky-tonk, where they only serve beer and the lights stay on bright all night, nothing sneaky allowed, I suppose. After that, Kate and I went skinny dipping in the city lake, the water was warm. We rode on the next day to just outside Austin, to Lake Travis where we found that the water was also very warm. Very different than the reservoirs we were used to in our part of the country. The Reapers were having their Labor Day run there at Lake Travis. Bobby Joe, Johnny and Frog all rode down for the run. Frog got separated from his riding partners and as he was studying his map, a pack of forty Bandidos pulled up next to him on the side of the road and the leader of the pack said, "Follow us prospect, we know where the party is." He didn't fall in and managed to find his way to the party, but not theirs.

Somewhere out in West Texas the four of us had stopped at a rest area and were enjoying the shade over a table we were sitting on. A Bandidos member from Washington stopped. I knew him from West Yellowstone, Bulldog's friends from Tacoma. We talked for a short time until two more Bandidos pulled up on their bikes and he drove on. The two on motorcycles had never met any Barons before. I broke out this really good pot that Savage and I had been smoking all the way from home. When we pulled away, the two Bandidos were lying on their sides on the table and were slowly waving good bye to us with big smiles on their faces.

The Bandidos had their Labor Day run just five miles down the road on Lake Travis. Knucklehead Joe stopped at the Reapers camp and partied it up with Johnny and invited him to come up to their camp. Johnny declined. With odds of 500 to 1, the chances of one guy not liking him were too great for even Johnny to ignore. After the week-end, Johnny, Bobby Joe and Frog went back home while Savage, Little John, Teepee, Kate and I rode to Teepee's parents place in Austin where the Texas Highway Patrol caught up to me with a message from my family in Tucson. My father had a heart attack.

Kate and I left the bike in Austin in Teepee's parent's garage. The two of us caught a jet for Tucson that day. We stayed in Tucson until dad was somewhat out of danger. That was my first experience with the miracles that is modern medicine. Dad recovered and later had a triple by-pass operation. He was just too mean to die. After seven or eight days we prepared to fly back to Austin, Texas.

The flight was to leave at 10:00 pm so we got dropped off at 9:00 pm at the front door of the Continental terminal. Before takeoff we were told that there was a problem with the plane. After waiting two hours until mid-night, we finally left for Austin. When we were safely landed in El Paso, our first stop, the pilot announced the plane was still screwed up so we were to transfer to another. The first thing everyone noticed about our new plane was that it was old, not new! Everyone was nervous as the plane careened down the runway and just as we were starting to lift off, the pilot shut it down and pushed hard on the brakes. With a chuckle, the pilot announced, "You're not going to believe this but the generator just went out on this plane." No one else thought it was funny when we returned to the gate and boarded our third plane in the El Paso airport. Making it to Austin that morning I came close to swearing off flying. Getting to the bike we were back in our element and on the road to Houston.

Savage had been in an accident on the Houston freeway at rush hour, a hit and run. The bike was all fucked up but Captain had two huge machine shops that usually built things for the oil industry and they were very busy, but work on Savage's bike was given priority. When Kate and I arrived, Savage was riding again and his bike looked great. Captain and his wife, Carol Ann took us out to a Greek restaurant on the water front on the Houston bay. Great food and a good time.

Checking out Houston one afternoon while Captain was at work, we found Telegraph Road. Lots of bars, we found one with a beer drinking buffalo penned up behind the joint. The buffalo liked long neck bottles of Lone Star, so we bought a six pack and went out back to have a few beers with the beast. The bartender warned us as we went out the door, "Don't give him any whiskey! He gets mean on whiskey." We didn't give him anything but beer. What was really strange about the buffalo was the fact that both horns turned down not up. He was an expert with those long neck bottles, he would take the bottle from your hand by placing his mouth over the neck, tipping his huge head back, he drained each bottle in very quick succession. After giving him four we started back for the bar but he started coming over the broken down gate. I don't know if the buffalo knew about 99 bottles of beer on the wall, but he sure knew that there were six bottles in a six pack. We hurriedly fed him the other two and moved on.

    Our next stop was much different. It was the middle of the afternoon when we pulled into a bar along Telegraph Road, a non-descript place. I have no idea why we stopped, we were the only customers except for a couple and three guys here and there in the bar. We were shooting pool and drinking a few beers, no big deal. Teepee brought my attention to a man sitting at a booth table alone with a pistol in his hand under the table. He was watching our every move so I went over and sat down across from him. I did not have a gun. Not knowing what was going on I opened the conversation with a challenge. Telling him that he could end up with that pistol shoved up his ass. That opened up the conversation, and then he motioned another loner at the bar to come over. I wasn't worried, my brothers were watching me. The newcomer sat across from me and next to the guy with the pistol, who was no longer pointing it at my gut. The newcomer turned out to be a police detective and he told me that in this bar about a year before, two Bandidos were in the bathroom talking to a undercover narc, who was selling them something they should not have been buying. He fucked up and they stomped him and took the money and the drugs. Got what he deserved but then he made a stupid decision. The undercover cop got up from the floor and got his pistol from his ankle holster. With the gun in his hand he rushed out of the toilet waving the weapon as he came forward with his beaten face, he looked very scary. Two harness cops who were walking their beat came through the front door just at that moment. They both saw the undercover cop come rushing out of toilet with the gun in his hand. They both drew their pistols and blew him away. The two Bandidos were arrested and ended up going to prison for life. Well, we decided we didn't care to stay any longer, and as we rode on I noticed a police tail so we split up and lost them and then went back to Captains house and waited for him to get off work.

Captain went all out and threw us a Texas Bar-B-Que. The T-bones were thick and delicious with all the trimmings, and the beer was ice cold. We had all over eaten and were full and satisfied when Ronnie Hodges, National President of the Bandidos joined the gathering. Ronnie brought along his Sergeant of Arms, he was big and quiet! Ronnie was a man whom I liked, he was always straight with me and this would be no different. Ronnie and I went out back next to the pool and he ate while we talked. The very first thing Ronnie said when we were alone was, "I've already told all the chapters that we will no longer pull patches because of the color of the patches." I was stunned when he spoke, this was and is a big deal. I was totally relieved. Ronnie was a visionary Bandidos leader who made a big mark on the Bandidos Nation. With the reason we came down to Texas having been settled I relaxed and we visited long into the darkness of the night. I liked Ronnie, when he died I was in federal prison. Willie, a former Bandidos chapter president from Washington came to me to inform me of Ronnie's death. That was 1993 and I will always remember Willy coming to my bunk and saying, "I know you and Ronnie are friends' so I thought you should know he died today." I was moved and sorry to see him go. Nice of Willy to inform me.

Our trip home was uneventful, the only thing I remember was a pit stop out in the Middle West Texas. Van Horn was somewhere near. While we were stopped, Savage was collecting small cacti for his cactus garden back in Utah. Kate and I were next to the motorcycles while Savage and his helpers Little John and Teepee were walking around looking for the correct cactus. Savage stored them in a helmet hanging from his sissy bar. Perfect timing, a Texas Highway Patrol car pulled up. The two patrolmen in the car ask if the Puma folding knife, on my belt, was a locking blade knife. It was and it is considered a fighting knife and as such is illegal in Texas. We were told to put our knives into our saddle bags. The next words out of his mouth were classic, "The border is two hundred miles, that way. Don't waste any time getting there." We didn't have to be told twice. We were in Farmington, New Mexico the next day and in Salt Lake City the day after that.

Kate had loved the trip to Texas. She was a doctors daughter with a I.Q. about half again as high as mine but the spontaneity and freedom of our lifestyle seemed to help make her fall for me. She was probably my first real love. She taught me a lot about women. How to understand and treat them with the respect they are due. Also how to love them and where the buttons are that turns them on. If my dad had used that script when he gave me "The Talk", my life would have been very different and so would have been the lives of several women in my early life. Kate was good for me.

*Excerpted from *Kick Start* by Ralph "Teach" Elrod (2013), ISBN 9781460221877.

The "70's" were wild and a little crazy, we were making the rules up as we went along. After over 44 years as a member of the Barons MC, I find those early years from "69" through "80" shaped my values and philosophy. I spent the 60's getting educated on a football scholarship at Boise. After four years of teaching elementary school, my wife took the kids and left. My fifth year as a teacher, I was also a Baron, in fact I was Road Captain of the Barons MC and principal of Wolf Creek Elementary School at the same time. My real education began at the end of that school year.

I learned how to take a motorcycle apart and put it back together, sometimes on the side of the road. I learned about the men who rode them, really rode them. I listened to the older riders, there weren't many. An old retired Galloping Goose gave me my nick name, "Teach". I was schooled by Kenny Means, an honorary Monk and later the founder of The Righteous Ones MC. I rode my "57" ridged framed, Panhead chopper all over the west. I met and became friends with many different clubs. Most of those ties still hold today. I became President of the Barons MC in 1972 and held that office for seven years. The extended family of clubs, men and women that we have built up over the decades is real and extensive, and so my education continues.

After being accused of three or four murders by the Salt Lake City newspapers and suspicion on the part of the cops, I moved to Montana, where I still live in the cabin I built. They always found the real killers, but they were too quick to look at me, so I left town. I've been married to my wife Jodi for nearly thirty years, truly the love of my life. She has stuck with me through the years. These days I have great grand children and I'm still active in the Barons as a Nomad. Sharing the stories and history of the beginnings of the clubs and their relationships with each other makes me feel like I am still teaching. I hope to keep riding for another thirty years. Nomader what!

Mayhem In The Midlands

By Tony Thompson

May 14, 1986

Daniel "Snake Dog" Boone had been a full member of the Warwickshire-based Pagans MC for a little less than a month when he got his first opportunity to kill for his club.

It had taken more than a year and a half of fierce dedication and determination for the softly spoken twenty-one-year-old to earn the right to wear the club patch on his back, and the experience had affected him deeply on many levels. Boone had been drinking beer and riding motorcycles long before it was legal for him to do either so it came as no surprise to anyone when, after leaving school and working a series of menial jobs, he started hanging out in biker bars and making friends with members of the local MCCs. Although he enjoyed the social side enormously, he always felt there was some-thing missing. For Boone, motorcycles were never just a hobby, they were a way of life and he wanted to be with others who shared that same level of passion. He found them in the MC scene.

An MC is a band of brothers like no other. During his eighteen months as a prospect, Boone had spent more time with club members than with his friends or family or even his girlfriend. The Pagans lived in each other's pockets, rode, fought, and fucked side by side. When Boone finally got his full patch, it was as though all his birthdays had arrived at once. The bonds between him and his fellow club members were deep, powerful and utterly intoxicating. The love, loyalty and respect they all felt for one another meant that each and every one of them would be willing to do anything for the good of the club. Even take a life.

Brandishing a sawed-off 12-gauge shotgun, Boone joined a five-strong, early morning raiding party as it smashed its way into the home of a leading figure from a rival MC that was threatening to destroy the Pagans. The men stormed up the cluttered staircase and made their way to the master bedroom where they found their prey sound asleep, alongside his girlfriend.

The terrified woman was dragged off the mattress, thrown into a corner of the room, gagged and then covered with the quilt so she would not have to witness the events that were to follow. While three of the team immobilized their target against the headboard, Boone forced the barrel of the gun deep into the man's mouth and began to squeeze the trigger.

The trouble had started a week or so earlier when the club had learned that a man living on the edge of its territory had become a prospect for their despised rivals, the Leicestershire-based Ratae MC. Maintaining absolute control over territory is the first order of business for all MC clubs, but also one of the greatest challenges. Each weekend and as often as possible during the week, the Pagans would gather together and try to get around as much of their turf as possible, partly to remind people that they were in charge but also to give potential recruits the opportunity to approach them.

A favored watering hole was a lively Irish bar called O'Malleys in Rugby, a few miles from the Leicestershire border. But with so much other ground to cover—more than 750 square miles—and none of their 30 or so members living close to Rugby, it simply wasn't practical for the Pagans to drink there more than once in a blue moon.

The Ratae, who had already expanded to the north and east by forging close links with bikers in other countries, were quick to sense an opportunity and started hanging out in the bar themselves.

It was while the Ratae were drinking in O'Malleys that they happened across a local biker who expressed an interest in becoming part of the MC scene. After letting him hang around with them for a while and checking into his background, the gang offered him the chance to become a prospect, an invitation he eagerly accepted.

Once Boone and the rest of the Pagans learned of this their objection was a simple one: if the man wanted to join the Ratae, he would have to move to Leicestershire. As a resident of Warwickshire with an interest in MCs, he should have approached the Pagans in the first instance (though he had now blown his chances of ever being accepted by them). His counterargument was equally simple: he never saw the Pagans in his area, but the Ratae were there regularly so he assumed the town belonged to them.

In truth, the prospect was being used as a pawn. The Ratae knew full well that O'Malleys was outside their turf and wanted to see how far the Warwickshire gang were willing to go to defend it. Anyone could make a threat, but did the Pagans have the balls to follow through? So far as Boone and the rest of the Pagans were concerned, their credibility was on the line, as was their place as the dominant MC in Warwickshire. The Ratae had left them no choice: they would have to take it to the next level.

Becoming a fully patched member of an MC is a lengthy and involved process that is the same for clubs all over the world. It is made deliberately difficult and unpalatable, partly to weed out the unsuitable and ensure full commitment to the lifestyle, but also to prevent undercover law enforcement officials from gaining access to a club in all but the most extreme circumstances.

The road to a full patch begins as an official "hangaround" (a prospective member who "hangs around" in order to become familiar to the club). To attain this status a biker might typically have met several members of a club through drinking at their regular bar, attending rallies or even being a guest of another hangaround at the clubhouse.

Compared to what follows, the hangaround stage is something of a honeymoon period. The club has no real claim on the potential recruit and cannot call on him to take part in anything more than the most rudimentary activities. Likewise, while the hangaround is able to attend certain club events and literally hang around in the clubhouse in order to get to know all the members of a chapter (and vice versa), they have no official association with the club.

It is at this stage that clubs are particularly on the lookout for those attempting to join with a specific agenda in mind. There have been countless cases of bikers who have been bullied or harassed in some way and decided to get their own back by trying to join an MC. They figure that once they are in they can take advantage of the "one in, all in" rule to drag an entire chapter into what is essentially a personal conflict. Such antics are deeply frowned upon: the rule is that if something develops while you are in the club, you will receive full backup. But anything that happens before you join is baggage that you must leave behind.

Some hangarounds have no intention of taking things further, others are eager to become more deeply involved. In both cases the only rule they have to abide by is that you can only be a hangaround with one club at a time. It is the first hint at the level of loyalty and commitment that is required to make it into an MC.

The hangaround stage typically lasts anywhere from a few weeks to a few months. Sometimes it becomes obvious to those in the club that someone isn't made of the right stuff to progress. At other times, the bikers themselves, having gotten a better view of what is actually involved, change their minds and withdraw.

To reach the next stage of membership—prospect—requires the sponsorship of a full-patch holder who remains responsible for the newcomer until he receives a full patch of his own. Bringing high-quality recruits to the attention of the club can enhance the status of a member, but if anything goes wrong—for example, the member turns out to be an undercover police officer—then the sponsor is likely to be severely punished. Or this reason, prospects are usually subjected to stringent background checks to ensure they are exactly who they say they are. To become an official prospect for the Mongols, for example, a candidate is required to fill in a three-page application form and provide his Social Security number, access to education and employment records, telephone numbers for relatives, hard copies of tax receipts for five years and, of course, a valid driver's license.

Occasionally there are prospects who rub some existing members the wrong way, but this rarely happens. The truly obnoxious recruits tend to fall at the first hurdle of the hangaround stage. Those who make the cut to prospect usually adapt in order to fit in with the club, often ending up as quite different people by the time they gain their full patch. This blending in with the brotherhood is one of the things that makes the bond between members of an MC so strong.

Most clubs distinguish prospects by only letting them wear the bottom rocker of their colors along with an MC patch, others have special "probationary member" jackets for prospects to wear. Prospects have no identity other than their lowly rank and having a separate dress code makes them all the more easy to identify. A patch holder rarely refers to a prospect by name. Instead it is "Get me a beer, prospect," or "Prospect, drive my old lady home."

As a prospect you are basically a slave and to all intents and purposes you become the property of your club. Whenever a full-patch member tells you to do something, it is an order that you have to obey without question. There is not much a full-patch member can't tell a prospect to do, so prospects find themselves getting involved in everything from stealing cycles and moving drugs to cleaning toilets at the clubhouse and polishing endless amounts of chrome. Some members have their prospects doing push-ups in the gutter simply to dominate them, others force them to take part in crazy stunts, like walking across hot coals during club parties.

For every ten prospects who sign up, on average around three will make the cut. Like most MCs, the Pagans always believed the credo that the patch does not make the man, rather the man has to make the patch. "You take a good man and bring him into the club in order to make the club better, Snake Dog," the club president, Caz, had told Boone. "It doesn't work the other way around. You can't become a prospect and then become a member and then become a better man. That's not what we're looking for at all."

Even in the case of a born natural, there is practically no way to avoid the prospect stage. Those who have been full- patch members of other clubs and left in "good standing" are still required to prospect for whatever new club they want to join, though in such cases they may end up getting their patches relatively quickly. One Pagan, Rabbi, had received his own patch in less than six months having been a full member of an MC called The Filthy Few a short time before. Boone had to wait a year and a half for his.

For a prospect to become a full member, the whole chapter has to be 100 percent in favor. Depending on the reasons put forward, a single dissenting vote may either mean the prospect is out of the club completely or simply has to continue his life of servitude for a few more weeks or months until another vote comes around.

In any MC, the moment a prospect receives his full set of patches is a high point of his biking life and something he will never forget, despite the fact that there is little in the way of an actual ceremony involved. After getting his, Boone spent the rest of the evening and most of the next day just riding around Warwickshire, flying his patches left, right and center, wanting to be seen by as many people as possible. The feeling of pride and satisfaction was so intense it almost made him giddy. All the sacrifices and hard work he had put in over the preceding eighteen months had finally paid off and he had won the ultimate prize. He knew there and then that his life going forward would never be the same.

As a full member, the club becomes your second skin. Each member is permanently on call. If other members are in trouble or need assistance, you are there for them. And between the weekly meetings known as "church" and group events known as "runs," you invariably have something going on that includes club members. Rarely a day goes by when you do not see one of your club mates for some reason or other.

The club is your extended family. The men become your brothers and their wives and girlfriends become your sisters. Their children will be friends with your own children. Some of the younger, single members share houses together. In every MC, if you cut one member, they all bleed.

Hence when, in the late spring of 1986, the Pagans heard that a Ratae prospect was regularly drinking at O'Malleys while brazenly wearing his patches, it was bound to lead to trouble. The more the prospect flew his colors within the Pagans' territory, the weaker their claim on the area. A series of increasingly threatening warnings failed to have any effect, so a decision was made to visit the new recruit in person and take his patches by force.

As it turned out, little actual force was needed. When the group of Pagans arrived at the prospect's door the following day, he offered no resistance. He knew exactly why they were there and exactly what they wanted. He handed over his patches without a single punch being thrown.

The Pagans returned to their clubhouse and waited for the Ratae to make their next move. Tradition dictated that their sergeant at arms would contact his opposite number in the Pagans and arrange a meeting. As separate MCs in separate areas, the proceedings would take place in an atmosphere of mutual respect. Ground rules would be laid out: typically the Ratae would agree not to have any members in Warwickshire and the Pagans would agree not to expand into Ratae territory.

But the men from Leicester had other ideas. Two nights after the prospect's patches were taken, a team of Ratae burst into the Warwickshire home where a popular Pagan named Rocky Jived with his wife. After pounding the couple into submission with fists, heavy boots and baseball bats, the Ratae dragged Rocky over to a corner of the room and forced him to watch while his wife was repeatedly and horribly brutalized right in front of him. He was then struck on the head several times with a ball-peen hammer so hard that part of his skull fractured and caved in. His attackers then fled into the night, leaving him for dead.

The attack had taken place in the early hours of the morning and most of the Pagans did not learn about it until much later in the day. They rushed to the George Eliot Hospital and learned that Rocky was in a critical condition, possibly suffering brain damage, and slipping in and out of a coma. His wife was also in the hospital being treated for various injuries of her own. Boone was particularly affected by the attack. Although he felt close to all the Pagans, Rocky, a five-year veteran of the club, had been his personal sponsor and the bond between the two of them had been particularly strong. In the waiting room, the corridors and the waiting room, the corridors and the parking lot, all the talk between Boone and the other Pagans centered on one topic: revenge.

The vicious attack made it obvious to the Pagans that the situation wasn't going to resolve itself without more blood being spilled. There had been plenty of incidents of interclub conflicts in the preceding years but this was something far more serious. Instead of the usual drunken Saturday-night fight, they were truly at war. Fully aware of the level of violence the Ratae had already employed, no one could escape the fact that there was every possibility that some of them might lose their lives, or find themselves being forced to take the lives of others.

Club president Caz called an emergency meeting that same evening to discuss their options and one of the members, a tall, heavyset man who had been around for longer than anyone could recall, stood up and said that he was going to leave. "Listen guys, I can't guarantee that I'm going to be there for you. I haven't got the stomach for this. It's just not for me."

He took off his patches and carefully placed them on the center of the table in front of him and then walked out of the room. No one ever saw him again. Caz quickly got back to the matter at hand.

A car had been spotted leaving the scene of the attack and, thanks to an associate working at the Department of Motor Vehicles the Pagans were able to match the license plate to an address. Early the following morning five full-patch members—Boone, Rabbi, Link, Dozer and Tank—

met up at the clubhouse, armed themselves with a variety of weapons and headed out into enemy territory.

The small, semidetached house was just a few miles into Leicestershire. After double-checking that they had the right target—the car used to trace the address was parked in the driveway—the men hovered about, unsure of the best way to get into the building, until Rabbi, tall and ruggedly handsome with a winning smile, simply kicked open the front door and led the charge upstairs.

The barrel of the gun was so deep inside the mouth of the Ratae that it was making the man gag. All Boone had to do was keep squeezing the trigger and it would all be over. But something was holding him back.

Murder had been in his heart throughout the journey to the man's house. His rage about what had happened to his friend and fellow Pagan was driving him on: more than anything in the world he wanted the man dead and gone. But at the same time, Rocky was still alive. Only just, but still alive. And that was getting in the way. Taking a life in return for having put someone in a coma just didn't seem to be the right thing to do. Boone didn't want to be the one to push things to the next level because of the potential repercussions.

He pulled the shotgun from the man's mouth and used the butt of it to club his victim across the side of the head. Then, without any words being exchanged between them, Boone and the other Pagans repositioned the man on the floor be- side his bed with his left arm stretched out, palm downward, in front of him.

Calmly and methodically, deaf to the screams of agony that echoed around them, Boone and the others used a heavy claw hammer to break each and every bone in the Ratae's hand. They finished him off by plunging a hunting knife through the back of his palm, pinning him to the floorboards while they made good their escape.

During the journey back, Boone was bitterly disappointed and more than a little frustrated about what had taken place. He'd been given a golden opportunity to kill one of the enemy to avenge the attack on his friend and he had failed to follow through. He just couldn't be sure if he had done the right thing.

There was precious little time to dwell on such issues as the Ratae were certain to respond with escalating force. Back in their clubhouse, a two-storied property in Leamington Spa, the Pagans began to prepare fortifications, boarding up the windows, sealing the door frames and sinking sharpened metal spikes throughout the back garden that would impale anyone who attempted to jump the wall. The work went on until the early afternoon and once it was complete, there was nothing to do but sit back and wait for the Ratae to make their next move.

*Excerpted from *Outlaws: One Man's Rise Through The Savage World Of Renegade Bikers, Hell's Angels And Global Crime* by Tony Thompson (2013), ISBN 9780142422601.

Tony Thompson is the bestselling author of *Reefer Man*, *Gangs*, and *Gangland Britain*. He has twice been nominated for the prestigious Crime Writer's Association Gold Dagger Award for nonfiction. He lives in the United Kingdom.

Church

By Peter Edwards

Kill 'em all, let God sort it out.
Sign in Wayne (Weiner) Kellestine's window

Jamie (Goldberg) Flanz didn't suspect a thing when the surveillance car slipped behind his luxury sport utility vehicle as he drove out of Keswick, north of Toronto. With him in the grey Infiniti FX3 was Paul (Big Paul) Sinopoli, a gargantuan full-patch member of the Bandidos Motorcycle Club, and when Big Paul was around, it was hard to notice anything or anybody else, since he all but blocked out the sun.

Flanz had just been a prospect member of the Bandidos, the lowest rung on the club's ladder, for six months. His lowly status meant he was required to be on call for round-the-clock errands like fetching hamburgers and cigarettes or chauffeuring full members like Big Paul. Prospective members like Flanz generally performed such grunt work without complaint, in hopes that they too would someday be allowed to wear a "Fat Mexican" patch on their backs to announce that they were full members in the second-largest motorcycle club in the world, behind only the Hells Angels.

Given their difference in rank, it made sense that Flanz had the chore of driving Big Paul to the emergency club meeting at Wayne (Weiner) Kellestine's barn in tiny Iona Station (population 100) in rural southwestern Ontario on the evening of Friday, April 7, 2006. Club meetings were called "church," "holy night," "the barbecue" or "dinner," and attendance at this particular gathering was mandatory, much to Big Paul's chagrin.

Weiner Kellestine's barn was a couple hours' drive from the Greater Toronto Area, where most chapter members lived, and Big Paul was only attending because senior members had made it clear that if he didn't, he would likely be kicked out of the club.

The York Regional Police surveillance team had been quietly tailing Flanz and Big Paul for almost four months, since shortly after a man walking his dogs in neighbouring Durham Region on December 8, found the body of a small black male bound, gagged and badly burned in a forested area near the York-Durham Region Line. The grisly corpse was all that remained of small-time drug dealer Shawn Douse. The reason Flanz and Big Paul were on the police radar was a simple one: the last time Douse was seen alive, he was stepping out of a cab late on the night of Saturday, December 2, to attend a party at a townhouse in Keswick owned by Flanz.

In many respects, Goldberg Flanz seemed an unlikely target for a police surveillance crew probing a particularly grubby and violent murder. With his shaved head, goatee, pirate-styled hooped earring and muscled-up football lineman's physique, Flanz looked intimidating enough. However, if you stopped to look into his eyes, the tough-guy effect quickly evaporated. Once you saw his smile and his eyes, his bruiserish appearance seemed nothing more than a carefully constructed persona, much like the performance of his namesake, the professional wrestler Goldberg. He was only playing tough.

Flanz was the rare Toronto-area outlaw biker who didn't have blue-collar roots or a trade that involved soiling his hands. In real life, he had far more money and social status than his biker mentor, Big Paul. Flanz's father, Leonard, was a senior partner in a prestigious Montreal law firm, specializing in insolvency cases, while Goldberg ran a small computer consulting business that provided on-site technical support to companies. While most of the Ontario Bandidos didn't qualify for credit cards and lived on the brink of having their cellphones cut off, Goldberg owned a couple of properties, one for his real family and another as a hangout for his Bandido friends. His "Goldberg" nickname was a not-so-subtle reminder that he was Jewish, which also made him an odd fit in his circle of friends in the outlaw biker work. It was hard to think of any other Jews in Canada's outlaw biker world, but there were hardcore anti-Semites, including the man they were going to visit that night, Weiner Kellestine, who once ran a gang called the Holocaust.

Weiner Kellestine was under two lifetime weapons bans, but remained an enthusiastic collector of Nazi memorabilia and military weapons, including machine guns, pistols, bayonets, knives and explosives. He encouraged rumours that he was a biker assassin by signing his name with lightning bolts resembling the insignia of Adolf Hitler's Schutzstaffel, the Nazi murder squad more commonly referred to as the SS. Lest that not be unsettling enough, Kellestine surrounded himself with skinhead white supremacists and once cut a massive swastika onto his farm field with a scythe. He ran a business called Triple K Securities, a not-so-subtle nod to the initials of the Ku Klux Klan. Triple K offered "complete electronic privacy," "telephone taps," electronic sweeps for hidden recording devices and "discreet professional service." When he gave Goldberg a business card, Kellestine wrote "SS" on the back with his phone number.

Many members of the Bandidos are considered by police to be criminals, but there was no sound business purpose for Flanz to be cozying up to the Bandidos. Truth be told, the Toronto Bandidos may have had the ambition, but most of the profitable crime was being committed by other groups, who worked hard at being criminals. Part of Goldberg Flanz's appeal to the Toronto-area Bandidos was that they could borrow money from him. The attraction the Bandidos held for Goldberg was harder to define. He might be a whiz with computers and have solid business sense, but he saw himself as more complex than that, and something about the dangerous image of an outlaw motorcycle club appealed to him in a way he couldn't fully understand.

Aside from Kellestine, most of Goldberg Flanz's Greater Toronto Area biker buddies didn't have a problem with the fact that he was a Jew. They might have cringed, however, had they read his profile in an Internet chat room, where he looked for love under the code name BigDaddyRogue. At the very least they would have teased him mercilessly, had they read how he wrote, using horrible grammar and spelling: "If you are stong [sic] enough to love you have more strength then most. I have that strength, the will, and the confidence to give what I expect in return. IM a diehard romantic who beleives in giving all of HImself when he finds that somone special." He went on to describe himself as "a strong Man" who was searching "for something most seem to have forsaken ... true love." He didn't exactly describe himself as an outlaw biker, but came close, writing, "This Man comes with a Harley." He also said in the online profile that he believed in happy endings, writing of himself, "He is a romantic diehard who still believes in finding His fairy tale."

There was no record of his friend and mentor Big Paul Sinopoli also being a diehard romantic, unless one counted an enthusiastic love affair with large plates of food and biker brotherhood. Big Paul was thirty years old, but still lived with his folks in a basement apartment of their ranch-style home, set among a thicket of trees in Jacksons Point, north of Toronto.

No one could remember Big Paul ever having a long-standing girlfriend, or any friends at all, for that matter, apart from other bikers. He was chummy with a few local Hells Angels, but kept this quiet, as Bandidos and Hells Angels were supposed to be mortal enemies. A one-time security guard and salesman at a sporting goods store, Big Paul dabbled in selling drugs, but didn't make enough money at it to move out into a place of his own. Those who knew him appreciated his quick, easy sense of humour and apparent absence of ego. Those qualities made his bulk less threatening, and some women who knew him called him "the big teddy bear." Once, he pointed to a black Bandidos T-shirt that was tightly stretched across his abdomen, smiled broadly and asked biker cops who were standing nearby, "Does this make me look fat?"

Privately, Big Paul was extremely insecure about his massive weight, estimated at somewhere on the hefty side of four hundred pounds. He had been teased about it since his childhood, when he emigrated to Canada from his birthplace of Argentina. He had occasionally talked wistfully about returning to South America to rediscover his roots, but his more immediate concern was shedding a couple of hundred pounds to stave off what seemed to be an inevitable heart attack. Although Big Paul was a full member of an outlaw motorcycle club, he wasn't particularly interested in motorcycles, and still hadn't paid off his second-hand Harley-Davidson. He was rarely seen on it, since it was in no better shape than Big Paul. Perhaps he also knew he would look like a bear in the circus riding it.

While Big Paul didn't love motorcycles, he revelled in his version of the biker lifestyle, which offered massive men like himself the prospect of respect, in addition to ridiculous nicknames like "Tiny" rather than the "Fatso" or "Hey you" they might hear in the outside world. A Bandidos patch had a way of covering over some pretty glaring imperfections. As fellow club member Glenn (Wrongway) Atkinson noted, "How many guys that weigh four hundred pounds get laid that often?"

That evening, Goldberg Flanz, Big Paul and the police surveillance team snaked their way south down Highway 404, west on Highway 407, and then onto Highway 401. When the Infiniti pulled close to the town of Milton, northwest of Toronto, the York Regional officers peeled off, leaving the pursuit to a team of five officers from neighbouring Durham Region. Those officers were in a minivan and tow trucks and took turns travelling in front of and behind the Infiniti, making them hard for the bikers to pick out, even if they had been looking.

The surveillance team lost sight of the Infiniti for almost half an hour, before finding it again at an Esso station just west of Woodstock at 9: 30 p.m. The bikers were none the wiser, and when the officers spotted Goldberg once again, he was talking with two other men. A police officer pumped gas into his tank nearby as the two men got into a silver Volkswagen Golf. Flanz didn't bother to fill his tank as he also drove away. The Volkswagen was already familiar to the Durham Region officers working on Project Douse, and they knew it was registered to Luis Manny (Chopper, Porkchop) Raposo, a full-patch member of the Toronto chapter of the Bandidos, who grandly called themselves the No Surrender Crew. Chopper was with another man they would later learn was Giovanni (John, Boxer) Muscedere, Canadian president of the Bandidos Motorcycle Club.

Chopper Raposo was a different sort of biker than Big Paul or Goldberg Flanz. Even though he was considerably smaller than the other two men, his eyes could take on a glassy, crazed quality, and at those times he looked like a man who would shoot first, and often. Chopper Raposo could be painfully polite and respectful, especially on the phone, but whenever he was photographed in biker social settings, he always seemed to be grinning dangerously and giving someone the finger.

It was a hard-edged image for a forty-one-year-old who still lived at home with his parents, in the upper floor of their brick home in Toronto's Kensington Market area. With its big-screen television, glass chandelier, full bathroom and kitchen, Chopper's place seemed like a tony urban loft, and it didn't hurt things that his parents paid for his motorcycle insurance as well. Chopper was a good-looking man, and there had been a number of women in his life, but none rivalled his mother for strength or love, although no one would dare call Chopper Raposo a momma's boy.

Raposo held the rank of el secretario, or secretary-treasurer, of the club's Toronto chapter, the only full chapter of the Bandidos in Canada. Despite his druggy demeanour, there was no doubt that he took Bandido club business extremely seriously and personally. That night, his briefcase contained club paperwork, including a membership list with the nicknames of all of the No Surrender Crew, as well as "Taz" and "D," referring to Michael Sandham and Dwight Mushey of Winnipeg. There was also a chart showing who owed what in terms of club dues, and a printout of an insulting email he had recently received from Taz Sandham, president of the probationary Winnipeg Bandidos chapter. Also in Chopper's briefcase was a loaded sawed-off shotgun, which looked like a pirate's oversized pistol. Club rules forbade such weapons at "church" meetings, but some instinct told Chopper he was justified in carrying hidden and deadly firepower this night.

Boxer Muscedere had agreed for the meeting to be held at Kellestine's barn, even though it was an inconvenient drive for the Torontonians. The No Surrender Crew didn't have a clubhouse to call their own, and Kellestine had pushed hard for the meeting to be held in his barn.

Boxer and Kellestine had been friends for decades, and Boxer was loyal to a fault where his friends were concerned. In Boxer's world view, Kellestine was his brother, warts and all, and nothing trumped brotherhood. Boxer could sense Kellestine was tense about something, but didn't seem too concerned. Kellestine was often tense about something. Unlike Chopper Raposo, Boxer went unarmed to the farm that night.

*Excerpted from *The Bandido Massacre* by Peter Edwards. © 2010 by Peter Edwards. Published by HarperCollins Publishers Ltd. All rights reserved. ISBN 9781554680443.

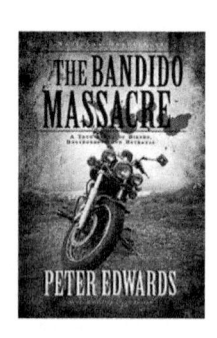

Peter Edwards is the author of eleven non-fiction books, most of which have been national bestsellers. He has also written for *The Toronto Star* for twenty-seven years, specializing in organized crime and justice issues. His most recent book is *Unrepentant: The Strange and (sometimes) Terrible Life of Lorne Campbell, Satan's Choice and Hells Angels Biker*, (Random House) which was published in the United Kingdom as *Satan's Choice: My Life as a Hard Core Biker with Satan's Choice and Hells Angels* (Sidgwick & Jackson).

The Bandido Massacre was reprinted in German by Statt Verlag and won the Hamilton Literary Award for non-fiction. Other books include *One Dead Indian: The Premier, the Police and the Ipperwash Crisis* (McClelland & Stewart), which became a Gemini-award-winning movie on CTV and won Edwards an eagle feather from the Union of Ontario Indians. *The Encyclopedia of Canadian Organized Crime* (McClelland & Stewart, with Michel Auger), has been in print for almost a decade. A historical work, *Delusion: The True Story of Victorian Superspy Henri Le Caron* (Key-Porter Books) was published in Britain under the title *The*

Infiltrator: Henri Le Caron, the British Spy Inside the Fenian Movement (Maverick House). Excerpts from *A Mother's Story: the fight to free my son David* (Doubleday, with Joyce Milgaard) were reprinted in *Reader's Digest* and *Reader's Digest Crime Files*.

Edwards has lectured on organized crime at several universities, including the Nathanson Centre for the Study of Organized Crime and McGill University, and has been interviewed about organized crime for the BBC, CBC, CTV and the *Mob Stories* Parts 1 and 2 and *Outlaw Bikers* series for History Television. He is currently writing his twelfth book with Italian journalist Antonio Nicaso on the Mafia wars of mobster Vito Rizzuto.

PART TWO
Fiction

The Offer

By Iain Parke

"It's like old Nick says right at the start, all clubs that have ever existed are either dictatorships; run by a top guy until someone comes along and knocks them off their perch, or democracies; run on the basis of consensus. They always have been, and always will be."
Damage 2008

Monday 25 April 1994

I killed the engine and instinctively let the big machine sink underneath me, the long side stand sliding across the cobbles of the courtyard until it found its stable resting place. Still sitting I pushed my goggles up onto the brow of my lid, pulled off my leather riding gloves and reached under my chin to release the strap of my helmet and pull my faded chequered scarf from across my nose and mouth. Then I swung the handlebars hard to the left, feeling the bike settle again in a sort of aftershock as its centre of gravity shifted, and turned the key in the ignition to lock the steering.

Only then dismounting, I turned to face the club house, squinting against the harsh light of the security lamp above the door which threw the bikes filling the yard into a jumbled network of black shadows.

Gloves stuffed into my lid, I pulled my scarf loose around my neck as I walked across the yard towards the warmer yellow light spilling out from where the steel security door was ajar, semi- silhouetting in a cloud of cigarette smoke Spud the striker who was on yard duty tonight. He stood aside as I walked up and nodded a greeting as I reached him that I didn't bother to return. He was wrapped in a thick fleece jacket under his cut off. He would need it, he would be there all night until the meeting broke up, keeping an eye on the bikes outside and acting as security.

Strikers always had to work their passage, demonstrate their commitment to the club by taking on all the crap jobs that came their way until after a year or sometimes two, they had a chance to be voted up to full patch status, if they ever made it.

As I pushed the door shut again behind me I nodded to Wibble, one of the other current strikers who was relaxed, feet up on the desk inside the door beside the CCTV monitor, and headed on into the warmth and noise of the bar.

The third striker, Fat Mick, was nowhere to be seen. I guess he was out on patrol as part of the security detail.

You never normally saw a striker sitting at all. It was all fetch and carry. Some of the guys just used them like personal slaves. They were deliberately treated like shit but they all knew what was coming, what they'd signed up for in taking a bottom rocker. As a tagalong they'd have seen how it worked.

It was also fun to watch. You could tell the smarter ones, they quickly developed a skill of just melting into the background when a particularly crap job was in prospect, being around and doing what they needed to, to serve their time and prove themselves, while leaving the dumber ones to catch the dumber shit. You could respect that, the nous to work the system. It was all part of the game, although it wasn't just a game. This was deadly serious. It was a test.

We wanted to make sure they had what it took, the total commitment needed to join the club.

So we would run them ragged, work 'em from pillar to post, fetching beer, cleaning the clubhouse, stomping round outside in the cold, night after night on guard duty, doing whatever the shit a member told them to do. It was a time of working like a dog and just sucking it up to show what they'd got, what they were made of. That they had the self-discipline and dedication we were looking for.

Would they pass the test?

To do so the club came in front of family, work, friends, everything. A striker had no friends outside the club any more.

But once they'd got patched, then they'd got that knowledge, that self-assurance that they had made it, that they had won their way through to a place in the elite; that from then on they weren't going to take any shit, any more, from anyone, ever again. Then that was what made it all worthwhile.

So seeing Wibble sitting with his boots up on the desk was a rarity. But then Wibble was nearly there, he'd done almost a year, he'd shown what he could do, what he could put up with, what dedication he could put in to making the grade. It was almost time to vote on him and I guessed Tiny, his sponsor, would be putting him up soon.

But he'd also shown he'd got the smarts. After all, he was the one sitting down. I liked that.

I wasn't sorry to see that Spud had drawn the short straw tonight again. He was an arsey little wanker, too cocky for a striker I thought, and that Butcher was his sponsor was the final straw as far as I was concerned. I'd be voting against him when the time came. It wasn't just that I disliked him. It was more than that. When you were deciding on whether a guy could become a full patch you were making a judgement call. You had to be sure that he would be there for you, to get your back whenever and whatever the circumstances. And if you weren't sure you shouldn't be saying yes.

Even though I was a well respected member, that on its own wouldn't be enough to keep him out, I'd have to explain my objections. But one more dissenter, one more black ball and that would be it. Two votes against and he would be out automatically and it would be another six months as a striker before he could reapply.

The club house was out in the wilds, right on top of the Pennines about five miles up into the hills above Enderdale, and as everyone said, it was a fucking good club house. We had bought it out of club subs as a half derelict ruin about five years ago just after the merger, and then we had all worked on it to get it right. Set back in a dip in the ground high up a track across a field from the road and screened by a thick belt of trees, the old farm house offered privacy, with the space in the fields below and above for partying when we hosted other clubs. The club house itself faced onto a cobbled yard that offered secure parking for the bikes, flanked along either side with barns that gave room to take them inside and work on them if needs be, together with the kennel for Wolf the guard dog.

Buying our own club house and the land around it had been a great move.

Whenever we were out in a bar or somewhere there always some tension. Not that we went looking for trouble when we were out. But not that we backed down from it either. If you acted with respect, you got treated with respect. But there would always be some wariness, someone with a potential attitude in the crowd, some dickhead, somebody who fancied themselves, someone who made a comment, someone who provoked and who had to be answered.

Because if you acted like an arsehole, you would get treated like an arsehole.

In our own club house, there was none of that. In the club house we could relax, josh, play fight with each other with no one calling the plod. In our out of the way old farmhouse with its bit of land in the hills we knew we could go and get wasted, party, and host other clubs without getting any hassle.

We got on OK with the locals normally. We were about two or three miles from the nearest village so there were only a few isolated farms around about us. We kept ourselves to ourselves and they didn't interfere so there wasn't any issue really. After all, a lot of us were brought up round here, Billy Whizz and I used to play in the woods below the road when we were kids for example, we'd been to school with the other local kids so he and I knew most of the local farmers and sorted out any problems that might crop up. They were used to the fact that on a couple of weekend evenings over the summer we would be hosting a bash and there'd be music and noise but otherwise we didn't cause any problems locally.

It had been a traditional uplands farm, with a small square two storey farmhouse and adjoining byre. Inside on the ground floor of the house there was a bar and a kitchen-cum-canteen while the byre had become a pool room with its visitors' wall decorated with plaques and badges presented by clubs we had hosted. Upstairs the bedrooms offered space for any member who needed to crash, while we had made the first floor of the byre into a meeting room big enough for club business. Which was why tonight we were all going to be here.

Beer in hand, I settled in to chat to some of the guys and wait.

Over the next twenty minutes the occasional roar of bikes pulling up outside in the courtyard announced the arrival of other members as the clubhouse filled up with patches. But tonight there were no tagalongs. This was billed as a serious meeting about club business so tonight it would be insiders only. Other than full patches the only people who would be here would be the three strikers, and they wouldn't be in the meeting, they would stay out of it, handling security.

By half past seven the bar was pretty full and I guessed we would need to get started soon. Billy Whizz said he thought Tiny was through in the pool room, so together we threaded our way across the crush around the bar and, bottles in hand, pushed our way through the adjoining door into the stairwell and then through the second door into the old byre.

Standing just inside the door, we could see that on the far side of the room Tiny, the President, and Butcher, Sergeant at Arms, were deep in conversation; with the one outsider who I had seen would be here tonight.

Most of the bikes outside were in variations on the Imperial colours of purple and gold, but I had seen the one parked up by the door suggesting that its owner had arrived early, its red and black paintwork harsh in the glare of the halogen. I knew the bike and its owner. It belonged to Dazza, President of The Brethren MC's north east charter for the last six or seven years although thanks to Gyppo I'd known him on and off for more like ten or twelve.

'What's Dazza doing here?' Billy asked quietly as we looked across.

'Beats me,' I shrugged. 'Not a clue. Thought you would know if anyone did?'

'Not me mate. Way above my level. In fact the whisper I hear is that he's moving up in the world. About to transfer over to The Freemen.'

The Brethren, otherwise known from their black and red colours as the 'Menaces', were one of the big six international clubs, up there with the Angels, Bandidos, Outlaws, Pagans and Rebels. Each country where there was a Brethren club had a national charter from the mother club in the US and so here their members wore a national bottom rocker saying Great Britain. Within the country they then had a dozen or so regional charters, but most were spread across London, the South, and the West Midlands, with Dazza's charter as a northern outpost.

Over and above these local charters were The Freemen, an independent charter in each country, not tied to any single locality. Each country was broadly left to run its own affairs but generally The Freemen charter's members were the national management of the club, they were The Brethren's elite, a club within the club and very much the top of the tree. They were also generally a self-selecting group, membership by invitation only and rumoured in many countries tending to be those within each national club who were into serious business.

Somebody had obviously said something or noticed that we were there as, looking up, Tiny raised his beer bottle and beckoned me over.

'See ya later,' I nodded to Billy, as I acknowledged the invitation and headed round the table.

'Yeah, watch yourself,' he answered, turning back towards the bar.

'And you know our Road Captain, Damage here,' Tiny said, as I joined them.

'Sure!' said Dazza, smiling and sticking out his huge hand for a surprisingly formal handshake that then opened up into a proffered hug that gave full sight of the leering blood red dyed ∫∫ style Totenkopf badge on the left breast of his cut off just underneath his President title, 'Yeah, I know Mr Clean and Organised here.'

I smiled at the familiar jibe. It was a long standing joke between us. As I say, I had history with Dazza, we went way back. We embraced, slapping backs.

He was right though. You have to be organised to be the club's road captain, sorting out the runs and all the hassle. The job also went to me because I had a relatively clean record since the road captain usually ended up dealing with any plod issues on a run.

'Not seen you since our last party back in the summer.'

'Hey I'm good. Busy planning next weekend.'

The May Day bank holiday weekend would be our first full club run of the year.

'Good to know, always good to have tight people around you.'

Patches and rockers of course were club property and the back of your cut off had always been strictly regimented as the club's uniform, proclaiming your membership and your charter. But in the early days there was a lot of individualism otherwise. Club officers would have their President or Sergeant at Arms tabs, and members might have some other club specific badges, but guys across all the clubs wore all sorts of other stuff on the front of their cut offs; bike logos, weed, swastikas, whatever they wanted.

But as clubs gradually became more disciplined these slowly disappeared so that the front of your cut off became more club focused while the club became ever more all involving and defining.

Flash nowadays was almost always just club business; you would only wear tabs awarded to you by the club. And since tabs were club business, no outsider to a club should ever ask a club member what a particular badge meant. After all, if it was club business, it was club business. But guys within affiliated or friendly clubs were always expected to just know as though by a process of osmosis. The Totenkopf tab on the front of Dazza's cut off declared, without saying anything, his membership of the feared Bonesmen.

And then it was time and the bar emptied as the crowd of guys filed dutifully and noisily upstairs to the meeting room, leaving Wibble in the lobby on the cameras and Spud outside in the cold.

As one of the club's officers, by tradition I was always one of the last in. Standing at the bottom of the stairs waiting for him, I heard Tiny say something to Dazza about roll call.

'No problem mate. We in The Brethren of all people respect other clubs' traditions. Just give me a shout when you're ready.'

*   *   *

Upstairs a few moments later the guys were packed around the edges of the room. There were about three dozen of us all told. As the biggest of the founding clubs, we ex-Reivers made up the largest contingent with about a dozen of us as the Borders cohort from the valley and the dales. There were ten of Gut's Westmorland cohort from over the border into Cumbria, another eight or so from Popeye's Northumberland cohort from up along the North Sea coast, and finally the half dozen of Butcher's feared Wearside cohort, universally known as the cleaver crew from Sunderland. Some were perched on a selection of battered chairs, some were standing. Billy Whizz was sprawled on the floor rolling a smoke. We could be raided at any time by the plod so the general rule was you could bring anything you wanted to the club, but only if you could swallow it if needed.

Butcher as Sergeant at Arms pulled the doors shut and the hubbub of voices died to a hush as he strode to join me, Gut the VP, and Popeye the secretary-treasurer, in flanking Tiny, standing behind two tables facing the assembled brothers.

Prayers, our weekly club meetings, were compulsory and unless you were down or incapacitated, if you missed more than one in a row, you could be fined. Miss more than two and you had better have a bloody good explanation or you could be looking at your patch. But since the empire covered such a wide area, each of the cohorts had their own weekly prayers. We only got together for High Church at the beginning, middle and end of the riding season, or on special occasions.

This was a special occasion, High Church, a full dress club meeting. Attendance was compulsory for all patches. That meant everyone had to be there, unless you physically couldn't make it like Prof laid up in hospital with a broken leg and Little Matt and Scottie, both on remand charged with GBH after a run in with The Hangmen last week.

Whether weekly prayers or High Church, every meeting started the same way, with the roll call as Tiny as President read the register in alphabetical order and we answered.

'Andy?'

'Here,' came a voice from the back.

'Damage?'

'Here,' I said.

Tiny continued to ask as he worked his way slowly and regularly through the list with replies returned from around the room until at last he got to, 'Gyppo?'

'On the road,' I intoned.

As Road Captain it was my responsibility to answer for each of the fallen brothers whose pictures adorned the far wall of the club room, in the same way that Butcher as Sergeant at Arms answered 'Down but not broken' for the guys that were inside, who were also always with us in spirit.

It was just strange that Gyppo was the first, in both ways.

With the register finished and the roll call taken, we waited in silence as Tiny closed the book on the desk. I and the other officers pulled out our chairs from under the tables and sat down.

Tiny remained standing, and seemed to take a moment to gather his thoughts before leaning forwards, knuckles planted on the table he announced, 'I've got something to say.'

This was it at last. The reason for the urgently called High Church meeting. You could feel the expectation in the air.

'You've all seen that Dazza from The Brethren is downstairs so you'll have guessed why we're here tonight as a club. Dazza called me last week and asked if he could speak to us. So according to our rules I need to ask you for your permission to invite a stranger to address a club meeting.'

*   *   *

A few moments later, Butcher escorted Dazza up. In silence, Gut ushered him to a space that had been made for him to stand beside Tiny who nodded in greeting, while Butcher closed and locked the doors from the inside.

Tiny waited for Gut and Butcher to resume their seats before speaking again.

'You all know Dazza here. So I guess I'll just let him say what he has to say.' He turned to Dazza and with a gesture gave him the floor as he pulled out his own chair to sit down.

Dazza nodded to him and looked out across the room, calmly meeting the guys' eyes as they stared at him.

Dazza had a presence. You could never deny that. And it was a very calmly delivered speech, very businesslike, almost a formal diplomatic address delivered to a hushed hall.

'Well firstly I'd like to start by thanking you guys for the opportunity to talk to you here tonight at your club meeting. I know you like to keep club meetings private, so do we in The Brethren, so I appreciate being invited in.'

Very polite. Very correct. We waited.

'We in The Brethren have known you guys now for many years, we know that you are stand up guys that we can respect and we've always had good relations.'

It was like hearing the ambassador from a powerful country address the parliament of a smaller, but fiercely proud, friendly power. He obviously had a message to deliver and would do so courteously but firmly, and despite being alone in this room, he was calm, protected by the knowledge of what an assault on him would mean.

I was still thinking about that Totenkopf skull and crossbones on his cut off and what Billy had said. Being a Bonesman didn't automatically entitle him to membership of The Freemen, otherwise he'd have been in what, six or seven years ago? But it was widely understood as being a necessary qualifier.

'Obviously some of us have long standing business relations with some of you, and we don't do that lightly.'

'Some of us' was a bit of a generalisation on his side of the house. I knew full well that Dazza was the main guy in the north-east charter who dealt. Since Gyppo, I wasn't involved in any of that any more but I knew he did deal with many of our guys as a way of moving his product into our club's territory. Billy for one, but Sprog and a number of others who either dabbled for a bit of extra bread, or dealt more seriously, mainly in whizz or blow as their main lines, together with acid and E for the dance crowds, although rumour had it that supplies of snow were starting to become much more available as well.

So what was coming here I wondered?

'I'm here to offer you guys a choice. The world is changing, you've seen that. The Duckies are organising in Scotland and now we hear that they have been talking to The Hangmen.'

There was a stirring amongst the guys. The Duckies were The Rebels MC, The Brethren's main rivals over here. In addition to Scotland, this side of the border they had charters that ran in a band across Liverpool, Salford and over the Pennines to Leeds where they ran into The Dead Men Riding, as well as down across most of Wales. Their patch featured a screaming eagles' head that The Brethren insultingly dismissed as looking like a duck.

The Hangmen however were very much our regional rivals and bête noirs. They had charters in Lancashire and South Cumbria so we regularly ran up against them in a border war that had been simmering and flaring up at odd intervals for the best part of ten years or so now. A link-up between The Hangmen and The Rebels could make us the meat in the sandwich and potentially lead to a serious escalation in hostilities.

But over and above our local beef with them, might it also mean that a wider war was in the offing? The Brethren were currently the top dogs nationally and they would refuse to let that change. If The Rebels absorbed The Hangmen that would strengthen their presence significantly and might even make them numerically the largest club in the country. The Brethren want to prevent that happening which meant that they might either be looking to recruit extra troops to fight, or just to ensure they retained numerical superiority.

'The regional independents are being rolled up – you've all seen it happening. So guys like you sooner or later are going to have to choose whose side you want to be on.'

So I could see what was coming. We and The Hangmen had in effect provided buffer states between Rebel and Brethren territory. If The Rebels made moves to absorb their buffer, then The Brethren would have no option but to respond in kind.

'You might say why do we need to choose? Why can't we just stay out of it, stay independent? Well that's a mistake. You can't.'

He certainly had balls coming in here and saying that to the guys' faces. If he wasn't who he was, he would probably have been stomped. And it wasn't that we were scared of The Brethren that was stopping anyone. It's difficult to describe to an outsider, but it was like I say, a respect thing. Almost as though he was here to parley under a white flag. He was an envoy. So it was like a tradition, his person was inviolable as he came here to speak. If we fought them later over this we would stomp him without question if we caught him. But here and now, we would hear him out and he would unquestionably walk out unharmed.

'If you try to stay neutral in a war, you will end up the losers. And the losing side in the war won't be able to help you, while the winner won't have needed you to win or have any reason to value you.

'But don't get the wrong idea here. I'm not here to threaten you guys.

'We don't recruit, we recognise.

'And I'm here to tell you, as guys we respect, we want you on our side.

'So as I say, I'm here to offer you all a choice.

'It's time to step up to the big time. Time to join the international Brethren world.'

Oh fuck, I thought, so that was what was coming.

'We want you to patch over. We want you to join us to expand the North-east charter across the region.'

Oh fuck. The what happens if you don't was unsaid. Once The Brethren had made an offer like this we were either in or against them. It was not a choice being offered but an ultimatum, however quietly and smilingly delivered. It was join us or disband.

And it was always a one time offer.

Once Dazza had finished, Tiny stood up to formally respond. He thanked Dazza for coming out to see us and for setting out what he had to say so clearly. Obviously there was a lot to take in and we as a club would need to consider what he had said; to consult; we would need to ask the brothers inside who weren't here tonight what they thought; we would need to come to a view.

'Of course,' said Dazza. 'That's only natural. Now I could hang around but I know that this is something you guys will want to discuss amongst yourselves so I suggest I leave you to it. Obviously you guys know where I am if there's anything you want to talk to us about.'

Butcher stood up to escort him from the room.

'But before I go, there is one thing I would like to say in conclusion.'

The room waited in silence.

'Just don't take too long.'

The storm of noise and voices broke after he left the room.

It was a heated discussion, freewheeling was always the way in the club. But immediately, it was difficult to put a finger on it exactly, there was already a bit of a change in atmosphere. The discussion was perhaps just a shade less open than it would have been normally. I just got the feeling that some people were being more careful about what they said than they would normally be. That this was serious, that the wrong words here could have serious consequences later on, of interests being assessed, of positions being considered.

Irrespective of what we thought of him or the message, as a representative he had clearly given a good impression for his club. As the evening wore on I heard a number of people say more or less the same thing:

'He has balls coming in here like that.'

'He was pretty cool about it.'

'You've got to admire his balls, walking into our clubhouse to deliver a message like that.'

We broke up that night without any formal decision being taken. I hadn't expected it would be. We were a strangely democratic group in many ways; we were brothers and we tended to naturally seek to reach a consensus. With most things Tiny would take soundings, discuss the offer with small groups, and gradually we would come to a view as to what we, as a club, would decide to do.

* * *

It was a crisp cold night under an inky black sky filled with millions of brilliant white stars and the ride home from the clubhouse took twenty minutes or so.

I loved riding on my own at night.

There was something about the blackness, the cold wind biting my face, the streaming smear of light on the road ahead, the howling solitude, the unthinking way that I followed the road, long grooved with memories, testing each familiar curve just one more time, that made me feel as though I was riding towards the end of the world; by myself in my own private bubble of time and space.

Alone in a dream I roared up and across the high empty moors. Then the dry stone walls started to close in on either side of the road's curves as I left the high ground behind and descended through the curves into the rolling foothills with their fields and occasional yellow-windowed dales farms.

Down here, the road home was along a mix of straight old Roman roads that just begged me to gun the motor, the wind whipping past my ears singing the strange music, and sudden twisting curves familiar through years of instinctive riding, requiring fierce braking at the last possible moment, the bike drifting, using all of the available road to get the right positioning to hustle through them, the bike heeled over to maintain the speed and set me up for the acceleration that pulled me upright again as I set up for the next bend. Before the glow of the first streetlight ahead signalled the start of the final drop down the long straight into the valley, the lights of the town opening up before me as the machine and I roared out of the dark.

It was the type of riding I always enjoyed. It was very Zen somehow. The speeding solitude, with just the sound of the wind, and the mix of unthinking instinct, and fierce full mind and body concentration required on the here and now of the riding freed my mind to wander, it gave me time to think.

But tonight was different.

It had been fascinating, sitting back to hear and see Tiny our pres, and Dazza theirs, in operation, and to mull over the difference.

All clubs are either dictatorships, run by a single dominant individual until such time as someone successfully usurped their rule, or democracies, run on the basis of consensus. They always have been and always will be.

We in The Legion were a democracy, certainly the ex-Reivers' part was, some other cohorts less so. That was why Tiny had called the meeting tonight. If there was something important to be said, we all needed to hear about it if we were to decide what we as a club were to do.

Dazza by contrast ruled his charter with a rod of iron. A bit like Butcher did with his boys down in Maccamland. I'd never been surprised that those two got on so well.

It was gone eleven when, bike locked up around the side, I walked in through the back door and parked my lid on the table.

'How did it go? What's up? Can you tell me?'

Sharon was an old school old lady. She knew that club business was club business and that sometimes I couldn't tell her everything.

I hadn't yet decided how much I would tell her. But I had to say something.

'In a word? Trouble. With a capital F!'

*Excerpted from *The Brethren Trilogy: Heavy Duty People* by Iain Parke (2010), ISBN 9780956161512.

Iain Parke imports industrial quantities of Class A drugs, kills people and lies (a lot) for a living, being a British based crime fiction writer. He became obsessed with motorcycles at an early age, taking a six hundred mile cross-country tour to Cornwall as soon as he bought a moped at the tender age of sixteen. After working at a London dispatch job delivering parcels on a motorcycle, he built his first chopper in his bedroom at university, undeterred by the fact that the workshop was upstairs.

Armed with a MBA degree, Iain first worked in insolvency and business restructuring in the UK and Africa, where he began work on his first thriller *The Liquidator*. The success of that novel propelled him to write a 'biker lit' trilogy about the Brethren Motorcycle Club, which has recently been optioned as a series for television in the UK. Today Iain lives off the grid, high up on the North Pennines in Northumberland with his wife, dogs, and a garage full of motorcycle restoration projects. He is currently working on a number of book projects, including another biker-based trilogy.

Meeting Up With Old Friends

By Edward Winterhalder & Marc Teatum

It took three rings before the girl picked up the phone at the Harley dealership in Springfield.

"Terreson's Harley-Davidson. How may I help you?"

"Can I speak to Fuzz?"

"Hold on a minute, please."

All it took was a quick phone call from one old friend to another, and Blues found out where Slinger and his crew were hanging out these days. After ten years of being away, Blues assumed that the old watering hole was either closed or under a different name, and he was right. Fuzz kept tabs on all the comings and goings of the motorcycle club community in the area. Since they were all his customers, he found it beneficial to know where they hung out, so that he could stop in and have a beer with them every once in a while.

*   *   *

By ten o'clock that night, Blues had found an opening in the long row of American steel that was parked in front of the Side Pipes Grille. Backing the machine into the spot, it felt good to blend in with all the other chrome and paint that populated the area. He kicked the stand to the pavement, and killed the bike in one smooth move that was just as natural as breathing to him. When he hung his bucket lid on the handlebars, he attracted absolutely no attention from the two vested prospects that were sitting on their bikes halfway down the line.

Going colorless into a bar that is full of motorcycle club members, uninvited and unaccompanied, is not the smartest move the average person should try. But Blues wasn't the average weekend warrior; he was a hard-core biker, the former president of a motorcycle club, and a man on a mission.

Pulling open the door, Blues was hit in the face with a raw energy of the rock and roll that screamed from the sound system. The noise of the crowd attempting to talk above the din, the smoke from the clientele ignoring state law, and the smell of a place that hadn't been cleaned since the last millennium were all so familiar to him. There were booths on one wall, a bar on the other, and a field of tables in between, running all the way to the back of the building. The requisite pool table was sitting just outside the bathroom doors, at the back of the bar not far from the rear exit door.

Ignoring the assault on his senses, Blues made his way to the end of the bar and found an empty stool. When the bartender approached him and asked what he wanted, he didn't hesitate for a second.

"A Coke."

The bartender just stared at him.

"And what else?"

"Ice, chief," Blues replied calmly, staring right back at the man.

"That's all."

As soon as he got his Coke, he focused on the task at hand, which was the large group of blue and silver patch holders that were gathered across the room. The one percenters had control of at least a half dozen four-foot by four-foot tables in the far corner of the room, and three of the tables had been pushed together to form one large one. One of the Skuldmen, who sat at the head of the three tables, seemed to be holding court, because he held everyone around him in rapt attention. Not far from the main group, Slinger sat at a table with two women and another patch holder, nursing a beer.

Sipping his drink and biding his time, Blues scanned the crowd, trying to categorize everyone into groups of hangaround, prospect, veteran, full patch, and plain citizen. Next he eyed the bright red exit signs that indicated a pathway to freedom and relative safety. If and when the shit hit the fan, he wanted to know where to go, and whom he might have to battle along the path to get there.

When his attention returned to the group of tables across the room, he could see Slinger looking at him from across the room. The Nomad, using hand signals, motioned to a prospect, and then pointed at Blues. When the prospect headed in his direction, Blues was not sure what was going to happen—he expected the worst, and hoped for the best.

"Slinger wants to see you."

Blues sat silently.

"Now," the prospect added.

Without saying another word, the prospect turned and headed back toward the crowd at the far end of the room. Blues just shook his head, picked up his drink and followed along.

When the pair got halfway across the room, Slinger emptied his bottle of beer and rose from the table. Nodding his head and using a hand signal, the blue and silver patch holder told the prospect that everything was okay. The prospect didn't go far, though; he stood against the wall a few feet away and watched Blues intently.

"I knew you'd come. I just knew it," Slinger said, grinning, when he came face-to-face with Blues.

"Hello, Slinger."

"So? You changed your mind, right? I knew you would. I just didn't think you would do it so soon, but I knew you would eventually."

"Wait a minute, Slinger, it's not what you think," Blues started to explain.

"Come on. The national boss is in town, and you need to say hi." Slinger pushed his way through the crowd as he made his way over to the head of the large table. When he got there, he made an announcement.

"Hey brothers! Shut the hell up for a second, will ya!" Slinger yelled.

When the conversation stopped and all heads turned in his direction, Slinger had the floor.

"I thought the best way to ensure the success of the new Springfield chapter, as it rises from the ashes, was to draw on its past, so I want you to meet a man who put some time in for the blue and silver many years ago. A man who wants to come back home and wear the patch again," he said, and then motioned for Blues to come forward.

Stepping up to the group of outlaw motorcycle club members, Blues was confident in stature, but uncertain about exactly what to say.

"Who the hell are you?" the national president asked tenuously.

Blues just stood there, not saying a word, as he sized up the situation. Taking a good look at his challenger, he suddenly realized that he recognized the man.

"When I was president of the chapter in Albany ten years ago, you were president of the Milwaukee chapter. I'm surprised that you don't remember me."

When the man stood, the chair scraped the worn wooden floor; everyone nearby went silent and turned their attention to the pair. Blues' heart felt like it stopped for a moment, as he wondered if he'd made a grave mistake. An error that might cost him, at best, a few front teeth.

"I meant no disrespect, Milwaukee Phil. And I'm not surprised you don't recognize me; it's been a long time. My name is Blues."

The men's eyes were locked—you could drive a motorcycle between the two and neither would flinch. Without looking at anyone else, they continued to measure each other up. After a few moments, it was the national president of the Skuldmen who spoke first.

"Holy shit! I remember you!"

The leader of the Skuldmen nation made his way over to greet his long-lost brother, the only way he knew how—with a traditional hug, and a slap on the back.

"Sit down, Blues. It's good to have you back."

Blues sat down at the table next to Milwaukee Phil, and the chatter that was going on among the crowd picked up exactly where it let off.

"This is Little Jimmie; he runs Maryland. He's in town to help launch the new chapter," Milwaukee Phil said, gesturing toward the Skuldmen patch holder who sat across the table from Blues.

Blues reached across the table and shook Little Jimmie's hand without saying a word.

"Blues, this is Jake," the Bossman continued. "He's also in the Maryland chapter, but he grew up in Boston, so he'll be here for a while helping Jimmie and Slinger get things going.

Blues reached across the table and shook Jake's hand without saying a word.

"So, is what Slinger says true? Are you here to pick your patch back up?"

The moment of truth had finally come for Blues. There was no way he would lie to anyone, especially a Skuldmen. When he was a patch holder, he would always speak the truth to his brothers, no matter what the consequences, for when it came right down to it, a man's word was worth more than anything. He learned that when he was a hangaround, and he held that same value in high regard as he rose through the ranks to become president of his chapter. He demanded it, and expected it, from every person who wore the patch then, and from everyone in his life since. This concept had been drilled and cemented into his psyche, and now was part of his being.

"I respect the patch. As you know, I lived for the patch, and I killed for the patch. But I'm not here to do it again," Blues explained. "We have some history, that's for sure. And although I have been asked to rejoin the club, it is not a journey that I'm ready to take at this time. I still remember the past, and what it meant to be a Skuldmen. But because of what happened to me when I wore blue and silver, I don't think that it's the best choice for me right now."

The national president nodded his understanding of the situation.

"Besides, I'm going to be reporting to a parole officer for quite a while; if I'm back in the club, you know it won't work out, and I'll get locked up again," he said, grinning.

Milwaukee Phil, Slinger, and Little Jimmie were a bit surprised at the words, but it was Slinger, looking to maintain face in front of both his national president and another respected member of his organization, who spoke first.

"Blues, we all know that you were sold out by assholes who didn't understand the concept of brotherhood, but don't let that cloud your judgment."

"There isn't a man who wears blue and silver who doesn't know of your loss and what happened to you," Milwaukee Phil added. "We still can't believe that your wife and child were murdered in cold blood. And we haven't forgotten Skip, and the courage it took for him to ride with you on what he probably knew was going to be a suicide mission of revenge. We feel your pain, brother, but we've changed a lot while you've been away."

Blues, Little Jimmie, and Slinger listened intently, as did the other club members who had gathered close to them.

"We're not the same club these days. We're a lot wiser, and smarter, in some ways because of your loss. Drugs, and drug use, are no longer tolerated. No more three strikes and then you get another last chance. Now it's one strike, and you're gone. That's the new rule. We're here for our brothers, all of our brothers. Because of this new policy, we're much stronger now than we were ten years ago."

Blues looked at Milwaukee Phil, Slinger, and Little Jimmie, then took a deep breath before he spoke.

"I really appreciate you guys giving me the opportunity to come back, but that's not why I'm here to see you tonight. Like I told Slinger the other day, the main focus in my life at the moment is my daughter. Until I make things right with her, and get off parole, I think I can do more for the club retired than I could if I was active."

"Then why are you here?" Little Jimmie asked suspiciously.

"For starters, if you guys had a clubhouse, wouldn't it be a lot easier to get this chapter up and going?"

"It wouldn't hurt," Slinger replied.

"Go on," the national president instructed.

"I work for some people who own a multifamily apartment over on the west side. Unfortunately the building has been taken over by gangbangers and is no longer in their control. The owners would be thrilled if they were evicted, but they can't use the normal channels to get the job done. You guys have the resources and ability to rectify the situation."

"And why would we get involved?" Little Jimmie inquired. "What's in it for the blue and silver?"

"If you guys do this, the people I work for will provide you with a place for a clubhouse in an industrial building they own in downtown Springfield. They would also be happy to give the club a five-year lease for three hundred dollars a month."

Milwaukee Phil and Little Jimmie looked at each other, and then they both looked at Slinger.

"What exactly are we going up against at the apartment building?" Slinger asked.

"Shit, nothing that you can't handle, that's for damn sure," Blues replied, smiling.
Pulling out two sheets of paper from the pocket of his plain leather vest, he offered them to Milwaukee Phil and Slinger.

"Here are the specifics. One page is all about the rental property, where it's located, and the gangbanger kids that have taken it over. The other one gives you the details about the property that's being offered for your new clubhouse."

Slinger took the pages from Blues, glanced at them, and then handed them to Milwaukee Phil. Little Jimmie got up from his chair and walked around behind the national president to get a look at the paperwork from over Milwaukee Phil's shoulder.

"Blues, why don't you give us a couple of minutes to talk about this? Go get yourself another drink, will ya? It's on me," Milwaukee Phil said, before he turned to the group of patch holders standing nearby and issued another mandate.

"Get me someone who knows this town real well. I want someone who knows everything about the west side, and the downtown area!"

Within seconds two men stepped forward; they were probationary members that Blues didn't recognize.

After Blues made his way back over to the bar, he caught the bartender's eye and held up his empty glass—the gesture caused the bartender to head in his direction.

"Let me guess. You want another one—with ice, right?"

When Blues nodded his agreement, the bartender turned around and walked away to fill the order. One minute later there was a fresh glass of Coke on the bar in front of him. While he was taking a sip, Slinger wandered up and sat down on the stool beside him.

"Looks like you're serious about making things right with your daughter."

"That I am. I sure owe it to her, don't you think?"

"After ten years in the can, it's going to be a tough row to hoe," Slinger replied.

"It'll be worth it."

"If I had a kid, I'm pretty sure I would feel the same as you. You probably missed her a lot over the years, huh?"

"Yeah, I did. I also miss the club, don't get me wrong. I miss having a room full of brothers around me, and I miss the camaraderie. But I miss my daughter more. She's all I have left in the way of blood now. At the moment, I want her back in my life more than I want to wear the patch again. If I went active, there's no doubt in my mind that I'd lose whatever chance I have now to heal the wounds between us."

"You do whatever you have to, and fix things with your kid. I just want you to know that we're here for you. We'll do whatever it takes to help you out, and if it means keeping our distance until you and your daughter get reacquainted, then we're all fine with that. I'll let all the brothers know what's going on with you, but if you need us for anything, you just make the call."

"I don't have your number," Blues said.

Slinger pulled a Skuldmen courtesy card from his pocket, and scribbled a cell phone number on the back.

"Here's my number. Don't hesitate to call if you need us. We're still your family, too."

"Thanks, Slinger. I appreciate it."

"Thanks for bringing us the clubhouse opportunity," Slinger replied.

"I guess in a way, helping you guys get a place of your own is my little way of staying connected."

Before Slinger could respond, Little Jimmie and Milwaukee Phil joined the pair at the bar.

"You got a deal, Blues," the national president said.

"Give us a couple of days, and then you can tell the owners they can come back to their building," Little Jimmie added.

*Excerpted from *The Moon Upstairs: A Biker's Story* by Edward Winterhalder & Marc Teatum, published by Blockhead City (2012), ISBN 9780977174782.

Edward Winterhalder is one of the world's leading authorities on motorcycle clubs and the Harley-Davidson biker lifestyle; his books are published in multiple languages and sold all over the world. He was a member, and/or an associate, of outlaw motorcycle clubs for almost thirty years. The creator and executive producer of the *PHASS MOB*, *Biker Chicz* and *Living On The Edge* television series, Winterhalder has appeared worldwide on television networks such as Bravo, Prime, CBC, Fox, National Geographic, History Channel, Global, AB Groupe and History Television. In addition to his literary endeavors, he is a consultant to the entertainment industry for TV, feature film and DVD projects that focus on the Harley-Davidson biker lifestyle.

Marc Teatum is an author of contemporary motorcycle fiction. Born in Brooklyn NY, he currently lives in Salem, Massachusetts. Formerly an editor of *UPDATE*, the Massachusetts Motorcycle Association member's magazine, Teatum began his career as a professional photographer, owning a studio that serviced the advertising and public relations industry. During that time, his work won numerous awards in both the photography and design fields. His personal fine art photography has been exhibited widely and is represented in both private and museum collections. He has served on the Board of Directors of The Art Directors Club of Boston as well as the Massachusetts Motorcycle Association, and is currently working in the publishing industry as a content licensing manager. An avid motorcycle enthusiast for more than twenty-five years, Teatum is active in motorcycle rights organizations in the Boston area.

The Garage

By Vic Shurtz

Hank stood at the base of the old cottonwood tree in front of a Texaco station. The sound of a Harley had caught his attention. It caused him to look west toward the sunset. He stared at the mirage of a warrior. He shook his head; the vision cleared and became a biker pushing his bike. Hank recognized the style. The fat bobs, the wide glide, and the throaty sound of an old '74.

Preacher saw the old man watching him as he brought his bike up to a standstill in front of one of the bay doors. The old tree was surrounded by a bench that had been built in the years past. Two trucks sat in the shade. This must be a resting spot for the locals, Preacher thought, as he took off his gloves and loosened his jacket. His black helmet sat on the sissy bar.

Around the base of the tree were a couple of old boys drinking soda, or whatever, and they were all looking at Preacher. Preacher shut off the motor, stood up, and stretched his back by arching it backwards.

"Excuse me," Preacher said, walking toward the tree, "is the owner around?"

Hank put his hands in his pockets, standard practice, prior to speaking. "That would be me," he said as he started walking forward.

"Glad to meet ya," Preacher said as he strode up to meet the hazel eyes of Hank, and offered his hand. "Preacher, Shasta County, California."

Hank looked at the offered hand. "Well, I don't know if I'm glad to meet you, but I do own this station, and if you're in need of assistance, you may be out of luck."

Preacher pulled his hand back. So that's how it's going to be, Preacher thought; okay, I can deal with this. In his most civil tone and manner, Preacher said, "Excuse me sir, but as you can see, I have a flat tire. I was hoping that I could fix it in the shade."

Hank looked at the bike. Yup, the tire was flat. "Do you have the fixens to repair that tire? If not, I might have to charge you for the patches."

Preacher smiled, "Yeah, I've got the fixens, but I would like to rent that milk crate over to the side of the shop."

Hank smiled and looked at the milk crate beside the station. Grass was growing up through it. As he looked up, he met the gray eyes of Preacher. "Son," he said, "you're welcome to the use of that milk crate, and if you need any practice, there are a half a dozen flats next to that tire machine that need fixen, that is, if you're of a mind to."

Preacher smiled as Hank turned his back and headed back to his cronies around the tree. He had seen his type before. One of the good old boys that acted grumpy. Most would see through it.

Slapping his gloves in his left hand, Preacher turned on his heel and strode into the sunset toward his bike. It was a '71 FLH originally: wide glide, bucket headlight, and fat bobs that would take you two hundred miles. Preacher had modified it to his height and to the length of his legs. His old girl was stretched one inch with six-inch over tubes on a twenty-one inch Avon. Ape Hangers finished off the triangle with grips that were tasseled with eight inches of leather on the end. The bike was black in color with a luminance of the paint that made it look like a dark rainbow in the sun.

As Preacher walked back to the bike, he took in the bays of the station. The first one, the one closest to the office and bathrooms, had a hydraulic rack that ran off of air pressure. The other side looked like a hodgepodge of flat tires, a soak tank, and oil drums. A path of sorts weaved its way through the collection.

The outside of the station was stucco, brown with dust to gray at grass level because of the years of accumulated grease. The milk crate stood next to one of the oil barrels outside the building. Last year's grass looked like straw sticking out of everywhere.

In the front of the second bay, Preacher saw a place he could nose his bike in. The soak tank was close, and the sun was going down, so inside was a good thing. Preacher took off his jacket, set it on the tire machine with his gloves and walked to his bike to push it forward out of the sun.

He made sure the bike was somewhat level before he went outside to retrieve the milk crate. God bless steel milk crates, Preacher thought, as he pulled it from the grass; they don't build them like this anymore. He pulled the grass out and banged the crate on the dirt. With milk crate in tow, Preacher started back to the bay.

*   *   *

The crew at the tree changed two or three times before Preacher got his tire fixed. Hank, however, had been watching the Preacher go about his business. In his cut-off T-shirt, Preacher had moved his bike into the bay out of the sun. As Hank watched, Preacher picked up the back of his bike, by the fender mounts, and kicked the milk crate under the frame. His shoulders and forearm muscles rippled as he worked, making his tattoos move as if they were alive. When Preacher pulled his spoons out of his saddle bags, Hank smiled and thought to himself, that man knows what he is doing.

Preacher stood up from putting his tools back in his tool pouch and looked at the sun. He had noticed Hank watching him throughout the afternoon and knew he had earned some respect from the old man. He blinked against the sun and looked back at Hank.

Hank stood looking at Preacher.

"Hank," Preacher said, "do you think I could pitch my tent next to the shop and head out in the morning?"

Hank sauntered over, stuck his hands in his pockets, and looked at Preacher with a smug look.

"Preacher," he said, "I will rent ya that space for the night and even buy ya supper over at the diner if you will fix those two split rims for me—them bastards hurt me every time."

Hank looked sideways at Preacher, "I hear they're serving meat loaf, mashed potatoes and gravy."

Preacher cocked his head, looked at the diner then back at Hank, smiled, and stuck out his hand.

"Hank, I think I could wrap myself around a good meat loaf," Preacher said.

This time Hank took the offered hand.

*   *   *

Maggie had been wiping down booths and tables when she heard the Harley. The sound was not that familiar out here in the middle of nowhere. Here, most traffic sounds were pick-ups and big rigs trying to beat the scales. Pulling the curtains aside, she glanced out the window. A biker was nursing his Harley up to Hank's station with what looked like a flat back tire. This ought to give them boys something to talk about, she thought.

Maggie had grown up in this little spot in the road. Her mother had owned this diner for as long as she could remember. The diner, station, and a small store/beer bar were the focal points of this country. The ranchers and the boys around the tree had been supporting this area for years. When you're the only spot in town, everybody knows everybody.

Maggie was a good-looking woman of about forty. Running the diner had kept her in shape. Standing 5'6" or 7", she had long shapely legs, a trim waist, a nice small bubble butt, and coffee cup sized breasts. Her hair was piled on top of her head in some sort of bun, and it was flaming red. She looked like Reba McEntire.

As she stood looking out at the events around the tree, she shook her head and smiled. "Well Hank, here's your broken wing," she said to an empty room.

"Did you say something?" came a voice from the kitchen.

"It looks like your dad has a new friend," Maggie said as she dropped the curtain and started toward the counter.

The diner had three booths under the front windows. They were the old vinyl type with the table running between twin benches. Against the sidewall were half a dozen tables with chairs, and a gleaming white counter with stools on chrome pedestals shone under the lights of the opposite wall.

Maggie had taken over the diner from her aged mother. She had a brisk coffee club business, which Hank was a member of, a fair lunch, and once a week she cooked a special. Her specials ran from barbecue ribs to fried chicken. Tonight it was meat loaf.

Tina came out from the kitchen, behind the counter. "What did you say? My dad has a friend?"

Maggie met her halfway between the booths and the counter. She looked back at the windows, "Yup, your dad has a friend, and the boys around the tree are going to be talking about it for a week."

Maggie looked back at Tina and said, "I don't know who I feel the sorriest for, you and me for having to listen to them or that biker for having to deal with them."

Tina walked over to the windows and looked out. "Well, Dad's walking back to the tree, and the biker is walking toward his bike, so it can't be all that bad."

"Yeah, well, your dad's famous for taking in broken wings. I'm surprised he doesn't get burned more often than he does," Maggie said.

* * *

Preacher turned around after shaking Hank's hand, to survey the mess around the tire machine. Several tires stood or lay, side by side in front of the old thing. The retractor on the bottom seemed to work as Preacher stepped on the foot valve. Other than that, it would be all muscle and iron to take the tire off.

Preacher looked at the two tires Hank had indicated; the first two in the row were 7.50 x 16's on split rims. The tread on both tires and the rims matched, telling Preacher that they belonged to the same truck. Not much mud, but Preacher could see the goatheads sticking out of the rubber. There's the culprit, he thought. He rolled one out and looked around for some tools. He found what he was looking for toward the back of the shop next to an old bubble tire balancer. The hammer Preacher chose was about the size of a four-pound single jack except it had a fin on one side that looked like an adze. The next tool he looked for was an old friend, the milk crate. He found the soap in a can by the tire machine and went to work.

Preacher broke the ring loose from the rim, walked it off with a pair of long screwdrivers and looked to see if it had a boot in the tire; it did. He picked up the tire and set it down on the tire machine, spun the collar down tight, stepped on the foot valve, and broke the bottom bead loose. He spun off the collar, picked up the tire, turned it over, and dropped the tire on the milk crate. When the rim collided with the crate, the tire came loose all around. All he had to do now was push the stem through, and the tire was off. Then, it was fix the tube and put it back together. The compressor was on the west wall of the second bay next to the dunk tank. Preacher started to fill the tube with air then stuck it in the tank. When he noticed the bubbles coming up from the tube, Preacher put his finger on it and stood up. As he did, he saw a BMX bicycle leaning against the wall. Its front tire was flat. I'm surprised Hank didn't ask me to fix that tire as well, Preacher thought. He chuckled at the idea.

*   *   *

As Preacher started on the second tire, he noticed a newer Ford truck pull up. A small boy, of about six, jumped out and came flying toward the station.

"Grandpa...Grandpa!" the child yelled excitedly, "I rode the mutton; I really rode the mutton." He puffed out his chest and said "I'm going to win that mutton bustin' contest at the rodeo." Beaming with excitement and pride, the boy strutted back up to the driver of the truck.

"Roy said nobody can beat me if I stick like glue. Ain't that right, Roy?"

"Isn't," Roy said, "and yup, if you stick like glue you can't be beat."

Roy wasn't a big man. He stood only about 5'10" or so with the slight build of somebody that spent a lot of time on the back of a horse. He had narrow hips, square shoulders, and forearms that rippled when he flexed his hands. His Levi shirt matched his jeans. His brown boots had seen a lot of wear. The boy was all but the spittin' image of the man, down to the small boots that he wore.

"Roy," Hank said, "Tina's going to be mad as hell at you for bringing Josh back this late."

"I suspect you're right about that, but Josh wanted to try it one last time. It was that last ride that Josh stuck for the time," Roy said. His voice wasn't apologetic, but it was that of accomplishment.

"Well you'd best explain that to his mother," Hank said.

"I think I'd rather get in a fist fight than do that," Roy said. "She doesn't think that highly of me anyway."

"Give her time, Roy," Hank said in a patient voice.

"I'd give her all the time in the world if she'd have me, but I think the devil will be selling snow cones before that happens."

*   *   *

While Hank and Roy were talking, Josh had wandered over to look at Preacher's bike.

"This your bike, mister?" he asked.

Preacher looked up and smiled at the boy. "Yup," he said, "that's my bike."

"Cool," Josh said. "Can I look at it?"

"Sure," Preacher said, "but remember the rule—you can look, but don't touch."

"That's what Grandpa says too," Josh said as he walked over to the bike. Look, but don't touch, and keep your hands in your pockets."

"I have a bike too," he said. "It's that one over on the wall, but it has a flat."

"I noticed," Preacher said as he went back to work on the tire.

This boy has been taught respect for other people's property, Preacher thought.

The boy was about as tall as a yard stick with dark brown hair cut short, and not as slight of build as Preacher had thought. He was a tight little bundle of muscle and sinew. This boy runs free and plays hard, Preacher thought.

"Are you working for Grandpa?" Josh asked, walking back from Preacher's bike.

"Only for a meal," Preacher said.

"Yeah," Josh said. "Grandpa does that a lot."

"We're eating over at the diner tonight too. My mom said we're having meat loaf and taters. Do you like meat loaf?" Josh asked.

"Yup," Preacher said.

"Me too; okay...we'll...see ya later," Josh said as he walked over to Hank and Roy by the tree.

*Excerpted from *Preacher: Do Unto Others* by Vic Shurtz (2006), ISBN 9781601450586.

Vic bought his first bike, a 1971 FLH, in 1977, and has traveled extensively throughout the western United States and Canada. The author of five books about the biker lifestyle, he is a ten year member of the United Bikers of Northern California, a 501C Organization, and the owner of motorcyclefiction dot com, the website for biker books.

Meeting Bill

By Max Billington

Connor had spent all day watching the clock. The hours seemed like days and the minutes seemed like hours. Connor couldn't remember the last time he had been out of the house and especially out of the house with Terry. Four-thirty finally came and Connor could start his escape.

Connor pushed the button on his key fob and unlocked his truck. His hands were shaking from the excitement of heading to Terry's place so much that he dropped his keys by the door of his truck. He reached down to pick them up and noticed that there was a quarter on the ground next to his truck. Connor grabbed his keys and the quarter, opened the door to his truck, put the ignition key in and roared the old beast to life.

After a very uneventful commute to Terry's, Connor pulled up into his driveway. Connor put the truck in park and shut the truck off. He looked up as the garage door at Terry's place opened and there stood Terry.

As the garage door opened, the various treasures in Terry's garage began to appear. There were two bike frames sitting on the floor, surrounded by motorcycle parts and old tools. The two neon beer signs hanging in the garage were turned off. Right next to the entry door into the house was a trash can that was completely full of mostly pizza boxes and beer bottles and next to it was the almond beer refrigerator covered with stickers. But the true treasure was backed in and sat right at the front, Terry's bike.

Terry rode an old Shovelhead Harley. Terry spent all of his free time and what little spare change he had keeping that bike in tip top shape. That bike was a biker's bike. She had 18 inch ape hangers, loud drag pipe exhaust, and tons of chrome. Connor always loved watching Terry kick that bike to life.

Terry came walking out of the house into the garage. He still had his work clothes on, which were permanently stained with grease and dirt. No matter how much he would wash them, those stains weren't coming out, and Terry could care less. His sleeves on his shirt were rolled up just below the elbow, which revealed two of his many tattoos.

Terry's left arm had a tattoo of a mermaid and his right arm had an eagle with wings wrapping all the way around his arm. These two, along with the rest, were not the new school fancy type tattoos, but they were not of the prison variety either. Terry's age and constant time in the sun had faded them quite a bit.

"What's up, Connor!" shouted Terry, as he crushed a beer can that he had just finished.

"Same ol' same old," Connor answered. "You ready to head out?"

"Yeah, let me grab another beer. You want one?"

Connor thought about it for a second. If Julie found out he actually had an open container in his car, she would be pissed. "What the hell? Grab me one."

Terry grabbed two beers from the almond fridge and hopped in Connor's truck. They both cracked open their beers and Terry hit the garage door opener button to close the garage.

"So, where are we headed, man?" asked Connor.

"The bike shop right off Elm Street," Terry replied.

Connor had driven by this bike shop several times. This shop was no modern style dealership. It was an old school mechanic's shop. At any time you would see a few motorcycles parked out in front and some bikers hanging around. The shop was strictly a service and parts place so Connor was a bit surprised that they were going to look at a bike to buy from there.

Connor said, "I thought you told me that Bill didn't sell bikes."

Terry replied, "He don't, but he lets folks leave them there."

Connor had always heard great stories from Terry about Bill, but had never met him, and really had no reason before to go up to that shop. Connor knew that Terry hung out at that shop every now and then and knew who Bill was, but Connor knew that Bill had no idea who he was.

"So I guess I'm finally going to meet this Bill dude," Connor said, with a hint of excitement in his voice.

"Yeah," Terry answered. "Don't worry though. He's cool. Just because you don't have a bike doesn't mean he won't like you, but if I were you, I wouldn't mention that you used to have a metric. He's not really a big fan of those type folks."

Since Terry and Connor had known each other for quite a while, it did not matter to Terry that Connor once rode a Japanese bike. Besides, Connor didn't have it anymore. Terry would always make comments about metric bikes and how they were inferior to the American made bike; that was Harley-Davidson.

Connor made the turn onto Elm Street and pulled up next to the shop.

"Park over there," Terry explained as he pointed to another pickup parked beside the building. There was no specific parking for cars or trucks, but there was a specific area roped off for motorcycles.

Terry walked towards the open sliding door at the front of the building and Connor continued behind him by a few steps.

The shop looked deserted. There were no bikes parked outside the shop and just the lone pickup, which looked like an abandoned vehicle, was parked beside the shop. As Terry walked into the shop, a small, black, mixed breed dog greeted him with a loud, growling bark as to try to convince anyone that he was more Doberman than a Terrier mix. The dog bounced up and down like a basketball. Terry finally reached down and put his hand gently on the dog's head. Then a voice came from around the corner of the shop:

"Get that son of a bitch, Chief. Get him. Bite his fucking nuts off."

That was Bill. Connor rounded the corner behind Terry and took his first look at Bill. Bill stood about 6 foot tall and probably weighed in the 250 pound range. He had on a black T-shirt with the sleeves cut off that had a phrase in white lettering on the front reading "Would you like a nice 'Fuck You' with those fries?" Bill's jeans were covered in oil and grease stains, and the boots that he was wearing looked like they were black at one time in the distant past. He wore a black bandana on his head, wire frame glasses on his nose, and had the remnants of a cheap drug-store cigar hanging out of the side of his mouth.

Terry reached into his shirt pocket, took out a cigarette, gave the smoke a light, took a drag and breathed out a puff of smoke as he spoke to Bill.

"So Bill, where's the bike that dude has for sale?"

"You mean the dipshit whose ol' lady won't let him have a bike?" Bill responded.

"That's the one I came to have a look see at." Terry answered.

"It's over here," said Bill.

Connor followed Bill and Terry as the made their way toward the back of the shop. Connor stepped over the grease and oil spills on the floor, as well as the smeared dog shit that was a few feet from a pile of old tires. Bill and Terry didn't seem to care, as they walked without paying any attention to what was on the floor.

"Well, there she is, Terry. She don't lack much. Hell, if I didn't have so many fucking bikes right now, I would buy her myself."

"Cool deal," said Terry. "It's pretty much as I expected. Oh shit, I forgot, this is my old friend, Connor."

"Nice to meet you," said Bill, as he extended his filthy grease covered hand out to shake Connor's hand.

Connor gave him a firm grip back, even though he hesitated to get his hand dirty. "You, too." Connor replied.

"So which one of you is going to buy this, Terry?" Bill asked.

Connor laughed. "Julie would kill me if I brought a bike home."

Bill then turned to Terry. "So, you want it?"

Terry scratched his head for a few seconds. Then, he crossed his arms and leaned back against the wall and seemed to disappear into deep thought. Connor was looking at Terry with baited breath as he was hoping that Terry was going to buy the bike. Connor always enjoyed seeing people make large purchases and when it came to things that he knew Julie would not let him have, he took every opportunity to live vicariously through whomever was getting to make the purchase.

"Man, I don't fucking know," said Terry. "Let me grab a beer. It will help me think."

"Help yourself," said Bill.

Connor looked befuddled. "Beer," he thought, "at a place of business. That's cool as hell."

Terry opened the refrigerator and grabbed three beers from the cardboard beer case inside. He tossed one to Connor, one to Bill, and cracked open the third. Rather than slamming down the first drink out of the can, as Terry normally did, he just took a small sip and swished the beer around in his mouth. This was exceedingly strange, as Terry never made a decision in his life with any thought. Terry lived for the moment, for today, not tomorrow.

"Connor, you should buy this bike and start riding again."

Connor laughed again. "Dude, Julie would kill me, you know that."

"Man," Terry replied, "Julie ain't as bad as you think she is. She didn't marry a pencil pushing sissy like she has made you into. Maybe if you put a little bit of bad ass back into yourself, then Julie would bang your brains out more often."

Terry's line of logic was typical of Terry, and Terry knew that Connor had the money. Terry knew that Connor knew how to ride and that knowing how to ride a motorcycle is something that you never forget how to do. Terry assumed that Julie would be a little bit frustrated with Connor if he bought the bike, but Terry figured that she would eventually get over it.

"Dude, your birthday is coming up. Why don't you just buy this bike and tell Julie that it's your birthday present and she doesn't have to buy you anything? Look, you buy the bike and I will fix her up a bit, get her nice and shiny, and come riding up on the bike in your driveway on your birthday with a big bow tied to the forks. You will never forget that birthday. Think about it."

The idea that Terry presented was very tempting for Connor. Connor took a drink of his beer and contemplated the feasibility of him getting a bike as the various scenarios were racing through his head.

"Bill," asked Connor, "what's the guy asking for it?"

Bill looked at Connor a bit surprised that Connor even wanted to know.

"The dude said he wants $3500 but I bet if you gave him three grand cash he would take it. You want me to call him?"

Connor hesitated. Terry and Bill were staring at him, each one holding their almost empty beer cans, anticipating a negative response from Connor.

"Sure. Tell him I will give him three grand cash today only. If he won't take it, then I ain't going to do it tomorrow. Terry, if he takes the offer, we will do what you said. Can you have it ready by this weekend?" Terry couldn't believe what he had just heard. This was definitely not a typical spur-of-the-moment decision that Connor would make.

"Dude, listen, Julie doesn't care that much for me as it is. I was just fucking with you." Terry continued, "Bill, I'm going to have to wait a week or so before I have the scratch to buy it so…"

Connor interrupted. "Dude, Terry, I'm serious. I want it. Bill, call the guy up and see if he will take three grand."

Bill walked away as he was dialing his cell phone. Terry looked at Connor as he crushed his beer can with his hands and proceeded to throw it into the trash can next to the refrigerator.

"It's your funeral," said Terry, "but I will hang on to it for you until the weekend. That should give me time to get the stuff done to it."
"Can Bill do it for me?" asked Connor.

"Yeah, but it will cost you some money."

"That's fine," said Connor. "I can't rely on you to always fix the bike so I might as well have Bill do the work on the bike since I'm guessing that I will be having him do all the service on it. I don't know how to do any of that shit."

"Okay," Terry replied, "Let's see what Bill says when he gets off the phone."

Terry reached into the refrigerator and grabbed two more beers.

Connor had about ¼ of a can left and he quickly downed the beer so as to keep up with Terry. They both cracked open the beer cans and watched as the dog brought in a plastic coke bottle that he was attacking like a stray cat. Just as the dog decided that he was bored chewing on the plastic bottle, Terry and Connor heard a voice behind them.

"What's happening, Big T?"

Connor and Terry turned around. Terry reached out his hand and shook the man's hand.

Terry greeted the man. "Hey Ratchet. What do you know good?"

"This and that and everything else."

Ratchet was a man of fairly slender build. He had long salt and pepper hair and a full beard that hung down past his neck. He was wearing a pair of blue jeans, brown work boots, a black T-shirt with no sleeves, and a black leather vest.

Connor took note of this black leather vest. The vest had three patches sewn onto the front of it. One patch had "Ratchet" embroidered on it, while one patch had a skull with broken wings on the side of it and the last patch said, "In memory of Trigger."

As Ratchet turned away from Connor to reach inside the fridge for his beer, Connor noticed the back of Ratchet's vest. There were three patches on the back of his vest. The bottom patch had "Kansas" on it, which was the state that they were in, the patch in the middle was a skull with a liquor bottle in its mouth, and the top patch read "Libertines."

Connor knew that there was a bike club in town called the Libertines. He had seen them riding on the roads, usually 4 or 5 bikes at a time. They all rode loud bikes and seemed to always be going to a bar. Connor envied their lifestyle as he considered his life dull.

Connor stuck out his hand to introduce himself to Ratchet. Before

Connor could open his mouth, Terry grabbed his hand and immediately made eye contact with Connor. Terry gave Connor a gaze with his eyes as to telepathically tell Connor to shut his mouth and stand still.

Ratchet turned back around and opened his beer.

"Ratchet, this is a friend of mine, Connor. Connor, this is Ratchet."

Connor said, "Nice to meet you, Ratchet."

"Same here." Ratchet extended his hand and Connor took it and they shook hands. Ratchet then wandered off and went back outside.

Terry grabbed a hold of Connor and whispered to him, "Dude, there is a whole etiquette thing with club members. You basically don't exist to them until introduced."

About that time, Bill came walking back into the shop with a manila folder in his hand. He walked up to Connor and opened up the folder. Inside the folder were a few pieces of wrinkled up paper and a Kansas motorcycle title.

"Gimme three grand bud. She's yours."

*Excerpted from *The Libertines Motorcycle Club: An Outlaw Is Born* by Max Billington (2011), ISBN 9780615542096.

Max L. Billington has worked in the insurance industry and as a consultant in the aerospace industry. He is an avid motorcycle enthusiast, has been riding motorcycles for more than 20 years, and is actively involved in community charitable functions and the organization of local motorcycle events. The writing bug bit him in 2011, after a good friend of his suggested that he should put his imagination to use by writing a book. Although his literary works are fiction, some of the subject matter is based on the biker culture of which Max is a part of on a daily basis.

The Run

By Iain Parke

Thursday 30 July 2009

I had been a crime reporter on the paper for over ten years now. It was how I met Damage and The Brethren in the first place. I had been to talk to him when he'd first been elected President of The Freemen, and then later when he was inside I'd interviewed him extensively in the last few months before he'd died. The publication and success of the biography that had come out of those sessions, Heavy Duty People, had made my reputation as a writer on both crime and biker clubs. So nowadays I often talked to both the police who specialised in this field, and other clubs who spoke to me with varying degrees of wariness or enthusiasm about the prospect of publicity.

On the police side of the fence, it helped that I'd known someone who was now one of my key contacts from way back when we were both teenagers. Bob and I had been at the same sixth form college together, had both been into bikes and so almost inevitably we'd both been part of the same small town social scene of pubs, discos, parties, bored suburban kids and girlfriends for four or five years or so. All normal teenage stuff, and one of my abiding memories of him was a night when we had cycled away at the end of a party we'd gone to on our tredders so we could get pissed; and him pulling away from me into the darkness while over his shoulder all I could hear was the sound of him fondly imagining he was imitating the noise of the black and gold Ducati 900SS that he had his heart set on as the perfect bike. Which would be quite a step up from the Wetdream he had at the time.

I'd moved away after university, up to London to follow my career and I'd lost touch with the crowd as I drifted away. I'd known vaguely that he'd joined the force and every so often heard a bit about his progress; off the beat and across into plain clothes, sergeant's exams, marriage to a Woopsie, inspector's exams and a posting as what he apparently described to one of our mutual acquaintances as the Sherriff of Uxbridge.

And then one day about six months or so ago, out of the blue we'd just met up again. I was at a SOCA briefing, the Serious and Organised Crime Agency that seemed to fancy itself as nascent British FBI, and there he was, up in front of me on the platform being introduced.

So I made a point of grabbing him at the end of the talk before I could miss him to say 'Hi', and we had snatched a coffee and a catch up for an hour or so in the canteen before it closed for the evening.

It wasn't surprising given the background we shared that biker crime was one of his areas of interest, and yes, he'd read my book. Useful background he called it. He had been particularly interested in asking what links I still had with The Brethren, and seemed disappointed when I'd told him, 'None, and given what was in it, I probably won't be having any anytime soon.'

Which at the time I thought was true.

We'd done some more social 'Do you remembers?' and 'Whatever happened tos?' and a bit more mutual professional quizzing and probing about 'What do you know?' and 'What can you tell me?' and that was it at the time. We were back in touch and we parted on the 'keep in contact' promise, which of course we both would. It was easy to see that we could be useful to each other in what we were doing.

So ever since then we had been dealing reasonably frequently. Telephone chats here, emails there, the odd meeting every now and then.

Of course there was a tricky balance to be maintained on both sides in this kind of set up. For a crime reporter a link into police sources, and particularly SOCA was vital, but while he could give me background, there was a limit on what he could say about the detail of any ongoing investigation, certainly for the record. From my side of the house, not only did I have a duty to protect my sources, but I knew full well what some of them might think if I started gossiping to the cops about everything they had said.

But we were both professionals, we had both been here before and we both knew the rules of the game. We knew what we were doing, and as importantly, what the other could and couldn't do.

So Bob was the obvious person to call once I'd got back to the office.

'Well,' he said once I'd finished, 'so are you going?'

'I don't know,' I admitted, 'I guess it depends on how safe it feels.'

'Do you think it might be a set up?'

'It's a possibility I suppose, but no,' I said on reflection, 'I don't think so. Like he said, if they wanted me out of the way they could easily have done that by now. They don't need to lure me out on some run to do it and to leave such a public trail.'

'I think you're probably right. If it was just a question of them wanting to settle business with you, then I'm sure they could arrange that without all this fuss.'

Well thanks, mate, I thought, that was comforting to know.

'Unless they want to get you somewhere to do it as a group thing,' he continued, 'to make an example of you as sort of a public spectacle within the club.'

Jesus, he was a cheery bastard.

'What about the cops? The Brethren wouldn't want to do anything with them around would they?'

'What cops?' he laughed, 'There won't be any on site. Never are. The Brethren police their own event. There's never any crime. Well, reported that is.'

'Christ.'

'So are you worried about going?' he asked.

'Yes of course I am,' I exclaimed, 'even before your jolly shit. Just because I'm invited by Wibble what guarantee is that? How can I be sure that one of the others won't just tee off on me on sight? Wibble said there were some pretty pissed off guys in the club about what I'd written.'

'But Wibble said he'd squashed that didn't he? And if it's Wibble who's inviting you, then I guess the first question is, do you trust what Wibble's saying?'

And it was odd but the answer to that, despite everything you might think or read about The Brethren, was yes. I think I did trust him and what he was saying. With my life? I reminded myself. Well possibly. And anyway, I thought to myself, I didn't have to stay long. If I didn't like the look of how things were shaping up I could always make my excuses and leave.

'And the second question is, do you think he can really control his guys?'

Well, having dealt with Damage for so long and learnt through him how the club ran, I thought I knew the answer to that one, and I was reasonably comfortable with it.

'Is it all peaceful now as far as your mob know?' I asked.

'Yes, about the big boys at least,' he said, 'there's nothing serious on the radar at the moment as far as we can tell, but that's only because they've got it all sewn up.'

'What about the stuff going on up in Lincoln?' I asked.

He seemed relaxed about it.

'Like I said, it's nothing to do with the big boys. Dead Men Riding and Capricorn have both got interests in the club trade out that way. There's been a bit of turf rivalry between them for years, there always is when you get a couple of clubs rubbing up against each other and there's business to be done. I don't know why it's flared up just now but I doubt it's anything too serious and nothing for you to worry about in terms of The Menaces, they won't be involved. A beef between two smaller clubs won't be on their radar, it's too small scale stuff for them.'

So Bob was confirming what I understood from my contacts as well. With the deal that The Brethren under Damage had refined with their main rivals The Rebels over turf and dealing, all was still quiet between the senior clubs at the moment. Everyone got on with making money and each generally kept their local, more junior, clubs in line in their own territories, albeit in the regions where there wasn't a senior club presence, like around Lincoln and the Wash, there could still be trouble brewing between the local boys. But while it might make for a potential follow up story, that wasn't my main concern just at the moment.

It was a bit odd this call just the same I thought, as I put down the receiver. Bob was a cop after all, and what's more, one with SOCA as well. Whatever anyone else thought about The Brethren and the other outlaw bike clubs, SOCA's view was crystal clear. The MCs were simply organised crime, full stop. So how come Bob seemed to be reassuring me about going on their run rather than warning me off, I wondered?

You would have thought a cop would only have one response to someone telling them the equivalent of 'I wrote a book which drove a cart and horses through the rules of omerta, and now I've been invited to a Mafia party,' which would be, 'don't go.' But it sounded as though Bob almost wanted me to be there.

I guess he must really think it'll be reasonably safe and he'll be hoping I might gather some intelligence for him, I decided. After all, I knew The Brethren were one of his key targets.

Well, we'd see. It would be useful to have some bargaining chips to trade with him if I could pick anything up on the day.

Saturday 1 August 2009

Of course it was their Toy Run. I had realised as soon as I thought it through while properly drinking my lukewarm coffee after Wibble had left.

An annual event, the Toy Run was one of The Brethren's main charity dos and an opportunity for them to present a positive face to the public who were always invited in for an open day and to see the bikes on show, and as much media as they could get to turn up. The local Brethren charters each took turns in hosting it on some kind of rotation, with all the other charters riding in bringing toys with them as donations that then went to children's charities. There would be beer tents and fairground rides during the day, a bike show and prizes, and then bands and decidedly more adult entertainment going on into the evening, as the rally turned into a more hardcore bikers' party which would go on through the Saturday night and well into Sunday morning.

I checked on the web. There was a booking site for tickets and to register for the run campsite for those who were going for the full on experience. This year I saw it was the Cambridge charter's turn to host. I wondered about going up into the attic and seeing if I could dig out my old tent to pack and then decided against it. I would take my sleeping bag just for show, but I didn't have any intention of using it. I was nervous enough about being there during daylight as it was. Sticking around until after dark when the beers would have been flowing all day just seemed to be asking to push my luck that little bit too far.

The meet for the run was in West London. I followed the instructions that Wibble had given me and so I rolled into the street in Wembley at about ten to ten the next Saturday morning. The Brethren clubhouse was the end pair of a row of shabby Victorian two-up two-down terraces a little way north of the Hanger Lane gyratory. The windows were covered in steel plates painted with The Brethren's black and red club colours, as was the front door of the further one, above which nestled a cluster of CCTV cameras covering the approaches from the front. The other front door had been bricked up so I assumed the houses had been knocked through inside somehow. A high brick wall topped with broken glass enclosed the yard to the rear which was accessed by a set of double steel gates, again in the same paint scheme, and which were, unusually I assumed, open, so that as I drew up I could see there were at least half a dozen Harleys there, parked but loaded and ready to go.

Not that The Brethren would be worried about security too much this morning. A further couple of dozen Harleys in various states of customisation were drawn up along the curb outside the yard and along the front of the clubhouse, all facing outwards, with their riders hanging around in groups, smoking and chatting as they waited for the off. The club's strikers had put out some police cones along the road to reserve space for themselves. Someone had nicked them, I guessed.

I read some bollocks somewhere a while ago, some journalist who had been fed a line that bikers always parked up so the bikes were backed against the pavement and facing away from the road so as to conceal the registrations from police observers. I had almost wet myself laughing. How the hell the pillock's informant had managed to keep a straight face with that one was beyond me.

It was just practical. If you were going to leave it on the side stand the bike was generally safer if you parked it that way so it couldn't roll forward. Christ, I despaired sometimes at the crap some people would believe.

Faces turned to check me out as I pulled up at the far end of the line where there were a couple of anonymous large Jap bikes tucked away as if out of sight. The nearest full patch guy turned away from a youngster he was talking to and fixed me with a wary glare.

'Yeah?' he demanded as I swung off my bike and he eyed the large teddy bear bungeed to the pillion seat of my bike, which I had indeed put on expenses for the day, 'And who the fuck are you?'

And a good morning to you too, I thought, but obviously didn't say.

As he'd turned I'd caught the flash across his chest, Sergeant at Arms above the blood red dyed tottenkopf tab. The head of club security. Shit, just the sort of guy you wouldn't want to have a problem with at the start of something like this.

'It's OK Scroat, that's the writer guy Parke. He's with Wibble,' growled a voice behind him that seemed slightly familiar, as I saw the man-mountain from the meeting at the service station walking across to where we were standing.

'We'll be off in a few minutes so you just fit in here at the back with us and the tagalongs and Wibble'll see you when we get there, OK?'

That was OK by me.

Scroat grunted and abruptly turned his back on me to resume his conversation with the kid he'd been talking to.

That was OK by me too.

The order in a club run is always the same. The club's officers would be at the front, the president and the road captain first, followed by the sergeant at arms and secretary, full patch members next, then strikers and finally the lowest of the low, tagalongs and very, very occasionally, a stray civilian like myself. Sometimes there would be a full patch tail end Charlie to keep an eye on the back of the column and a support truck if there was one bringing up the rear. The pack would ride close together in pairs and with this number of bikes on the road, a couple might take it in turns to ride ahead as shotgun so as to block traffic coming out of side roads while the column passed to prevent the pack getting split up by intruding traffic.

The only variation today was that it seemed as though Scroat and the man-mountain were fixing to ride at the back with me and two young looking guys.

I looked around and caught the eye of the kid standing next to the bike beside mine. From his unadorned jacket he was presumably a tagalong and I assumed also the owner of one of the Jap bikes. The other one must belong to the other lad I decided. After all, no self respecting full patch Brethren would turn up for a formal run of this importance on anything other than their hog.

It was the slickback's first time I guessed and I wondered if he realised how much he was giving off waves of pure nervousness, as though he was trying to look tough, pleased and serious all at once. It wasn't working. And it was the sort of thing I thought that someone like Scroat would pick up on like a shark smelling blood in the water.

He smiled at me, I think in recognition of someone who was less of a threat and introduced himself as Danny.

They would call him 'Danny the Boy' I thought, I could see it now.

'Hi,' I said and nodded at him, 'Iain.'

He had obviously heard what man-mountain had said and he was a bright kid. He immediately put two and two together.

'Hey,' he asked, 'are you the guy who wrote that book? You are, aren't you?'

'Heavy Duty People?' I asked.

'Yes, the one about Damage.'

'That's right,' I admitted quietly, looking around to check out any reactions. It really wasn't a subject that I was very comfortable with him talking about right now thank you very much.

I guessed that Scroat for example might not be much of a fan.

'Hey it was a great book.'

'Thanks,' I said, wanting to shut the conversation down, 'Glad you liked it.'

'I've read it loads of times. It's one of the reasons I wanted to ride with the guys.'

Oh God, I thought.

'So how come these guys are at the back with us lot?' I asked him as a way of changing the subject, but also out of curiosity.

'Shouldn't they be up front with the others?'

'Don't know,' he said, 'this is my first time out with the guys and Bung's my sponsor so I guess he's going to keep an eye on me.'

He gestured in the direction of man-mountain, so now at least I had a name.

'And Scroat?' I said nodding in Mr Surley's direction.

The kid just shrugged. 'Guess he's Charlie's sponsor,' he said nodding at the other kid who was now standing off to one side, quietly watching what was going on and ignoring us completely.

Given that he looked as though he couldn't be more than twenty or so I was shocked to see that he already had a bottom rocker marking him out as a striker, someone working his passage and on track to be voted on for a full patch after a year or so. It seemed extraordinarily early. The Brethren was a very adult organisation, in all senses of the word. Most of its active members were in their thirties, forties, even fifties, with a few grizzled veterans even older than that and still riding and rolling with the crew. While one of the byelaws said that no one under twenty-one could become a full member it was almost an irrelevance since in practice no one ever got put up for membership until they were in their late twenties or early thirties anyway. The Brethren wanted solid guys, people who had done their time, in various ways, who had proved themselves. So what was this kid doing on his way at this age I wondered, filing it away in the interesting-things-to-follow-up-at-some-time category.

Danny the Boy didn't look as though he was about to introduce me and given Charlie's attitude I decided that I didn't think that was looking like any great loss.

Just then there was a sudden wave of anticipation and movement that swept its way down the crowded pavement as fags were dropped and riders started towards their machines. An instruction had plainly been given from up at the top of the line and we were about to move off.

As I turned back to my bike it suddenly struck me that there was something odd about the crowd mounting their bikes this morning. The Toy Run was a charity gig and a major club party event. But all of the guys here were single packing. Why was no one planning to take their old ladies today? Yet another thing to file away in the corner of my mind marked things to worry about. Perhaps the girls were making their way over separately, I wondered?

That would be good, I thought. But it seemed unlikely as I started to worry.

There were only two reasons to single pack on a party run that I could think of. The first was because it was going to be the sort of a party that you didn't want to take your old lady to as she might cramp your style. But on the annual Toy Run, as a semi public event, that seemed unlikely.

And the second was because you thought there was going to be trouble.

The kid next to me hadn't clocked any of this, I could tell from his attitude. I wondered why he was here. The kid was worried about how he would hold up in this crowd, he hadn't picked up on the vibe that there was something going down here at all. He was an innocent who just smelled of wannabe and that was never going to wash with this crowd. The other kid, Charlie, the one who'd blanked me completely when I'd arrived; he felt more right, watchful, arrogant, unfriendly. He already had the air of apartness that characterised some of the guys. Despite his age, you could immediately tell that he was right as a striker. He'd fit straight in, I thought, if he stayed the distance. Damage had talked once about recognising, not recruiting, and with these two I could see just what he meant.

'Hey,' Danny the Boy shouted across from astride his bike as he did up his helmet, 'Are you writing another book? About the club I mean. Is that why you're here?'

That was a very good question, I asked myself. A very, very good question. So as I pushed the bike upright off its stand, turned the key and pressed the starter button for the bike to crob into throbbing life, I smiled back at him and shouted across the honest truth to the kid over the roar of the engines firing up all along the kerbside.

'The thing is kid, I really don't know.'

*   *   *

The run, the ride there, wow that was something else, like nothing else I had ever experienced.

I'd ridden with other bikers before of course. As kids my mates and I had hung around together and ridden together as we graduated up from our fizzies and AP50s onto our first real machines, our two-fifties, Bob on his Dream, me on my GS250T, Cliff on his RS. We'd all taken our tests and ridden these throughout our student years, blasting up to town to the Hammersmith Odeon for Sabbath gigs, or to the Marquee for Girlschool, racing each other round Surrey lanes and south west London's streets, or cruising down in a group to the west country to join the rest of the lads, with their assortment of second hand minis and parents' cars borrowed for the week, at Croyd or Perranporth for our drunken surf and zider holidays.

And then as we'd each got jobs, the first purchase had been the bigger bike, the seven-fifty, the real thing.

'It's like falling in love with motorcycling all over again,' Bob had told me when I first got mine, and he was right, it was.

And for the next few years we did all the same things on them as we'd done on the two-fifties, only bigger and better and faster. The trip to Devon or Cornwall was a complete thrash, one which cost me my first three points somewhere on the A303. The biking holiday one year for three of us was a seventeen hour and fifty-six minute blast leaving from Lands End at just gone five-thirty one beautiful July dawn and pulling into John O'Groats just before midnight that evening having realised as we zoomed past Carlisle and headed to the border that we were only half way.

And when we headed down to Box Hill on a sunny weekend we needed to be careful to dodge the speed cops on the dual carriageway.

I'd ridden on MAG demos in London, we'd joined in semi organised runs from Box Hill to Brighton on an August bank holiday.

Courtesy of Bob, I'd even been out a couple of times years ago with his local police motorcycle club, and fun rides they were, mind the speed limits in town and don't cross solid white lines but once out onto the unrestricted roads, it was every man, and one woman in skin tight leathers riding a bright yellow café racer Kwacker special, for themselves.

But none of those was ever anything like this.

Damage had talked to me about the discipline, the presence of an outlaw pack. But hearing about it and being part of it, even in such a tangential way at the back, was such a different thing.

Wibble had been right about one thing though. There was no need to wear anything fluorescent, not riding with this mob.

No one, not even the blindest Volvo driving twat, was going to do a sorry-didn't-see-you-guv-pull-out on an outlaw convoy like this.

The lights were red as we came to the junction with the North Circular so as I pulled in at the back of the pack behind the two staggered lines of slowing bikes in the column, I was just bathed in the noise washing over me of the clattering and banging rumble of the overruns as The Brethren braked.

The Japs had copied the look of the Harley, they'd even produced some fantastically close looking clones, but it was all surface. They had never managed to capture the souls of the machines, the feel, the heart, or most gloriously, the noise. That indescribable deep melodic throaty booming rumbling burbling growl emanating from the mouths of the slash cut shotgun exhausts.

Ahead of me I could see rear mudguards shaking and juddering from the Harleys' tick overs as we waited at the lights, a sound that at idle always seemed to clutter almost to a ragged dying halt, before tumbling over in its cycle again, the inimitable uneven mechanical heartbeat of the big V twin.

I was the only one in a leather jacket. The Brethren didn't tend to go in for the traditional British biker uniform, distaining its practical safety aspect. Black bomber jackets or donkey jackets were their riding outfit of choice underneath leather waistcoats bearing their sacred patches.

So the riders ahead of me were a contrast of black, red and steel. The high widespread handlebars of the big bikes putting the riders into a wide shouldered stance that flew their colours in an arrogant and open challenge to the world, while below the fat bulbous chrome steel dome of the primary drive cover hanging out low down on the left side of the bike, shining proud behind the riders' feet and hanging ponderously low, close to the rolling tarmac beneath, giving the bikes and riders that classic Harley profile from the rear.

Then the lights turned green and the noise picked up into a full throated roar as the heavy machines launched forward again in pairs and swayed in a heavy curve through the corner and out onto the main road.

*   *   *

A couple of hours later we swept through the high street of what would otherwise be a quiet Cambridgeshire fenland town like an invading army, the bikes' reflections flashing in the windows, and the harsh bark of the exhausts bouncing between the buildings, heads turning at the approaching guttural noise, the bikers' eyes fixed rigidly ahead, ignoring the everyday Saturday morning shoppers as they stopped and turned to watch the convoy rumble past like some kind of fearsome pageant.

Our destination was a rugby club just on the outskirts, where once through the gates we rode along a tarmaced track through a small orchard and then out at the edge of an open playing field with the sets of posts at either end, and a reasonable sized red brick built club house behind which the first bikes were pulling in.

We were here.

As we parked up at the back of the pack, Wibble was already striding straight across towards us, pulling off his lid as he did so.

'Alright?' he asked with a friendly grin as he reached us where I was settling the bike down onto its side stand and swinging myself off it. 'Enjoy the ride?'

'Yeah, it was great thanks,' I replied honestly, grinning right back. It was true. There was nothing like riding in a pack like that and feeling the world's eyes on you. It just did things to you. It was like an old biker saying, If I had to explain, you wouldn't understand.

'OK then,' he said, as I hurriedly stuffed my gloves into my lid and clipped it to the lock on the bike while he pulled his gloves off and quietly surveyed his dismounting horde before turning back to see how I was getting on.

'Well at least it's a V-twin I suppose,' he observed looking at my bike, 'even if it's an Eyetie one.'

'And at least he doesn't ride it like a twat,' the big Brethren chipped in from behind me to my surprise. 'Can't stand these fucking "born again bikers" wobbling round the corners like they're a thruppenny bit.'

It was an old Guzzi California, one of the original ones, with the black barrel shaped tank and huge creamy white trimmed buddy seat. I don't know why but its semi CHiPs styling had always appealed, I had just always wanted to ride a bike with footboards for some reason. I'm quite tall and lanky and I'd worried before I'd got it if it would be comfortable or whether I'd find myself banging my knees on its pots but it had been fine. Long legged and easy to live with had been the strapline on the gloriously sexist bike mag ads back in the eighties that I had ripped out and bluetacked to my bedroom wall, as long haired models in drapey slit-sided skirts lolled languidly and suggestively in front of the gleaming bike. And it wasn't a half bad choice of description either, the torquey 850 shaft drive was easy to live with and with plenty of grunt mado for a comfortable, if a bit squishy long distance cruiser, ideal for those summer trips over to France with my mates in my early twenties, boys abroad with tents bungeed onto the rack with one gallon plastic cans for red wine en-vrac at what seemed like pennies a time.

'Looks in good nick though for its age,' Wibble added approvingly.

Nowadays, it wasn't as sexy or as urgent as it had been when I was younger, it was an older affair, comfortable and relaxed, it felt like an increasingly middle aged reminder of a freshness and youth I'd never recover.

His ride, when he showed me later, was a very different proposition indeed. I guess someone who didn't know bikes, and I guess quite a few who did, would have taken a glance at it and just assumed it was a mildly customised Harley. But they would have been wrong. From its 2000cc S&S motor with RevTech coils, single-fire ignition, carburettor and pipes, its hand built frame, twin cap mustang style tank and classic chopper chrome Bates headlight, right down to its hand laced chrome spoked wheels and billet forward controls it was an entirely custom built, purpose filled machine. He told me the only original Harley components on it were the gear box and the traditional tombstone taillight, and afterwards I wasn't even too sure about that. Not that I could really tell all those details either. I was too long out of the serious bike scene to be able to pick it apart like that, but I only had to ask Wibble a single question about the bike to get the full ground up build and spec run through.

Mine was a comfortable old classic and well worn, but off the peg number.

His was a sharp edged, tailored high spec machine.

It was country tweeds suit versus hardnosed city slicker.

It was casual versus very, very serious.

'Ready?' he asked. I nodded.

'Come with me then,' he said, 'there's some people we need to meet first,' and turned away to walk off.

Well I thought, since I was here today, it was obviously time to go to work.

The kid who was standing next to me looked awestruck.

'See you round,' I nodded to him as I left and headed to catch up with Wibble.

'Yeah see you,' I heard from behind me.

*   *   *

'Where are we going?' I asked.

'We're here, so we need to meet the locals,' was his cryptic reply as we strode out, with some of the other Freemen falling in behind us.

The show cum rally cum party ran over the weekend. It wasn't in the same league as the Big Two's events, the Hells Angels' Bulldog Bash or the Outlaws' Rock and Blues Customs Show and Ink and Iron festival, the premier events in the UK biking calendar, but even so, The Brethren were determined to put on a good show.

Round the front of the clubhouse was the show. To the right of the pitch was a street of tents. Looking down the lines along which a small crowd of bikers and apparent tourists were drifting, I could see from the signs that the closest were hosted by a friendly support club, the local Harley dealer, a T-shirt seller, a Triumph owners club and traders in leather jackets and helmets. Beyond that the line curved round in an arc that lead back to the top end of the rugby pitch where there was a small cluster of other stands which from this distance looked like some kind of autojumble.

Ahead of me a giant beer tent and a row of burger vans from which I could just about smell the frying onions, marked the far side of the pitch; while behind them ran a hedge beyond which were the camping fields where a mass of tents of every colour, size and design had sprouted like a forest of demented toadstools, interspersed with parked up bikes and fluttering club flags.

The pitch itself had been cordoned off with a waist high screen of portable metal railings since it would be being kept clear for the day's events. At the moment the half to my right was being used as a showground for a guy doing unbelievable tricks on a trials bike, his commentary booming across the field from speakers on poles at each corner as he rode up and over seemingly impossible obstacles without bothering to ever actually use the front wheel of the bike.

Early in the afternoon there would be the formal ride in by The Brethren, followed by the other clubs and independents in order of precedence, up onto and across a stage that had been organised at the far end of the pitch on my left, to present their toy donations to the charity. Those bikes that were being entered for the 'show what you rode' would be parked up on the pitch for display and judging while the stage would be set up for the evening's bands.

Show awards would be at six, the music would kick off at eight and go on into the early hours. It was one of the reasons for holding it well out of town.

Should be quite a night.

And then further off to the left, behind the stage and beyond the pitch itself, was a single large marquee. There were two flagpoles outside the entrance each flying The Brethren's colours and even from here I could see a cluster of what were obviously strikers on guard at the entrance, one of them striking in the other sense of the word from the bright white sling his arm was in. He'd obviously had some kind of a shunt but as a patch, striker or tagalong, you'd have to be pretty fucked up and totally bedridden to miss today I knew. Still, I wondered how much slack, if any at all the sling would get him as a striker? Not much, was my bet.

This would be the members only tent.

Wibble headed straight towards it.

'Locals?' I asked, although I'd guessed what he'd meant.

'The Cambridge crew.'

I had been wondering whether he was going to take me into the marquee but as it happened we didn't need to get that far as a small posse of Brethren emerged from within as we approached and came forward to meet us.

The two groups stopped, facing each other a few feet apart as Wibble and Thommo, the local charter president, stepped forward to embrace in the usual formal backslapping bearhug and expressions of solidarity, while their respective crews eyefucked each other across the gap.

'So who's this?' Thommo said looking at me with an openly hostile stare as they broke apart again.

'He's a journalist,' Wibble replied calmly.

'You brought a fucking journo here? This weekend? What the hell for?' Thommo demanded.

'PR,' Wibble answered simply, 'He's here to see how nice we are right? So treat him nice yeah, you hear?'

It didn't look as if this news was endearing me to Thommo any more than before. Then Wibble really twisted the knife, 'You might have heard about him. He's the bloke who wrote the book about Damage.'

'Oh it just gets better doesn't it?' Thommo said, giving a surly snarl towards me.

Well thanks a bunch Wibble, I thought, that's just fucking great. Are there any more psychopaths you want to wind up and set on me?

'Yeah sure,' Thommo said, the edge of sarcasm obvious in his voice for all to hear. 'Why don't you just feel free to snoop around, just see what you find to write about?'

* * *

'What the fuck was all that about?' I whispered, as we walked away again towards the food stops, Wibble looking pleased with himself.

'Ah, just winding Thommo up.'

The subtext was clear. Thommo hated journos so Wibble imposing one on the party on his turf was really just Wibble rubbing Thommo's nose in his authority.

'Tell me, he's not a fan of yours anyway is he?'

Wibble raised eyebrow at me. 'What was it Damage used to say sometimes? You might very well think that, I couldn't possibly comment?'

Despite everything I laughed. That was Damage alright, from one of his favourite shows.

But still I wondered, if Thommo wasn't a fan, why make him mad? Surely Wibble already had enough to do watching his back, without provoking Thommo's hatred. Wasn't that just making unnecessary trouble for himself?

'So was that just a pissing contest then? Showing him who's top dog?'

'Could be. Does him good to be put in his place every now and then.'

Great, I thought, with me as the post to piss on. Thommo didn't look like the kind of guy to let it lie and if he couldn't get back at Wibble directly I reckoned he'd have no qualms about getting at me if he could. I'd need to be very careful about keeping away from him and his guys, I decided, both today and in the future.

But as it turned out, it seemed as though Wibble had thought of that too as the next thing he did was to organise me a minder.

'OK, so what happens now, what do you want me to do?' I asked.

'I've got some stuff I need to do first, so how about Bung shows you round?' he said, indicating over his shoulder with a jerk of his thumb to where The Brethren I had already recognised was standing. Even if Danny hadn't already dropped his name, I couldn't miss who Wibble was talking about, it would be hard not to. At six foot two or so, in most directions as far as I could see, he was the man-mountain who'd got me coffee at the services, and so presumably was one of Wibble's personal bodyguard.

'Bung, come over here for a minute willya?' Wibble shouted over to him.

'Bung?' I asked Wibble quietly as he ambled towards us.

'Short for Bungalow,' he answered.

Wibble introduced me with a, 'You've met.'

I could see why the nickname had stuck, although looking at the sheer size of him, Brick Shit House might have been closer to the mark.

'Stick with Bung here for a while will you? He'll show you round, let you meet some of the guys, keep an eye out for you, and then we'll talk.'

That was OK by me again, and so I headed off with the lumbering giant.

Over the next hour or so Bung walked me round, introducing me to The Brethren as we went, although I couldn't help but notice that the ones he took me to talk to were mainly the other Freemen and some of the ride ins from other charters. I didn't really do any interviews as such, more just a bit of chit chat. There was a bit of a tense atmosphere and for a while I couldn't put my finger on it.

At first I thought it was just me. After all, Thommo was hardly alone within The Brethren in what he thought about writers and so I thought the hostility was personal, not helped by who I was specifically and my history.

Then I realised how separate Thommo's local charter and some of the other ride ins were keeping from the Freemen and those that were hanging with them and so I decided that the tension I could feel stemmed from some animosity between these two groups. But after a while that simple explanation didn't feel right either as the tension seemed to be ratcheting up as the day wore on, without any noticeable interaction or overt incidents between the two clusters who simply seemed to be keeping themselves to themselves.

There was something else going on. But for the life of me I couldn't work out what.

As a civilian I knew I wouldn't be particularly welcome riding in after the patched clubs to make my donation, so after checking the form with Bung we made our way back to where I'd left the bear on my Guzzi.

As Bung and I wandered back past the clubhouse and the rows of parked bikes I spotted the two kids I'd ridden in with. They had obviously been told to stay with the strikers guarding the bikes as the start of their long apprenticeship ladder that might one day lead to a Brethren patch, and after a morning that felt a bit as though it had been spent bothering smiling tigers in their cage for interviews, I decided it was time for some light relief.

'Hey,' I said as I freed the stuffed toy from where it had been riding pillion and handed it to Bung who was gathering up a three foot high panda from one of the other non-club ride ins, 'do you two fancy talking for a bit?'

Danny smiled at the approach, but gave a slightly uncertain glance at Bung as if for approval that this was OK. The other kid just shrugged as if it wasn't worth making the effort to open his mouth.

As I began to talk to Danny, Bung roped in first a striker and then a grumbling Scroat to complete the collection and then, having made sure I was ensconced for a while, marched them off to deposit the toys on the stage, Scroat still moaning about 'Fucking teddy bears,' as he went, the three foot girth of mine edged under his left arm.

At first I tried to include the other kid in my questions as well, but all I got was a glowering look and occasional grunts so eventually I thought, well screw you chum, and concentrated on Danny.

I felt uneasy at how proud as punch he seemed to feel to be there. A bit of guilt perhaps that I was a little bit to blame, that I'd helped to glamorise The Brethren, although God knows it wasn't as if they were famous or infamous enough before I'd come along, after all they had a string of newspaper headlines stretching back since the early seventies in this country that had given them their public reputation.

I asked him anything and everything I could think of. Why was he here? How had he first met The Brethren and got involved? What did he think about The Brethren now he'd met them? What did he think about their reputation? What did he think he was getting himself involved with? Did he think it was worth the risks? What did his family think?

I suppose I was asking him the questions I would want him to ask himself before it was too late. Before he got too committed to something from which as far as I could see it was very difficult to back out of later.

With a heavy heart I realised that whatever I was saying, I wasn't getting through to him. And as I looked up from where we were sitting on the grass to see Bung bearing purposefully down on us, I realised I had run out of time.

'Well, if you ever want to talk kid, about all this I mean, come and see me.'

'Hey yeah, will do. Listen, but like with all the questions, you are working here aren't you? Writing I mean? That's what this is all about right? Isn't it?'

I could see how his mind was working. None of my question had done any good at all, had raised no doubts. The only thing he was thinking about was that he might end up being in a book about The Brethren and wasn't that going to be just cool.

That was the only time that the other lad decided to get involved. He could see it as well and he didn't like it.

'That's not what it's about. It's not about being a poseur,' he dismissed the prospect with barely concealed hostility and contempt, 'and you don't talk to anyone about the club without the club's say so. Club business is club business you understand? Because if you don't get that then you're never gonna make it.'

Danny fell silent and his face flushed red.

'Time to go,' said Bung, and I stood up and walked away.

*   *   *

Wibble wanted to see me.

'You're staying the night,' he said bluntly. 'Don't worry, Bung here'll look after you and I'll sort you out properly afterwards.'

He must have seen the look on my face.

'No, not that sort of sort you out. Protection I mean.'

I didn't know what he meant by that, but I didn't much like the sound of it.

It seemed as though I was free to come and go as I liked around the site, but given what had happened with Thommo, straying too far from Bung and the Freemen didn't seem too smart a move. Still it wasn't as if we were joined at the hip so I had a chance to think as we took a stroll round the site.

Bring a sleeping bag Wibble had instructed me when he'd given me the details of the run, so I had, just so as not to piss him off. So it gave me an excuse to head back over to where they were all parked up although what I really wanted to do was surreptitiously check out the situation by the bikes again. Of course, there were strikers on guard. If they had been told I wasn't to leave, there was no way I was going to be getting my bike back out the gates, and anyway, there were strikers on them as well under the control of a quiet watchful pair of patches, collecting the ticket money from the faithful as they arrived and stuffing it into plastic carrier bags that every so often would be collected by a posse of full patches and carried off back to the members only tent.

'So where are you guys sleeping?' I asked Bung as I unhooked my bag from where it was bungeed to the bike's buddy seat.

'Crash tents. Some of the strikers have come in a transit and they're busy getting them up now.'

'The ones behind the beer tent?'

'Yeah, it's all TA gear, Widget and his lads have borrowed it for the weekend.'

So that explained the gang I'd seen laying out a row of large green army tents.

As we made our way back across the showground so I could drop my gear off, I was still keeping my eyes open for possible escape routes.

There was a fence around the rest of the site facing onto the road and hedges and smaller fences elsewhere. Even if I gave Bung the slip, I'd be seen if I tried climbing over any of them during the day so if I wanted out, I resigned myself to the fact that it looked like the best bet might be to wait for dark anyway.

While Bung stopped to meet and greet a posse of bikers from some support club that he seemed to know and want to chat to, I took the chance to wander out of sight for a moment and whip out my mobile.

Thank Christ, Bob answered on the second ring. Breathlessly I filled him in on my situation and asked what he thought I should do.

'Nah, you'll be safe enough I'd think,' he said, 'It's the Brethren's main public event of the year, a big money spinner and a shop window for them. They aren't going to want to compromise all that with a murder. Not when they could do it any other time. Why have the hassle?'

So it looked as if my chances of rescue from the outside weren't great either.

'OK?' asked Bung as he caught up with me as I chatted with the guy at the next stand about his charity which involved getting disadvantaged kids to build ratty but working bikes.

'Yeah fine,' I said cheerfully, but I remember thinking as I did so, show any fear and you'll never going to fucking get out of here alive.

But as it happened, as the afternoon wore on, despite my misgivings, I did start to feel safe enough in the Freemen's company to unwind a bit and begin to enjoy myself.

The sun was shining. People, by which I meant The Brethren and their cohorts, were, in the noticeable absence of the Cambridge crew who it seemed had taken themselves and their grudge off to a beer tent on the other side of the field, relaxed and friendly.

I supposed there must have been some underlying issue with Thommo's charter that the Freemen had thought might lead to trouble, but now that seemed to be off the agenda they just seemed determined to bask in the crowd's attention and have a good time.
There'd been no mention of The Brethren in connection with the local punch-up between Capricorn MC and Dead Men Riding MC or any suggestion of a link that anyone had made to me so far, so I didn't think it had anything to do with that, although I supposed perhaps Thommo and his boys were under a bit of pressure from the rest of the club over it. It was clear that part of the reputation of a senior club like The Brethren rested on the expectation that they would keep the more junior clubs on their turf under control. After all, no one wanted any unnecessary trouble since trouble was bad for business, and a war, even between two junior clubs was trouble since it could lead to all clubs, senior and junior, coming under the spotlight. So I guessed The Brethren would be looking to Thommo and his boys to get this thing under control which might explain the obvious needle between Wibble, as president of the Freemen, and Wibble as the local charter P.

'Spliff?' Bung asked.

'You want to roll up here?'

'Nah,' he said, before adding in best Blue Peter fashion, 'here's some I made earlier,' surprising me when he flipped open a pack of cigarettes from his cut's pocket to reveal half a dozen or so tailor-mades and a handful of twisted doobie tips, and tugged one out.

He cupped his hands around his lighter as he flicked the wheel with his thumb and sucked in a deep breath to draw it into life. They were huge hands I noticed as I watched the performance, darkly tanned with the blurred and faded blue-green of old tattoos dark against the skin under the hair on the back, the fingers encrusted with a selection of heavy and ornate silver skull and patch themed rings that probably did well as an impromptu set of knuckledusters when needed.

Then he all but disappeared in a huge puff of acrid white smoke as he exhaled and took a second toke. He looked around the field approvingly as he held it in for a moment, giving an air of complete contentment.

'Lovely,' he said as he exhaled slowly and proffered it to me.

I had to take it. There was nothing for it but to do what I had to do.

I'd smoked a lot at uni, In my day it was resin, eighths of hash, gritty but soft and crumbly Leb black, or rock hard nodules of Moroccan red that needed to be melted with a match before you could sprinkle it onto the baccy; or so our little league dealers told us. Grass was a rarity and anything else was an occasional experiment as and when it presented itself. That was how I had first actually spoken to any of The Brethren, when a trio of them were selling ten quid wraps of speed outside the doors of a Motörhead gig at uni. Not that I remembered much after that other than borrowing a fiver from a mate to roll up and heading straight to the bogs to do the lot. It was evil fucking stuff I have to say.

But I'd been a reasonably regular stoner as and when I could catch it, right up until I'd had a bad trip while under the influence; panic attack, hallucinations, shit it shook me up. And then I left uni and suddenly I wasn't around the people I knew who could get it and so I just sort of stopped. It wasn't that I gave up as such; it was just that I wasn't bothered. And then I'd given up smoking period.

And much to my surprise I'd beaten the habit, at least other than the odd guilty fag or café-crème once in a blue moon and nowadays I didn't even smoke ordinary smokes really anymore, let alone joints.

I lifted it to my lips and took a hit.

'Jeeeezus!' I swallowed a cough as I concentrated on keeping the smoke down to get the full hit, even as the harsh hotness of the raw weed caught at the back of my throat. Then I let it out again in a long stream as a definite buzz hit me. 'What the fuck are you smoking?'

Bung just grinned as I spluttered and gasped while I handed back the joint.

'It's good shit isn't it? Our local Cong's sensei special.'

'I can see why they call it skunk,' I said, 'Christ it stinks.'

The Cong were the growers, I knew that already from Damage. Cannabis farming had become something of a Vietnamese gang speciality with rented houses gutted to make way for intensive cultivation under hot lights by trafficked peasants using stolen electricity until the smell, the heat or the occasional fire when someone got careless with the wiring gave them away.

But with the plants cropping in batches every few months and continuous cycles of batches coming through, the occasional lost crop was just a cost of doing business as far as they were concerned, while intensive cultivation was inexorably raising the strength of the weed's THC.

What the Cong didn't have was the distribution networks to retail the gear or the muscle to control dealing territory which was where other operators, like the bike clubs, and others, were a natural fit.

And if you were dealing in the shit and had a taste for it the way Bung obviously did, naturally you would keep some of the best stuff for your own personal use.

Whether it was the strength of it, or whether it was just that I was now so unused to it after all these years, after only a couple of tokes I realised that Christ, I was actually pretty bloody stoned already.

'Shit, I need a beer,' I said.

'Now you're talking,' agreed Bung and together, the man-mountain and I shambled across the field towards the bars.

As we went inside and a path opened up in front of Bung towards the bar I slipstreamed in behind pulling out my wallet as I did so, it was my shout I reckoned; I had a brief moment of clarity. Probably one of the last for the day if I'm honest looking back.

Advice or no advice, thanks to taking that first spliff, it was pretty bloody clear by now that I wasn't going to be leaving. I would be staying the night with The Brethren and if I was going to be under Bung's protection from whatever Cambridge's beef was, then I needed to stick to him and keep him onside.

And then I plunged on in before the crowd could close in behind him and separate us.

*   *   *

So for the rest of the day and into the evening I tagged along with Bung, meeting the other Freemen and those of The Brethren who were attaching themselves to Wibble's crew. As the day wore on I was introduced to a generally friendly parade of names that I tried to keep track of, from the Bills, Steves, and Mikes of various descriptions, to the Smurf, Gollum and Viking.

It was a tricky balance to try and pull off. As a reporter my natural instinct was to observe, learn and record. But as the beers flowed and the spliffs circulated during the afternoon that ambition became more and more impossible, while I also knew that having notes taken about them wasn't exactly a favourite activity as far as most Brethren were concerned and so if I was too obtrusive I ran the risk of changing the atmosphere fast in the wrong direction.

And since it seemed as though my health and safety depended on these guys' goodwill, discretion very rapidly took the part of valour and I stuffed the notebook away early doors, promising myself that I'd write up some notes when I crashed for the night.

Some hope.

As a result, looking at the scrawls in my notebook it was true when I wrote at about midnight: As it is, all I have are some very fragmentary notes and increasingly fractured memories of the night.

Cambridge crew are keeping themselves to themselves, but Bung and the other Brethren, with me tagging right along after them, are mingling with visiting clubs. Patch, side patch, MCCs. Come to show their colours and/or pay their respects? Even a women's patch club, The Psyclesluts MC. Very scary crop haired women with ears that looked as if they'd been in a nail factory accident. Why should the guys have all the fun?

Seems they've all read Heavy Duty People. Bung at pains to tell me that he'd nicked it, not bought it. Long surprising discussion with two Brethren, nicknamed Eric and Ernie, about twentieth century English novelists, a dismissal of D H Lawrence as really just an Edwardian writer and an appreciation of the oeuvre of Virginia Woolf. Astonishingly well read but then a real surprise. Open University English degree. BA Hons, the both of them. On the road and inside, Eric explained, Not a lot to do inside but read. Ernie: He waited 'til he got out to graduate y'know, so he could go up on stage with his colours under his gown.

Impressive camaraderie and self assurance. People who trusted each other bond of brothers. Explanations of their philosophy. We're not called The Brethren for nothing. The name wasn't picked by chance you know? These are my brothers, my family. Then more serious. Our trouble is we make good villains. The lament on the proffered business card, When we do good no one remembers, when we do bad no one forgets.

Bad munchies. Mars bar, chips, and a coke from a van.

Bonfires of tyres from neighbouring field after dark. Party atmosphere, faces emerging from the black, lit up by the fierce yellow stinking blaze. Laughter as one of the strikers rips the arse of his jeans on the barbed wire of the field as they struggle back over the hedge bearing a dead tree for the bonfire. Ribald and very concerned inspection reveals that the family jewels are intact.

The music from the sound system in between bands. A cracking set. A lot of stuff I don't recognise, some stuff I do. Anti Nowhere League's driving rasping gargling version of Streets of London running straight on after John Otway's Beware of The Flowers, Dumpy's Rusty Nuts, A Burn-up On My Bike, Christ, not heard that in years, and then ZZ Top, Blue Jeans Blues.

Roaring noise in my ears. Stagger out of main tent, not sure if it's the skunk, the generators, the booze or the bands. I'm sodden. Around midnight, Bung had had Wurzel and one of the others wrestle me down into the mud amongst the press of the beer tent towards the bar. My first Brethren party so he said I had to be baptised. Half a dozen of them pouring pints over my head, laughing while I buck against the weight and grip of the bikers and call them bastards!

Back at the huge roaring bonfire, all red, orange and white heat against the blackness of the night, Brethren and others sitting and lying around the upwind fringes to avoid the driving acrid thick smoke coming from off the burning tyres.

People increasingly wrecked. You need to write this down all about how we came together as a band of brothers to ride free and go out righting wrongs. Laughter from further round the fire at the bullshit. Protests: no I'm serious!

*Excerpted from *The Brethren Trilogy: Heavy Duty Attitude* by Iain Parke (2011), ISBN 9780956161529.

Iain Parke imports industrial quantities of Class A drugs, kills people and lies (a lot) for a living, being a British based crime fiction writer. He became obsessed with motorcycles at an early age, taking a six hundred mile cross-country tour to Cornwall as soon as he bought a moped at the tender age of sixteen. After working at a London dispatch job delivering parcels on a motorcycle, he built his first chopper in his bedroom at university, undeterred by the fact that the workshop was upstairs.

Armed with a MBA degree, Iain first worked in insolvency and business restructuring in the UK and Africa, where he began work on his first thriller *The Liquidator*. The success of that novel propelled him to write a 'biker lit' trilogy about the Brethren Motorcycle Club, which has recently been optioned as a series for television in the UK. Today Iain lives off the grid, high up on the North Pennines in Northumberland with his wife, dogs, and a garage full of motorcycle restoration projects. He is currently working on a number of book projects, including another biker-based trilogy.

Brothers Of War—Forever United

By Edward Winterhalder & James Richard Larson

FBI Agent Mitchell Gates keyed his radio, checked in again, and relaxed back in the plush leather seat of the big Buick four-door sedan. Earlier, he'd seen Yousef Bahari enter the apartment building, followed shortly thereafter by three others of Middle Eastern descent, two men and a woman. Gates recognized one of the men as the professor Ali Barush. Later still, Zarah Bahari, the sister of Yousef, entered as well. After ten minutes or so, Zarah emerged from the apartment building entrance, returned to her car and drove away.

Zarah returned half an hour later with grocery bags. When she was about to enter the apartment building, she hesitated at the sound of a car horn. When she turned, she smiled and decided to wait.

Gates noticed that another car had entered the lot, but his full attention was on Zarah. When the car doors opened, a Hispanic woman got out of the passengers side. When the driver got out of the car, Gates sat up in his seat, suddenly alert. He reached for his field glasses to be sure.

There was no mistake about it. The man was Scott Conlon.

What in the world is Scott doing with these people? Gates wondered.

Baffled, Gates saw Scott accompany the two women inside. A few moments later, Yousef Bahari, Ali Barush and the unidentified couple left the building.

* * *

Zarah, relieved that her brother and the others were gone, said, "Please, Isela and Scott—make yourselves comfortable. My brother has business to attend to, and he won't be joining us for dinner."

"Nice place you have here," Scott said. Although the apartment reeked of strong tobacco with smoke still hanging in the air, the rooms were spotless.

"I told you, Scotty," Isela said. "Check out the view from the patio window—it overlooks the park."

"I do like it here. But please—forgive the smoke," Zarah said. "I don't smoke myself, and my brother smokes too much, as do his friends. I don't particularly care for it."

"Why don't you make him smoke outside then, or on the balcony?" Isela asked.

"Our men smoke. They talk, they drink tea, and they smoke. Sometimes I think that's all they do."

Later, relaxing on the patio chairs, Scott said, "The dinner was excellent. When I was in the service I spent a few months in Kuwait and about a year in Iraq. I found out that I really liked Middle Eastern food—all kinds. Man, I'm stuffed!"

This earned a smile from Zarah. "I am so pleased that you liked it. Please forgive me for not providing liquor, but it is against our beliefs. Can I get you another Coca Cola?"

"I don't think so, Zarah. It's getting late. It's time we went home," Isela said. "Remember your promise—you're going to have to come to our place now."

"That's very kind of you. I'll make sure I do that," Zarah said.

"Well, how about next week? We can make it Thursday after work. What do you say?"

"Yes, I'd like that very much," Zarah said.

"Bring your brother if you like," Scott said. "He's welcome too."

"I'll be sure to let him know," Zarah said. "Thank you."

At the front door, they said their goodbyes. When they were gone, Zarah went to the bedroom and retrieved the recorder. The night was mild, and she took the unit out to the balcony.

Seated in the deck chair, she sat the recorder on the small table and keyed the machine to play, and gently rocked to and fro. A neighbor crossed the street to the park, his big German Shepherd pulling on its leash. Zarah relaxed, leaned back, and listened. She clearly heard the Pakistani woman say, "We thank you so much for your hospitality."

The rocking stopped. Her eyes saw nothing as she heard the conversation, the talk of explosives, of murdering innocent people, of bombing a stadium where thousands would be killed and maimed. Some of the conversation by Mina and Uddin was in Urdu, but for Ali's benefit, the majority was in English, understood well by the four plotters.

In shock, Zarah reached to turn off the machine. The scraping noise startled her, and she spun around, thinking it was her brother. To her right, from the next apartment, the middle-aged woman had opened her patio door and had come out on to the balcony.

Zarah was in no mood to converse with the chatty woman. She nodded to her before the conversation could begin, took the recorder in hand and quickly went back inside the apartment. Slowly, like a zombie, she walked to her bedroom. Placing the machine beside her on the bed, she stared at it, disbelieving, as if it was a sick joke, as if it was something that would vanish, and things would return to the normality that had existed only fifteen minutes before.

I knew he was up to something but I can't believe he'd actually think of doing a thing so terrible as this she thought. *It has to be Ali's influence over him—that must be it! Yousef is so impressionable, but this? This madness? Allah what do I do? Who do I turn to? I know one thing. I will not let it happen. I can't allow my brother to be party to something this evil. What in the world is the matter with him?*

* * *

Isela quickly wrapped the towel around her head and nearly tripped on the carpet on the way to the living room. She got to the phone just before the answering machine began.

"Hello?"

"*Hi. I'd like to speak to Scott if he's around.*"

"Yes, who's calling?"

"*This is Mitchell Gates.*"

"Oh, hi Mitchell. Geez, we haven't heard from you in a long time. What did you do? Fall off the world or something?"

"*I've been out of town,*" Gates said. "*A temporary assignment in Washington, D.C. It's good to be back. How about you guys? How's everything?*"

"Oh, we're doing all right, I guess. I'm still working at the hospital and Scotty works for Waddy's. Ah, he's not here right now. He's down at the clubhouse. Church is tonight. Do you want me to tell him you called?"

"*Church?*"

"Oh, you know," Isela said. "It's what the Skuldmen call their weekly meetings. Don't ask me why."

"*He's in the club now?*" Gates asked. "*Wow. I guess I haven't kept in touch. I knew he was interested in some way but to be honest I didn't think he was that serious about it.*"

"He didn't tell you?" Isela said. "He's been patched in the club now for quite a while."

"*No, I didn't know that,*" Gates said. "*Well ... does he have a cell phone?*"

"Ah, no, he doesn't. He never carries one. I've tried to get him to buy one but I haven't convinced him yet. But I'll tell him you called."

"*That's fine. Well, I'd better get going. Thanks, Isela. Nice talking to you again.*"

"Same here, Mitchell. Goodbye."

*   *   *

At church, T-Bone felt his phone vibrate. The text message from Isela read *Have Scotty call me no emergency.*

When church was over, T-Bone flagged down Zipper.

"Isela buzzed me," T-Bone said. "Call her back. When are you going to break down and get a phone, you cheap fucker?"

"Probably never," Zipper said. "I had one once. Every time I needed it the damn thing was dead. I get along fine without it."

"Yeah," T-Bone said. "Well, here's a news flash. You have to plug 'em in and charge 'em up. One of these days you'll break down on the side of the road and you'll wish you had one. Just wait."

"It happened to me already," Zipper said. "The phone was dead."

Zipper hopped on his bike and went to the pay phone at the Laundromat a few blocks from the clubhouse. Using the clubhouse phone for personal calls was frowned upon. The club had to be careful. Big Brother was always watching and listening.

"Hi babe. I got your message. I figured it must have been important if you called Ramon at church. What's happening?"

"*Mitch called.*"

"Did he say what he wanted?"

"*No. But he's a fed. I don't know what it's about but why does he want to talk to you?*"

"It's probably nothing. I'll call him from home and see what he wants. He might just want to bullshit or something. I don't think it has anything to do with the club."

"*The way it sounded I don't think it could be about the club. It was like he didn't know, unless he was trying to get information out of me. He said he had been out of town—in Washington D.C. He claimed he didn't even know that you were patched, but I think that's a lie. Oh geez, Scotty, maybe I shouldn't have told him where you were. I know he's your friend, but …*"

Scott was keenly aware of Isela's dislike of Gates. The men in her life were one percenters, and law enforcement people were the enemy.

"Don't worry about that, babe. I was going to tell him anyway. We just can't be seen together. Mitch has to understand that now. Some of our guys wouldn't understand."

"*I know. You coming home soon?*"

"Two hours."

"*I have something special planned for you tonight.*"

"Oh yeah? Like what?"

"*I guess you'll find that out in two hours.*"

* * *

The next day, when Scott called Gates, they agreed to meet for lunch at El Conehito's Mexican Cantina on 6th Street, a favorite of police officers and law enforcement workers.

As soon as he entered, even though he had dressed casually and had covered his tattoos, Scott felt the unease of being around so many law enforcement types. Nevertheless, he navigated through the busy restaurant and bar. Gates was already there when Scott arrived, seated exactly where he said he'd be, at a table for two in the back dining room.

Gates stood when Scott approached, and the two friends gave a quick hug as they always did. When a man saved your life, you didn't forget him.

"If you like Mexican food, this is one of the best places around," Gates said.

"So I've heard."

"I thought about linking up with you—hell, I didn't realize how much time had passed," Gates began. "I was in D.C. for quite a while working a case. I guess that's a poor excuse for not keeping in touch."

"Hey, no problem," Scott said. "Life goes on. And I'm sure we've both been busy. Either way it's good to see you again."

"Isela said you were patched with the Skuldmen MC," Gates said. "I don't know if I should congratulate you or what."

"It's something I've wanted since I was a kid."

"Yeah. I know that. I'll be honest. I never understood it, but you are who you are, I guess. Far as I'm concerned you're still the same person—although from where I'm sitting, it kind of puts us in different camps. You must know that law enforcement regards the clubs these days as criminal enterprises. From what I've seen on this end, that's exactly what they are."

"That's the misconception the press pounds into the public, with the police waiting in the wings to hassle the bikers, especially the club guys, and put them in their place," Scott said. "It couldn't be further from the truth. We're not criminals, no more than any other groups are—and by the way, that includes the cops. When a cop commits a crime, they don't consider the entire police department a criminal enterprise. When a biker commits a crime, they do. The club never committed a crime or broke a law. Individuals might, but not the club."

"You don't really believe that, do you?" Mitch said.

"It's the truth. Look, Mitch. I know something's on your mind. And I know you didn't ask me to come here to reminisce. Before you say anything, this doesn't have anything to do with the Skuldmen, does it?"

"No. It's nothing like that. Not my department, y'know?"

"Well—that's a relief," Scott said. "My loyalty is to the club. I take that as serious as I did when I gave my oath as a soldier—as serious as my loyalty to our country. One thing you'll find about patch holders—a lot of us are vets. We don't take our freedom for granted."

"You can equate the two? No B.S.? You really mean that?" Gates said.

"Yeah, I do. It's a brotherhood no different than when we were in the service. So—what's this about?"

"Well, here it is," Gates said. "And I'm sure you have an explanation. I saw you enter a residence. I was doing surveillance and there you were. And it appeared as though you were with the people we're interested in. It doesn't make sense to me."

The wheel in Scott's head spun like an old Rolodex out of control. *Be careful what you say. Gates knows something—if it isn't about the club, then what?*

"What in the world are you talking about?"

Gates kept his voice down. "Do you know an Iraqi student by the name of Yousef Bahari?"

So that's it. It's something about Isela's friend's brother. The big mouth.

"Yeah, sure. Isela works with an Iraqi woman named Zarah. Yousef's her brother. He goes to the University of Southern Wisconsin. What? The feds are interested in this guy?"

"He and a few others," Gates said.

"Well," Scott said, "From what little I know of him, he's got a big trap—and he's nothing but a whiny little piss ant. Zarah's okay. She's Americanized, you know? But her brother is an asshole. Like most of them foreign cocksuckers he thinks the U.S. owes him. He moved in with her a week or so ago. Quit his job. He's a fucking leech as far as I'm concerned. Isela doesn't like him either."

"There were others as well, when you entered the apartment building," Gates said. "Did you see them or talk to them?"

"Yeah. I saw them, but I didn't talk to them. They were leaving as we got to Zarah's apartment. Zarah invited us over to dinner. That's all. The others all seemed to be in a big hurry to leave. Her brother, two other men and a woman. I think Zarah said the older guy is a college professor."

"He is. His name is Ali Barush. He teaches at the university—Sociology, History, Middle Eastern studies. We're not sure who the other two are. Not yet. You weren't introduced to them? They didn't say their names?"

"No. But I can find out easy enough. All I have to do is ask Zarah. What? Are these guys wanted for something?"

Gates hesitated. The waitress came, took their order, and moved on to another table.

"I can tell you this much," Gates said. "I'm working on a case under the jurisdiction of Homeland Security. The FBI keeps tabs on certain foreign organizations considered enemies of the United States."

"You mean terrorists?"

"Yes. That's exactly what I mean."

"Yousef? Those others? You gotta be shitting me."

"It's not Yousef we're interested in—at least not yet. But Professor Ali Barush is a different story. We've known about him for a long time. He hasn't broken any laws. He has ties to an organization. We have information that Ali might be up to something."

"Organization?" Scott said. "What organization?"

"They call themselves the Jamaat. It's Urdu—Pakistani. The word means the circle, or the group."

"I've never heard of them."

"You'd be surprised at the number of our enemies," Gates said. "Like the book says, their numbers are legion. This group, the Jamaat, originated in Pakistan. They've been around for decades. Most are intellectuals, so they blow a lot of hot air and we've always believed they're relatively harmless. It seems that lately a more militant faction has taken over leadership of the group. They're itching to make a name for themselves. They make no secret of their hatred of the Israelis which means they hate Uncle Sam just as much."

"I saw enough of that when we were over there," Scott said. "You don't need to remind me. It happens time and again. We go over there and pull their asses out of the fire and they turn around and fuck us the first chance they get. The only ones we could really trust over there were our own people. By the way—did I ever thank you for saving my sweet ass?"

Gates grinned. "A million times. Ah, here's the food."

They ate in silence, stealing glances at the young Mexican waitresses.

"I think I'll have another beer to wash it down. Damn good food," Scott said.

After the waitress brought their beers, Gates said, "Is Isela close to Zarah? Are they good friends?"

"Yeah. Zarah doesn't have many friends. The Middle Easterners seem to be kind of weird that way—they tend to stay with their own kind—especially here in the U.S. But Isela gets along pretty well with her."

"Zarah's brother lives with her," Gates said. "Do you think Isela can keep her ears open? See her a little more often? Maybe the brother will slip. It sounds as though Yousef can't keep his mouth shut. Maybe when he's rattling his trap he might reveal something. Maybe the brother isn't involved at all. Who knows? But we have a reliable source that says something is going down with Ali. We just don't know what it is. They're meeting. That means they're planning something."

"I'll explain it to Isela and see if she wants to spy on her," Scott said. "That's what you're talking about, right?"

"If you want to call it that, then yeah. But this has to be confidential, Scott. You know that. Neither one of you can say a word of this—not to anyone."

"I kind of thought you were going to say that. Don't worry—we won't say a word—either one of us. If we learn anything, I'll let you know. But you gotta understand something, Mitch. You and I can't be seen together. If one of my club brothers even knew that I had a friend in the FBI they'd look at me in a whole different way. None of them trust cops. None of them. I shouldn't even be here. Isela knows about you—she knows about our friendship—but I swore her to secrecy. Her brother is a full patch Skuldman. I trust her to say nothing—not even to him."

"I understand," Gates said. "But I also understand that a lot of your club brothers are veterans, too—veterans who love their country as much as the next guy, probably more. And that's what this is about, no different than we were fighting together in Iraq. But this time, it's on our turf.

"I'll tell you what, Scotty. I won't contact you. You contact me. That way, I won't compromise you in any way. We'll set up a meet somewhere, that's all. Happens all the time in my line of work. I just want to know what Ali's up to. I'm sure it's no good, whatever it is. I need all the information I can get, however insignificant it sounds."

Reluctant, but reminding himself again of the debt he owed his friend, Scott said, "OK Mitch, I'm not making any promises, but I'll look into it. If I learn anything, I'll let you know."

*Excerpted from *All Roads Lead To Sturgis: A Biker's Story* by Edward Winterhalder & James Richard Larson, published by Blockhead City (2009), ISBN 9780977174713.

Edward Winterhalder is one of the world's leading authorities on motorcycle clubs and the Harley-Davidson biker lifestyle; his books are published in multiple languages and sold all over the world. He was a member, and/or an associate, of outlaw motorcycle clubs for almost thirty years. The creator and executive producer of the *PHASS MOB*, *Biker Chicz* and *Living On The Edge* television series, Winterhalder has appeared worldwide on television networks such as Bravo, Prime, CBC, Fox, National Geographic, History Channel, Global, AB Groupe and History Television. In addition to his literary endeavors, he is a consultant to the entertainment industry for TV, feature film and DVD projects that focus on the Harley-Davidson biker lifestyle.

James Richard Larson lives in Wisconsin and is a United States Navy veteran who served in the Vietnam War. An electrician and an avid Harley Davidson enthusiast for his entire life, he is the author of multiple books that feature the Viking lifestyle and Nordic mythology.

On The Road

By Troy Mason

The party around the campfire that night was just as crazy as the ones in Laconia. While the bikers smoked joints and drank beer, Jason slipped away from the pack, laid his bedroll in the shadow of his bike and tried to get some sleep. He no more than dozed off when Bull came by and kicked him awake. "Hey Prospect! Get your pansy ass up. You don't sleep till the Patches sleep. Now go out in the woods and get some more dead limbs and shit for the fire. We're running out."

Jason rose wearily. He and the other Prospects had gathered enough wood for two nights when the IRON KINGZ first pulled into the campground, and he knew Bull was just proving a point. Prospects were slaves to the Patches, and he was exercising his authority. Such was the price of membership.

Pulling on his boots, Jason staggered aimlessly through the campground looking for firewood. Outside the confines of the IRON KINGZ' area, the families who thought they were enjoying a nice summer camping trip were trying to get some rest. It was after midnight, and most of the lights in the campers and RVs were off. As Jason surveyed the scene, he noticed smoldering embers in a fire pit next to a pop-up camper. No one was around, and there were several oak logs next to the pit. "Fuck it," he thought. "They can spare a couple of these, and it'll get Bull off my ass for the night. He probably doesn't even remember he told me to do this."

He grabbed an armful of split oak firewood and started up the hill towards the IRON KINGZ' area. A dog inside a nearby motorhome started barking, and two lights came on. The first was inside and the other was over the door on the outside. Jason ducked behind a pickup truck as the door came open. An older man wearing pajama shorts and a white undershirt stood in the entrance. He was only about ten yards away, but he could not see Jason peering through the truck window in the dark. "What is it, George?" a woman's voice behind the man asked.

"Nothing I guess. I don't see anything."

"Those bikers are still up there," the woman said.

"Yeah. I'm going to complain tomorrow to the owners. They've ruined our whole night. It's like they don't even care that there are good families here, and nobody can sleep around those damn bikes and all the noise they make. I'm going to tell the owners they won't be seeing us here ever again if that's the kind of people they let in here."

"You should call the cops. They're disturbing the peace."

"I don't want to cause any more trouble than I have to."

"If you don't call them, I will. I am NOT going to have my vacation ruined by a bunch of criminals with absolutely no regard for anybody but themselves."

"Oh, to hell with it. I'll call them." He closed the door and walked back inside.

Jason hurried up the hill and found Lex. "Hey man, I just heard somebody down the hill say they were calling the cops on us. You might want to start stashing things in case they decide to search when they get here."

"No shit? Fuck those motherfuckers," Lex said. He was high, and Jason knew this was not going to end well for the IRON KINGZ if the cops found them all sitting around with drugs and guns in plain sight.

"Listen Lex. Unless you want to bail out about half the nation in the morning, you need to get the guys to hide their shit."

Lex did not answer; he just staggered away and sat down by the fire. He pulled a joint from behind his ear, and lit it with a stick from the edge of the fire. As he passed it around, Jason walked up and said to the crowd around the fire, "Listen up. The cops are going to be here in about five minutes. They're going to talk to everybody. Maybe run warrant checks. Even if they don't, all they have to see is you guys burning a joint around the fire, and they'll have cause to search. What do you think will happen then? You need to get your shit together unless you want to wake up in jail." It was a rare thing for a Prospect to speak to a Patch like this, and to speak to a nearly fifty Patches at once was suicidal. A normal reaction would have been for all of them to bull-rush the belligerent Prospect and beat him down, but instead there was stunned silence.

As the light of recognition began to dawn in a few eyes, they began to stir and move off toward their sites. Others were awakened, hushed whispers were heard, and the sound of saddlebags being opened, and things being flung into the woods resonated throughout the area. Within ten minutes, the entire site was clean as a whistle.

As the cleanup was ending, two patrol vehicles entered the campground winding their way through the sites towards the IRON KINGZ' area. When they approached, only about a dozen members were left around the fire. Except for Lex, they were all sober, and Jason was among them. The first deputy exited his car and walked toward the group. "What's going on guys?"

"Not much, how about you?" one of the patches replied. His name was Weird Eddie and he was the Treasurer of the Kentucky Chapter.

"Got a call about some noise up this way."

"Well," Weird Eddie answered, "that may have been the case a while back, but as you can see, it's pretty quiet now."

"Uh huh," grunted the deputy in reply.

The second deputy had joined him now. "You guys been drinking?" he asked.

"Sure, we've had a few. Getting ready to go to bed now, though."

Both deputies were shining their lights around the various campsites now occupied by peaceful, sleeping bikers. "You guys don't have anything illegal in here do you?" the second deputy asked as he continued to scan the area with his light.

"No deputy we don't," came the answer from one of the other patched members.

"Then ya'll won't mind if we look around, will you?" the deputy said.

"Actually, we would mind that very much," Jason said, stepping forward. We've got a long ride tomorrow, and our guys are trying to get some rest. There's no noise up here now, and there won't be any more tonight. There's nothing for you to see here, and nobody's going to consent to any searches."

This caught both deputies off guard. They stared at Jason, and the second deputy spoke again. "I need to see your ID."

"Why? I've done nothing wrong and you ain't got no reason to see it."

"Listen smartass, I can have a dozen cars here in twenty minutes. We will search every inch of this area, and we will charge everybody here with public drunkenness and disturbing the peace. And that's just for starters. Once we find dope and guns, that ups it all to felonies, and then we'll run warrant checks on your entire crew. My guess is a bunch of those will come back as WANTED in a bunch of different states. So once you're done serving your felony time here, you can go to the next state and start the process all over again."

He continued: "Your other option is to cooperate now, and maybe I can go easy on you and your friends. The choice is yours. The easy way or the hard way. Now what's it gonna be?"

Jason stood his ground. He knew the law better than either of these guys, and he knew this small-time department in middle of nowhere probably did not have a dozen cars on the entire force. He figured these two guys were probably the only two on duty in the entire county, and there was no way they were going to waste their entire night rousting a bunch of bikers who were leaving in the morning. "Call 'em in," he said. "We still won't consent to any search."

The deputies huddled together and spoke in hushed tones for several minutes. The bikers stood around the fire and watched. Lex was there, and he was looking at Jason very closely. Jason saw what he thought looked like a new attitude in Lex's eyes: Respect.

When the deputies again turned toward the bikers, the first one spoke. "We're going to be near this area all night. I don't even need anyone to complain again. If I hear anything louder than a mouse fart from this campground, I'll arrest everyone here for disturbing the peace. In either case, I'll be back here in the morning, and there better not be so much as a trace of you guys. Pack your shit and hit the road early."

Jason could see the anger rising in Lex. He was not in the habit of taking any lip from the law, and he did not intend to start tonight. Knowing any challenge to the deputies at this point would only invite trouble, Jason was quick to step forward and speak. "We got it, deputy. All you're asking is that we do what we're gonna do anyway." He gave a quick glance over his shoulder at Lex to make sure he had stopped. "You won't hear anything out of this camp tonight, and we're outta here in the morning. Y'all have a good night." He turned back toward Lex and said, "Hey Prez, these guys were just leaving. How about I get you a cold one and then we'll hit the sack?"

"Get us all a beer, and we'll watch these guys drive off."

Jason turned back to the deputies, and there was a momentary stare down before they began walking back to their cars. Breathing a sigh of relief to himself, he walked over to the nearest cooler and retrieved several beers for the bikers. Lex was the first to speak. "Prospect, you handled that pretty well."

And that was about as close as any Prospect would ever come to getting a "thank you" from a patched member. Without even finishing his beer, Jason grunted an acknowledgement to Lex and walked back toward his bike. He was tired and ready for some sleep.

*Excerpted from *Outlaw* by Troy Mason, published by Outskirts Press (2013), ISBN 9781478711759.

Troy Mason is a retired United States Marine, Iraq War Veteran, and an avid biker, logging over 20,000 miles per year on his Harley-Davidson. He lives in Virginia. This is his first novel.

Too Many Questions

By Vic Shurtz

Preacher mingled with the brothers while he ate a hot dog and drank tea. He would have a beer once in awhile after a hard day's work in the sun, but preferred his tea. He stood chatting with a friend when the young hang-around shoed back up.

"Dale, who is that kid?" He's been watching me all night long?"

Dale looked over at the young up-start. "I don't know his name, but he's always around. He doesn't say much, but he rides. I've seen him a couple of times by himself. Want me to ask?

"If you wouldn't mind. I'd appreciate it."

"Sure," Dale replied.

George and Preacher were sitting on the porch when Dale returned. "Preacher, I think you have a new hang-around. He asked a couple of discreet questions about you?"

Preacher offered Dale a chair with a wave of his hand.

Dale sat down.

"Who you're affiliated with, and where you're going."

Preacher smiled. He knew that if someone asks a question, and it really isn't any of their business, bikers won't tell them the answer.

"Is he getting any answers?" he asked.

Dale smiled. "No."

"Good." Preacher responded.

Dale looked over at Preacher. "Where are you going?" he asked.

Preacher smiled. "Denver."

Dale sat back. "Would you deliver a package for me?"

"Sure," Preacher responded. "Where am I taking it?"

Dale smiled. "Probably the same place you're going. The clubhouse."

"That works for me. I'll be leaving the day after tomorrow, early."

Dale nodded his head. "I'll have it here tomorrow."

The kid strolled by.

"Hey kid," Preacher hollered. The kid looked over.

"Me?" he asked.

Preacher waved his hand. "Yeah, you. Come here."

The kid out his hands in his pockets s he walked up to the porch.

"Yes sir?" he asked.

Preacher smiled. The kid was respectful. He liked that.

"Do you have any papers?"

The kid beamed. "Yes, sir," he said as he reached into his cut off Levi jacket and retrieved his pack. He offered them to Preacher.

"No, I want *you* to roll me a doobie," Preacher said. He slid his hand into his scrodie and produced some good California green bud.

"Sure," the kid said as he took a bud and started breaking it up. Dale, George, and Preacher watched. The kid's hands shook. When he was through, he handed Preacher back the smallest pinner he had ever seen. He smiled.

"You keep that for yourself. Now roll me a good one,"

"Sorry," he said.

This time he took his time and produced a nice round cigarette.

"That's better." Preacher said as he handed the doobie to Dale.

"Sit down for a minute. I want to talk to you."

"Yes, sir," the kid said as he sat down.

"I understand you're asking questions about me. Don't you think it might be a good idea to ask me, instead of sneaking around?"

"Sorry," he said.

"And quit saying I'm sorry. Never say you are sorry."

The kid nodded his head.

"Okay……" Preacher sat back. "Now ask."

"Well, sir, I was wondering where you were going."

"Why?"

"Cause I was thinking of asking if I could ride with you."

Preacher sat up. "Why would you want to ride with me? You have some damn good people right here to ride with.

"Utah doesn't fit me. I always feel out of place. I was thinking that if I went with you, I might find a place to call home."

Preacher studied the kid.

"Does it matter where I'm going?"

"No, sir. I've saved up a couple of dollars for gas."

"Does it matter when I'm going?"

"No, sir. I have a poncho and liner on my bike and a couple pair of clean socks in my saddlebags."

Preacher looked to the right at George. "Can you believe this?"

George was smiling. "He has all the right answers."

Preacher looked to the left of Dale. "What do you think?" he asked.

Dale was grinning. "If he fucks up, you could always kick him to the curb."

Preacher looked back at the kid. "Plan on staying here tomorrow night. We'll leave at sunrise, but tonight we're going to the bar and play some pool. I want to meet this guy who has been asking all the questions about me."

*   *   *

George and Preacher arrived at the club about an hour before the pool tournament started. George had made his call, and the bikes out front denoted their presence. A prospect stood watching over the bikes. Preacher knew a few of the old boys. His strategy was explained to the Brothers. They took their positions. George and Preacher picked a dark corner.

The bar held a reputation around town as being where a person could get into trouble. It also had the best pool team. Roger was part of that team. That fact alone told Preacher that the kid could shoot. Preacher, however, wasn't concerned with the kid's pool skills. He was worried about his own reputation. The kid was acting disrespectful. It was up to Preacher to discipline him. If he didn't the boys would loose their respect for him.

Roger swaggered into the bar like he was God's gift. He stood in the entrance. The light from the door behind him made him a perfect target. The pool tournament was not scheduled to start for another hour. Roger was here early. That fit into Preacher's plans perfectly. Roger was a good-looking kid. Clean face, short hair, and a twenty-five year old body that he had taken care of.

George glanced over at Preacher. He was watching Roger. Roger laid his case on the bar.

"Ernie, I'll have a cold beer."

The bartender reached into the ice and extracted a Miller Lite. Roger opened it and guzzled the first half.

"Run a tab for the night, will ha?" Ernie nodded his head. Roger grinned. "I think I'll practice for awhile."

"You do that." Ernie said.

Ernie was an old hand in the business. He had watched the patch holders converse with the older biker. He had also noticed the positioning of the prospects. He had survived in this bar as long as he had because he understood bikers. He knew something was going to happen. He called one of the older patch holders over.

"I don't want any trouble," he said.

The old biker replied. "Then stay out of it."

Ernie looked over at Preacher. "Okay," he said. He leaned back against the counter and cash register with his arms folded.

"Anybody want to play a friendly game?" Roger asked as he screwed his cue stick together. George looked over at Preacher, and nodded. George stood up. "I'll play you a game," he said.

Roger looked over at George. "Haven't I seen you before? You look familiar."

George took a cue from the rack on the wall. "I've been around," he said.

Roger stuck out his hand. "My name is Roger," he said.

George offered his hand. "George" was all he said.

Roger grinned. "I'll let you break," he said as he racked the balls.

"For a dollar?" George asked.

"Sure, I'll take your money."

George nodded his head. He set the cue ball off to the left side of the table. The balls all but exploded when George sent the cue ball down the table. Two solids and one stripe fell into the pockets. Without saying a word, George proceeded to clear the table. The eight ball was tucked behind the nine ball. George managed to kick it out toward the corner, but it didn't fall.

Roger was impressed. "You shoot a pretty good stick," he said as he stroked his stick. The cue ball glanced off the nine and bumped the eight, but it didn't fall. The cue held tight to the rail. George would have to try a bank shot. George put some high right English on the cue as he sent toward the opposite rail. When the ball struck the far rail, it came back on an angle that had the ball touching the side rail and tapping the eight ball into the corner pocket. George won. Roger pulled out a dollar and laid it on the table.

"Thanks for the game; care to try again?" he asked.

George shook his head. "No, but my partner might want a try."

Roger grinned. "Good, I'll take all comers."

George nodded toward Preacher. Preacher stood up. "Sure, I'll try you," Preacher said as he strolled over to the table.

Ernie had been watching the game and by play. None of the bikers had ordered a drink; they just sat and watched. When Preacher stood up, he noticed one of the boys step out of the front door, and one of them step out the back. They closed the doors. Roger noticed as well. Roger looked back at Preacher. His grin was forced.

"Name's Roger," he said. He didn't offer his hand.

Preacher nodded. "I'm glad to finally meet you, Roger. I've been hearing a lot about you. They call me the "Preacher."

*Excerpted from *Preacher: Thou Shall Not Lie* by Vic Shurtz (2006), ISBN 9781601451064.

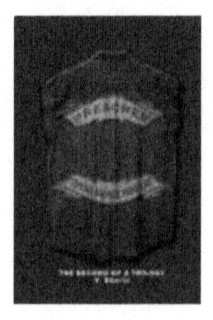

Vic bought his first bike, a 1971 FLH, in 1977, and has traveled extensively throughout the western United States and Canada. The author of five books about the biker lifestyle, he is a ten year member of the United Bikers of Northern California, a 501C Organization, and the owner of motorcyclefiction dot com, the website for biker books.

A Night Out With The Boys
By Edward Winterhalder & Marc Teatum

The ride to the bar went smoothly for Jake and the Skuldmen; not one of the bikers broke the pack formation along the way. Years of group riding experience translated into smooth acceleration, smooth deceleration, silky turns, and steady breaking. A consistent side-by-side pattern was the modus operandi of this bunch. Even in the encroaching twilight, the Skuldmen rode with confidence—but they were not overconfident. Like any seasoned rider, keeping a constant eye out for other motorists, especially those in the four-wheeled vehicles, was par for the course.

The Lobster Shanty was a small wooden structure plunked down in a marketplace at the edge of town; the shopping center had been created during the urban renewal craze of the late sixties and early seventies. Unfortunately, just like a farmer's cash crop that didn't flourish, the area it was in never quite thrived. It was one of the longest-surviving businesses in the pint-sized commercial village, which counted all of ten buildings— other tenants had come and gone every year or so. As they rode into the parking lot, Jake noticed that four of the buildings were empty; another one, Larry's Bait & Tackle, had a hand-painted going-out-of-business sign taped to the glass front door.

The Shanty, as the locals called it, was one story tall and had several sliding glass patio doors running along three sides of the building. On warm nights like this the owner of the joint opened the patio doors, alleviating the need to invest in air-conditioning. Placed outside were half a dozen plastic patio tables surrounded by plastic chairs, with folded Miller Lite shade umbrellas stuck in the center.

Although it was a warm night, no one was enjoying the great outdoors. Jake and the Skuldmen rode up on to the cobblestone surface, which permeated the marketplace, and carefully backed up their Harleys to the side of the building that didn't have any patio doors.

When they entered the bar, which wasn't licensed to hold more than ninety people, not including the patio, they became the business rush for the night. A lone pool table, basking under the glow of a triple hanging light bar, stood at one end; a postage-stamp-sized stage was nestled into a corner at the other end. There was no band or standup comic gracing the stage tonight, just the sound of an evening television talk show host greeted them. The décor, not surprisingly, consisted of some old lobster traps, a harpoon, what looked like a plastic marlin, and a fishing net tacked on one of the walls, to which were affixed some seashells and starfish.

There were four patrons inside when the crew arrived—two middle-aged couples enjoying what Jake assumed to be the specialty of the house, lobster. When Jake and the Skuldmen entered, the diners looked up but quickly returned to their meal, not wanting to make eye contact with the bikers.

The beer flowed like a brisk breeze through flowering fruit trees on a spring night. Jake was engaged in small talk with Moose, while Oilcan and Mad Dog were watching Big Keith and Little Jimmie play pool for five bucks a game. When Big Keith was all tapped out, it was Mad Dog's turn. After Jimmie had beaten Mad Dog, he looked around for another opponent—there were no takers. He motioned with his pool cue for Jake to come over and play a game.

"I need a bit of cash for some head work that I want to do to my bike. Feeling lucky?"

Jake shrugged. "I thought luck was for losers."

"Then step right up and show us all you're not a loser—it's real easy," said Mad Dog, grinning.

"It's just eight ball," added Moose, smiling.

"Come on, Jake. Put down a fin and I'll even let you break," said Jimmie.

Jake pulled a five-dollar bill out of his wallet and placed it on the edge of the table. Grabbing a cue from the rack he checked to see if it was good enough to play with. When he found a fairly straight one, he stepped up to the table and chalked the tip before he broke the rack. The crisp clacking sound from the impact of the porcelain spheres cut through the room as the balls scattered across the felt-covered plane.

At the last second, just as Jimmie was thinking *all power, no balls—a rookie's break*, a solid-colored ball dropped into a corner pocket. Surveying his next shot, Jake scanned the table for a good shot, while Jimmie turned his attention to a television ad for the local Democratic politician who was running for office.

A swift stroke of the pool cue knocked another one of Jake's balls into a corner pocket, while Jimmie focused on the message being delivered by the candidate. When the thirty-second spot ended, Jimmie was obviously irritated.

"The system makes me sick. The Democrats come up with bad ideas and the Republicans come up with concepts that suck; they are all just along for the ride on the taxpayers' back," Jimmie said, as he watched Jake sink two more solid-color balls on purpose and one striped ball accidentally.

"Man, that's a fact," Jake replied.

"Those that are elected are too busy looking for their next big score or kickback from some special interest group. They spend half their time campaigning for reelection and not doing their jobs. They only listen to the ones that give them the most return for their effort," Jimmie continued, as Jake finally missed a difficult bank shot.

"I think everybody in the world would agree with you on that," Jake responded as Jimmie surveyed the table and chalked up his cue.

"To make the situation worse, most citizens out there are brain dead and don't know it. They just go along with the system day in and day out. They listen to a government that is either too local and small-time to do anything worthwhile, or is too large to be in touch with the people they are supposed to serve," Jimmie explained.

Turning his attention back to the game for a minute, Jimmie sank the fourteen ball on his first shot. As he checked out the table for his next shot, he continued his tirade against the establishment.

"The politicians want to get on to certain committees, not for the good they might do, but because the more committees they're on, the more money they get in their pocket. The only time they are in favor of a project is if it benefits a company owned by either someone they know or someone who contributed a good chunk of cash to their campaign. Our forefathers would be rolling over in their graves if they could see what today's politician is all about."

Finished with his rant against the system, Jimmie lined up the twelve ball, aimed for one of the side pockets, and hit a home run.

From that point on, the game rapidly deteriorated for Jake. He might as well just have handed the money to Jimmie and spared the embarrassment of getting his ass whipped—he was no match for the one percenter, who proceeded to clear the table in short order.

Jimmie left the cue on the table as he pocketed Jake's five-dollar bill.

"Better luck next time, partner. Or maybe you need to practice a bit. Like you said, luck is for losers," he said smiling, rubbing salt into the wound.

"I was a bit off of my game tonight, Jimmie. But you're right. I need to practice a bit. Maybe someday you'll give me a rematch?"

"Sure, whenever," Jimmie said with a grin reserved for those who know they're the best at what they do.

"I think it's time for one more before we hit the road."

While Jimmie sauntered off toward the bar Jake put the cue back in the rack, then headed back to his stool, where he grabbed what remained of his beer. Just as he downed it in one hearty glug, Oilcan walked up to Jake and slapped him on the back, almost causing Jake to spit it back out.

"You did good work today—pulled your own weight and then some. Thanks for the help."

Oilcan then called out for the bartender to get Jimmie and Jake each a beer before he headed for the bathroom. It was about as close to a blessing as you might get from someone like Oilcan—it was his way of saying that Jake was okay. Not that Jake needed to hear it or was looking for it, but it was nice to feel a little like a part of something, especially at this particular junction in his life. All that he knew and cared about seemed like a world away and a lifetime apart.

"Everyone pay up! We're outta here, the fun is over," Jimmie called out, as soon as he and Jake had polished off the fresh round of brews.

Addressing the bartender, Little Jimmie said, "Thanks, Andy, see you again soon."

The Skuldmen dropped cash in the tip jar for Andy as they headed out the door to the iron horses waiting patiently outside; all were quite coherent and able to walk a fairly straight line.

"Thanks again for your help, Jake. Maybe we'll see you around sometime," Big Keith said as they got ready to start their bikes in the parking lot.

"You never know," Jake said, smiling. "Thanks for letting me hang out for a while."

Jake shook hands with Jimmie, Big Keith, Moose, Mad Dog, and Oilcan, then jumped on the kicker of the Shovelhead and climbed into the saddle for the last ride of the day.

Within minutes, everyone had mounted their Harleys, fired up, and pulled away. As those left behind inside watched from within, the Skuldmen roared away into the night.

*   *   *

A few miles down the road, Little Jimmie led the small pack into a deserted shopping plaza closed for the night. Without shutting off their motors, they all pulled around the boss in the dim light.

"Jake, thanks for your help, again. It's been a long day. I'm heading home and suggest you all do the same. And hey, don't forget. Church is the night after next at 8 PM—don't be late."

As he pulled in the clutch lever, Jimmie looked at Jake and said, "Follow me until I give you a signal at the blinking red light. After the blinking light, the next right will be the road that Angela lives on. If you miss it, it's on you!"

* * *

Jake arrived at Angela's just as he had the day before. It was dark again but he could still feel the land, marsh, and sea around the house; its smell and the lapping of the waves on the shore titillated his senses.

Jake began to chuckle a bit as it all seemed to be familiar in a strange sort of way. He stopped by the spigot, rubbed his hands under the cool water, and threw some of the refreshing liquid in his face. He wished he had a toothbrush; it seemed like ages ago that he had last brushed his teeth. *Talk about jungle mouth,* he thought, reflecting back to the mouthwash television commercial of his childhood days. He cupped some water and brought it to his lips, drew it into his mouth, and gargled.

Once again Jake climbed the steps, making sure the screen door did not slam behind him. He sat down on the couch and took off his shirt. As he slipped out of his boots he heard the house door open. In the pale light of the single bulb overhead, Angela stood in the doorframe. She was wearing an oversized white T-shirt, and he judged from the way her nipples were protruding against the cotton that there was nothing much more underneath.

"Hey, I hope I didn't wake you," he said a bit sheepishly. "Tried to make as little noise as possible."

"You didn't wake me. Did the guys show you a good time?"

"Absolutely. They're a pretty decent lot. Considering I'm an outsider they treated me like one of their own."

"I told you they were the best. They may be a little rough around the edges at times, but they're solid as granite," Angela said, as she slipped into a slightly worn chrome and leather armchair. No doubt one of the castoffs she brought home from her job, Jake figured.

"Listen, Jake, you should know something."

Jake drew a breath in the silence that followed. His mind raced as he thought about what she was about to say—he was pondering all sorts of possibilities.

Angela shifted in the chair and leaned forward.

"I'm not interested in being Mother Teresa and supporting any drifter that comes along. I have enough on my plate keeping my nose clean, and my little girl safe and happy enough so that prick of an ex doesn't haul my ass into court. So if you think you're gonna sit back here and have the ride of your life, you better think again."

Taken completely by surprise with a confrontation of this type from a woman who at this moment looked so soft and sexy, Jake could do no more than stutter a few guttural syllables.

"What? Well, I wasn't …"

"As long as you pull your weight, you're welcome to stay. But there's no free lunch here."

"I'm not looking for a free lunch."

"Look, it's late, I need my sleep and we can talk about this some more in the morning."

"Sure. No worries. Good night."

Angela got up, turned, and stepped back through the door as quietly as she had arrived. She doused the light on the porch, leaving Jake alone in the dark for the second time in as many days.

Sitting on the couch, he started thinking that if he had somewhere else to go, he would. *I don't need to take any crap from anyone,* he thought, *much less some woman I rescued.* Slightly disgruntled he threw his shirt across the porch into the armchair. He stared out into the darkness for a few moments, wishing he was anywhere but here. Just over two weeks ago his world had been about as normal as could be for a single guy with a good job, a place by the ocean and not a care in the world.

He stretched out on the couch, covered himself with the blanket that Angela had provided, and settled in for the night. After the hard work that day and the beers at the bar, sleep came easy.

*   *   *

Morning came with a drop in temperature and change in weather. It was several hours past sunrise and the previous night's dampness had turned into a drizzle. Jake woke to the sounds of music from the kitchen and the light chatter between a mother and her daughter making its way to him from a slightly open window. Although he suffered from a little case of dry mouth, Jake was glad he didn't have a hangover. Suddenly the front door opened ever so slightly and Lydia stuck her head out from around the doorframe.

"Hey, Mamma, you were right. Our talking did wake him up," she yelled over her shoulder, giggling.

"Was that you in there or did you invite a Girl Scout troop over this morning?" Jake asked the little head staring at him from the door.

"Oh, come on, we weren't that loud. Were we?"

"No. I've heard worse," Jake said, grinning.

"Mamma says if you get up and make yourself presentable, you just might get a cup of coffee."

Jake hauled himself off the couch, shivering from the cold and damp that greeted him now that he was out from under the blanket. He pulled himself together as he walked across the room to grab his shirt. Putting it on, he entered the house and walked into the kitchen.

"Good morning," he said.

"Good morning to you, too, Jake," Lydia said in return, giving him a big smile.

She was still dressed in her jammies, which featured images of SpongeBob—on her feet were a pair of pink bunny slippers.

"Morning," Angela said, flashing a quick smile. "The bathroom is over there. I'm sure that you can use a shower. There's a fresh towel hanging on the rack. I'll have coffee for you when you get out."

"Thanks, I could really use a shower—it's been a couple of days. It probably would be a good idea to put on some clean clothes, too," Jake replied.

"I'll say," Lydia quipped. "You kinda smell a bit."

"Lydia," Angela said, in a mild reprimanding tone.

"She's right. I do kinda smell a little. Maybe more than a little," Jake said as he turned around to fetch some clean clothes from his duffel bag, which lay on the porch floor next to the couch.

On the way back through, he smiled at the girls and headed to the bathroom for a long-overdue shower. The room, which wasn't much bigger than the average apartment-size bathroom, was a work in progress. Its blue walls had been patched here and there, the white plaster sanded smooth but waiting for a coat of primer and fresh paint. The floor had been stripped of its tiles, showing the rough plywood surface beneath. A vintage claw foot tub, which needed refinishing, hugged one of the sidewalls. An old shower curtain hung from a suspended elliptical copper rod above the tub. A refinished wall-mount vanity with new ceramic basin and matching side cabinet lined the opposite wall next to the toilet.

Ten minutes later Jake emerged looking like a new man. He made his way over to the big table and sat down, just as Lydia set a cup of coffee on the table in front of him.

"Do you want some scrambled eggs?" Lydia asked politely. "Mamma says she'll let me make them for you, if you want some."

"You know, I'm not really much of a breakfast eater lately, but if you've got something that resembles toast, that would be just fine," Jake replied. "But thanks anyway, Lydia," he added.

"Okay. You're welcome."

Lydia turned to Angela.

"Mamma, since I'm all done, can I go up to my room and watch TV for a while?"

"Sure, honey, that will be fine," Angela said.

Lydia dashed off up the stairs to her room while her mother continued cutting up what looked like a ton of mushrooms, and placed them on cooking sheets.

"Look, about what you said last night," Jake began.

"Before you say anything, don't be getting mad at me," Angela interrupted. "I just wanted to set the rules down right. I didn't know what condition you were going to be in, or what you were expecting, so I was just protecting myself by saying what I said."

"Not to worry, Angela. I understand. I appreciate you letting me hang around for a few days. I trust I earned my keep all right. And just so you know, I'm planning on moving on today."

"Well, unless you like swimming, you aren't going anywhere. There's a storm coming in. A really big one, too, judging by the size of the front that's out there," Angela said, gesturing out the big picture window toward the front of the house.

Jake took his coffee cup, got up, and walked out the door. He stepped outside onto the top of the front porch stairs, where he could feel the light rain and hear, for the first time, the thunder. Out on the horizon beyond the marsh and the ocean, huge gray clouds loomed in the distance; they were heaped up in picturesque disorder like piles of steel wool. They were stacked up in a straight line running from north to south as far as he could see. Jake knew from living near the sea most of his life that while a storm might be slow to come, it can be equally slow to leave.

"You're stuck here with us for the duration, I think," Angela said quietly from just inside the screen door behind him.

"It's going to be here for at least thirty-six hours."

He turned and faced her.

"If I leave right now I might be able to outrun it."

"It would be a foolish thing to do. You won't make it, so don't even bother."

"In addition to being a great pool player and a great cook, should we add good-looking weather girl to your résumé?" he said with a grin.

"You could. But it's because I've got something that you don't have."

"Isn't that supposed to be a guy's line?"

"Honey, don't kid yourself. Women will always have what you guys want," she said, smiling and staring straight into his eyes. "Come on inside. There's something I want to show you"

Making sure the screen door was latched securely, he followed her across the porch and back into the kitchen. She led him over to the counter near the double-door refrigerator.

"What I'm talking about is this," she said, picking up a small radio that was about five inches by seven inches, and about two inches thick.

"It's a weather radio, in case you've never seen one before. Here, listen."

With a click of the switch the radio came to life and a computer-generated voice informed them that the current conditions for the eastern shoreline of Maryland were deteriorating.

"Barometric pressure is twenty-two millibars and falling. The wind is out of the east at seventeen knots with gusts to twenty-five knots," the voice said.

Angela turned the radio off.

"See? Regional weather conditions, twenty-four hours a day, seven days a week, updated every half hour straight from the National Weather Service. This is where the television, radio, and Internet folks get their information. Mad Dog, the club's road captain, gave this to me. He uses one just like it to cover the boys when they go on a run. It's better than any dot-com weather site, and if you don't have electricity, it runs on batteries."

"Expensive?" Jake inquired.

"Under twenty-five bucks at Radio Shack. So it looks like you ain't going anywhere today, buddy boy," she added.

"So what am I gonna do now?"

"It just so happens that I have a big catering job to do tomorrow, and one of the staff just let me know he isn't going be able to make it. So here's your chance to help me out and make a few bucks in the process."

"I'm a carpenter. I don't know anything about catering."

"No, but you do know how to work with others. I saw that when you were working with the guys on the deck project. Look, it will be real easy for you. All you have to do is help me load the truck, drive it across town, then set up tables and stuff. Then after the gig is over help everyone clean up, load up the truck again, drive it back, and unload it again."

Angela explained that the total time involved would be about ten hours, and mostly indoor work. Only the loading and unloading on this end would have to be done in the rain, since the facility at the other end had a covered loading dock.

"I'll give you fifteen dollars an hour in cash, the day after the event. Maybe more if the client gives all of us a good tip. What do you say?"

Accepting her offer for him to stay until the storm passed was a good idea, and besides, he needed the money and obviously had nothing else to do at the moment. *If I'm going to continue living life on the run until I figure a way out of the situation I'm in, this is something I'm going to have to get used to,* he thought.

Before this odyssey began Jake pretty much knew what he was doing day to day. But now he had no home, no job, and no one to rely on. No one except Squire, that is. It was then that he suddenly realized it had been days since they last talked. Squire was his only link to the old world, the one that hunted and haunted him.

"I guess that'll be fine with me. You're right, I need to stay. And I do need to make some money. But before I do anything else, I've got a phone call I need to make. Do you have a phone I can use? I've got a prepaid calling card so it won't cost you anything."

"No problem. You can use the phone in my room upstairs."

"Lydia, honey," Angela shouted up the stairs, "Jake is coming up. Please show him where the phone is, will you? I'm up to my elbows in mushrooms."

Lydia greeted Jake at the top of the stairs and took him to Angela's room, which was just past the bathroom that separated the two bedrooms on the second floor. Like the rest of the house a simple touch had been used to finish and decorate the room. Exposed beams that had been whitewashed accented the ceiling—a polished floor with a woodstove in the corner helped fill out a space that was sparsely furnished with a large bed, a nightstand, and two dressers. A large picture window looked out westward to the salt marsh beyond.

Lydia left after Jake thanked her, and thoughtfully shut the door closed after her. He pulled out his wallet, found the phone card, and started stabbing out the two dozen numbers required to get through to his lifeline. Three rings later, he heard a familiar voice.

"*Hello.*"

"Hey, Squire. Anything special on the menu today?"

"*Hey, buddy, how are you?*"

"I'm doing okay, for the time being. The ride out of Boston turned out to be one of those situations where you jump from the frying pan into the fire, if you know what I mean? As a result I had to get off the wagon in the middle of nowhere. I put some miles under me after that, but I'm not really sure how far I traveled or exactly where I am. The only thing I know for sure is that I am looking at a lot of water."

"*Well, at least you're all right. I spoke with your RIDE HARD, DIE FREE savior the other day. Things are complicated, but I'm sure between the three of us we can work things out.*"

"Now that's something I like to hear, because right now I feel more hopeless than a school of fish trapped in a trawling net."

"Keep the faith, man. How are you getting along? What are you doing for scratch?"

"I've got enough for now. Since you're in touch with our friend, we really need to get moving on clearing my name and getting me back to where I was, Squire."

"Like I said, we're working on it. But it's going to take some time. Just keep a low profile and stay in touch."

"Don't worry, I will."

*Excerpted from *One Light Coming: A Biker's Story* by Edward Winterhalder & Marc Teatum, published by Blockhead City (2011), ISBN 9780977174751.

Edward Winterhalder is one of the world's leading authorities on motorcycle clubs and the Harley-Davidson biker lifestyle; his books are published in multiple languages and sold all over the world. He was a member, and/or an associate, of outlaw motorcycle clubs for almost thirty years. The creator and executive producer of the *PHASS MOB*, *Biker Chicz* and *Living On The Edge* television series, Winterhalder has appeared worldwide on television networks such as Bravo, Prime, CBC, Fox, National Geographic, History Channel, Global, AB Groupe and History Television. In addition to his literary endeavors, he is a consultant to the entertainment industry for TV, feature film and DVD projects that focus on the Harley-Davidson biker lifestyle.

Marc Teatum is an author of contemporary motorcycle fiction. Born in Brooklyn NY, he currently lives in Salem, Massachusetts. Formerly an editor of *UPDATE*, the Massachusetts Motorcycle Association member's magazine, Teatum began his career as a professional photographer, owning a studio that serviced the advertising and public relations industry. During that time, his work won numerous awards in both the photography and design fields. His personal fine art photography has been exhibited widely and is represented in both private and museum collections. He has served on the Board of Directors of The Art Directors Club of Boston as well as the Massachusetts Motorcycle Association, and is currently working in the publishing industry as a content licensing manager. An avid motorcycle enthusiast for more than twenty-five years, Teatum is active in motorcycle rights organizations in the Boston area.

The Big House Crew

By Iain Parke

I'm a dead man talking, I know that. Realistically there's no way I'm getting out of this alive. The only thing I have a choice about is when I stop writing.

And despite that, and despite the fact that whatever he says, I still think it was Wibble who really got me into all of this shit, the weird thing is, he's also the only slim hope I have of ever getting out.

Saturday 13 February 2010

The fight had been all over the Press of course, TV, radio, papers, everything. So much so that even here, hiding out in the back of beyond, we had heard about it during the week.

I had my coffee in the small panelled back bar as I read the story in the week's worth of papers I had collected that morning, my shopping including the family fun pack of Fluoxetine, sitting on the chair beside me. There were the usual slightly blocky and pixelated pictures from CCTV cameras which always made me wonder how much use they could ever be for really identifying anyone doing anything.

But then it was an airport, so if there was anywhere that was going to have a lot of CCTV coverage, that would be it.

On the other hand, as the Home Office spokesman had pointed out, it was also a place crawling with armed police. So if you were going to go at it, I'd have thought that there were plenty of other places you would choose. Not that it had put them off, obviously.

A fourth man had now died in hospital, with another two apparently still on the critical list and under armed guard, so the toll could still rise.

As I read, the latest development was the Home Secretary's statement to the House, telling MPs how all overseas members of The Brethren and any known associated clubs would be barred access to the country. You could almost hear the sounds of sanctimonious cheering and see the order papers being waved in righteous indignation. There was debate about how this could be enforced in practice against citizens of other EU countries, and worries about how the authorities would identify, or even what would constitute, being 'a known associate' of any of the clubs to be named and shamed.

As if!

It sounded like a policy heading straight towards a hearing at the European Court of Human rights at some point to me, but then what did I care?

Frankly, given what getting messed up with them had done to me and my life so far, they could all kill each other to their hearts' content as far as I was concerned, just the sooner, the better.

Anyway, the end result at the moment was that Wibble et al were all currently in theory helping the police with their enquiries, although I could make a fairly shrewd guess how helpful they were actually being.

*   *   *

By about 11am I'd finished everything I'd intended to do and it had stopped raining at last, so I began the walk back up the road.

Climbing the hill out of town eventually I turned and picked my way between the muddy puddles along the rutted dirt farm track leading towards our cottage.

It should have been the quiet that warned me.

As I reached the gate and turned the end of the hedge, I looked up the slight rise towards where the cottage was set back on the plot.

They might as well have hung a sign out.

Right in front of the front door sat a classic outlaw hog, all the current bagger style with springer forks, apehangers and chromed risers, a set of flame painted fatbobs, footboards, forward controls, an open belt drive, fat back tyre in a soft tail frame, tombstone tail light, and slash cut exhausts spattered in mud.

Beyond it was a green Range Rover with tinted windows blackening out the interior. A real hood's car if ever I'd seen one.

I stood stock still for a moment, wondering what to do; options and scenarios, and plans I'd been thinking about constantly for the last year or so came racing and tumbling through my mind.

With the car there was no way of knowing how many of them there were, or where they were for that matter; there'd be some in the cottage no doubt, but the others? There could be some behind me in the lane, ready to grab me if I tried to make a getaway.

No. There was no point running I decided. I doubted there ever had been. And so, dreading what I might find inside, I walked up the drive and stepping round the bike, opened the door which led directly into the kitchen.

She was sitting there at the wooden table facing the door, looking directly into my eyes as I came in, quietly terrified, but just about keeping it together.

Sitting opposite her, with his back to the door so his Union Jack patch was clearly visible, was one of the outlaws. Another biker with long blond hair tied in two Viking style pigtails was lounging off to the left hand side of the room, perched on the edge of the thick windowsill, his blue, white and black colours reflecting in the cottage window behind him.

What was he, and where did he fit into the picture I wondered? Escort? Ally? Observer?

The third biker in the room was a striker who also had his back to me as he was at the worktop pouring water from the freshly boiled kettle into the teapot.

'Hi there Bung,' I said to the seated figure as he swung his head around at the sound of the door opening. 'How are you doing? I've been wondering whether you would show up one day.'

*   *   *

He grinned as he saw me, 'Oh really? And here I was wanting to give you a surprise!'

'Well that's one word for it,' I said, as I pushed the door closed behind me.

'Are you OK?' I asked Eamur urgently, but as calmly as I could, locking her eyes with mine.

She didn't say anything, just nodded and then her eyes fell away.

'Fancy a cuppa? We're having a brew,' Bung asked, as though nothing had happened and shouted over to the striker at the worktop, 'Stick another one out will you?'

I knew the Irish biker's colours. He was with the club that was top dog locally, the *Fir Bolg*. Their bottom rocker claimed the old kingdom of

Connacht, but given the border they weren't restricting themselves unnecessarily and so had also added the old Ulster county of Donegal to their turf.

'So are you here to look after them? Or me?' I asked him.

He looked supremely relaxed. 'It's nothing to do with me fella. I'm just here to keep an eye on things while yer man there does whatever the fuck it is he's here to do, and to then make sure he fucks off home again.'

'But I thought you guys were part of the confederation. Pledged to remain independents and to stay out of this international type of shit?

'So who's getting involved?' He shrugged as the striker passed him a steaming mug, 'They just wanted a visit so they asked nicely if they could come and you can't very well refuse when they do that, now can you? It wouldn't be polite would it? So like I said, I'm just here to show them where they wanted to go and then show them on their way.'

'You're their chaperone?'

'Escort is more what I'd say now, but something like that.'

'I couldn't have put it better myself,' added Bung, as the striker plonked a steaming mug of tea on the table in front of him, and then another one in front of an empty place across the table.

Bung motioned for me to sit and so, reluctantly, I slid into the chair opposite him. There didn't seem to be anything else to do.

*   *   *

Despite myself I had to give a wary smile. Bung was exactly as I remembered him, a huge scruffy bear of a man. His jacket with his colours over it was draped across the back of his chair, and he was wearing a black hoodie with the words *Gangland, Film this!* surrounding a graphic of a hand 'flipping the bird' American style.

'Nice,' I said, nodding at the logo as I sat down.

'D'you like it?' he asked, glancing down, 'I picked it up at a bash in the States last time we were over.'

'Would you get me one next time you go?'

'Ah well, I don't think that'll be for a while now,' he batted it back to me with a conspiratorial smile. 'So how's life been treating you then?'

'Not bad I suppose up until a few minutes ago, I was quite getting to like a sort of normal life again.'

Bung shook his head dismissively, 'Over rated that mate, if you ask me. I tried to be normal once, it was the most boring two minutes of my life.'

The Irish biker gave a snort and then there was silence other than a slurping noise as Bung sipped from his mug and studied me over the rim, sitting there like some tattooed, silver skull-ringed, Buddha. It was typical Bung, he was always a bit of the club joker. On a good day, he could be one of the funniest guys I think I've ever met. It was just that for some reason I wasn't really in the mood at the moment.

It seemed as though it was going to be up to me to make the running I decided, to start with at least.

I was surprising myself by how calm I felt. I'd had six months or so to think about this moment, to anticipate it happening I suppose, and to prepare, if I ever could. Ever since I'd got out, Bung, or one of his ilk, turning up to take care of business had always been a possibility, something that might happen someday, something that I'd have to be ready for. It had been a constant shadow, sitting on my shoulder.

The only surprise really, I thought, was that they had come themselves.

We were off grid here out in the rolling damp hills above the village, and quite cut off from the world. No mobile signal, no telephone line, no internet. It was the way I liked it, part of the attraction of the place. But back down the hill, stuck at the back of one of the shops cum bars that lined the straight main drag of the village, there were a couple of desks with PCs on them that constituted the local internet café, and which ever since we'd arrived had been a strict part of my routine on my weekly walks in.

The one-percenter bikers had gone online alongside everyone else, and so I kept a close watch on the biker websites, forums and newsgroups that shared those essential snippets of news about busts, bust ups, rats and undercover LEOs amongst the postings and announcements. So I kept tabs on the boards, reading between the lines, although sometimes I didn't even have to do that, it had been clear for a while that a power struggle had been developing between Wibble and Charlie for control of the English part of the club, with Stu and the Scottish crew under his command sitting on the sidelines waiting to see how they played it out between them.

But one of the club turning up themselves wasn't what I'd been expecting. As well as keeping abreast as far as possible with what was happening on the club scene; the alliances, the patching in and members out in bad standing announcements that made up the outlaw versions of hatched, matched and dispatched notices, I'd also been looking for something else. Something that might sound innocent, even innocuous, but something that would actually have a deadly intent; it could be something as simple as a greeting, something like, '*Hey a big Irish Blue and White hello to all our Union Jack Bros and anytime you need anything just give us a call.'*

But from the time I'd spent with Damage and then watching Wibble at work, it was the way these things worked. Favours exchanged. No obvious link between victim and killer to give the cops something to pursue, and no actual involvement by anyone from the club in making it happen. Just a dead body and a series of dead ends.

With Bung here now though, I had mixed emotions. Despite everything that had happened, on a personal level I actually still liked the guy. Like I said, he could be fun, friendly and funny. But then I'd also seen what he, and what the rest of his club, could and would do without hesitation when it came to taking care of business. And of course, there was also what they had done to me, the reason I was stuck here, in hiding, trying to rebuild my life from scratch and living in long term fear for it.

So I tried to keep my anger in check. Anger about what I'd seen and knew, anger about what they had done to me, anger about what I'd had to do, and anger about how I was sitting here, now, having to deal with this shit again.

Besides which, we had a deal, I told myself. That was what I was clinging on to in some corner of my mind. Wibble and me, we had a deal, one that made sense for both sides. A deal that gave me some protection from the club in their own interests. So why would they want to screw it up now? What had changed?

'So what is it then Bung?' I asked, 'Let's get on with it then. What the hell are you here to do?'

'How do you know I'm not just here to see you?'

'A social call? Is that it? You should have let me know,' I said, an edge of bitterness in my voice, 'I'd have baked a cake.'

Which led on to another question of course.

'Who else knows you're here Bung? Christ, more importantly, who else knows I'm here?'

'Oh everyone,' he said casually.

'Everyone?' I asked, shocked, 'But I've been in hiding for Christ's sake.'

'Oh all the key guys know you're here and what you're up to, Charlie, Wibble, Toad, the lot.'

'So a fat lot of good being stuck out here has done me then,' I observed. Eamur had been right all along. If they could spy on me in an empty café back in London, they had obviously been able to keep an eye on me here across the water and over the border.

'Oh I wouldn't say that,' replied Bung, sipping his tea and smiling in what I guessed he intended to be a reassuring way at Eamur, 'the plod ain't got you for instance. And so long as the guys knew you were shacked up here nice and cosy, and keeping your head down, then they were happy enough.'

The trouble was, however avuncular a grizzly bear was feeling, to someone who met them the first time they were still a big scary animal, so I didn't think Eamur was quite getting the message.

*   *   *

'What about Robbie?' I asked, remembering the snout guided furry missile I had been relying on.

'The dog,' I added, since it was obvious from the puzzled looks this generated that they didn't know.

Bung laughed. 'Oh don't worry about him; he's in the shed snoring off a steak full of tranqs. He'll have a bit of a headache when he wakes up, but he's all right.'

'So what about her?' I said nodding at Eamur, 'she's got nothing to do with this.'

'What about her?' Bung shrugged. She obviously hadn't really entered into his calculations at all. 'She's nothing to us. They said you'd got yourself a good looking ol'lady.'

'So what about her?' I repeated.

'Oh don't worry about her; we'll take care of her.'

I didn't much like the sound of that.

'Thanks a bunch,' I said, 'That's what I'm worried about.'

*   *   *

'Oh come on,' protested Bung, 'now you're hurting my feelings.'
There was a snort of derision from the direction of the Irish biker but Bung didn't turn a hair.

'Don't be like that. Here we are just having a quiet chat. You know that if we'd wanted to cause trouble we'd have done it already.'

He had a point, but it wasn't one I felt like conceding just at that moment.

'More trouble than just turning up you mean?'

He chose to laugh at that.

'You're a bit bloody cool about it aren't you?'

'So what do you want Bung?' I asked. 'You're not here to snuff me I guess. As you say, if you wanted to do that then either you'd have got his mob to do it,' I said, nodding across the room to where the *Fir Bolg* patch was perched on the windowsill, cradling his cup in both hands and looking dubiously out of the window and up at the sky as if judging the chances of more rain, 'or you'd be on with it by now. So if it isn't that, what do you want?'

'Oh that's easy. They want you.'

'They want me? Who's they in this conversation Bung?'

'Wibble...

And Charlie,' he added, almost as an afterthought.

So Bung was still working for Wibble I decided, not that I'd ever expected anything different.

'I'm not sure I fancy that. Don't forget I've had Wibble's offers before, and look where it got me.'

He laughed at that too.

But meanwhile I was thinking furiously. Wibble and Charlie? That surprised me. One or the other I could understand. I wouldn't much like it but I could understand it. But both of them? That didn't make much sense.

But was Bung really suggesting that they had agreed they wanted to see me? Or was it just a coincidence?

'Jointly or separately?' I asked.

'Well they're both inside,' he said, 'but they're at different clinks...'

'No,' I interrupted, 'I meant, do they each want to see me separately, or is this a joint request by both of them?'

'Well, that's a bit of a tricky one,' he rubbed his beard thoughtfully as he decided and then said. 'Well I reckon it's sort of jointly, if you see what I mean.'

Which I didn't at all, but I let that pass for the moment.

'So why have they asked you to come Bung?'

'Because they thought there'd be more chance of you coming if I popped along and asked nicely.'

'What, rather than have Scroat pitch up for example?' I asked.

'Well yes, now you mention it. He'd be Charlie's choice.'

I bet he would, I thought, suppressing an inward shudder at the prospect.

'So why me Bung? Why do they want to see me? What can I do for them, what do they want me to do?'

'Negotiate,' he said simply.

'Negotiate?' I asked, 'Negotiate what? With whom?'

'A deal,' he shrugged as if it was a daft question, 'What else do you negotiate?'

I still didn't get it, what sort of a deal I wondered, about what?

Then Eamur chipped in for the first time, 'they need someone to act as a broker between them, that's it isn't it?'

Bung nodded.

'They want someone they both know to sort out a deal between them,' she continued, 'that's what this is all about isn't it?'

'You see, your bird here's smart, she gets it,' he said approvingly. Out of the corner of my eye I could see Eamur bristling at him although Bung seemed completely oblivious, 'They need to sort out a deal and they want you to help them do it.'

Christ, so that was it, shuttle diplomacy? I'm Henry sodding Kissinger now, I thought.

'Why me?' I asked. 'To what do I owe this honour?'

He counted the reasons off on his fingers, and as he did so they had a heavy inevitability about them.

'Well first off it can't be someone in the club, it has to be someone who has a bit of independence of either side and so can be seen to be neutral.

'But at the same time it's got to be someone who knows enough about the club and how we work to be able to talk sense.

'And finally of course, it has to be someone who'll keep their mouth shut about it and that we know won't go blabbing to the cops.'

And on the last point of course I couldn't, courtesy of Wibble. 'So you've got a fairly short list of candidates then?' I asked.

'You've got it.'

It was taking my mind a while for this development to sink in.

'So indulge me on one question then, just out of interest,' I said, 'What if I don't want to come?'

Bung was having a good day, I could tell he was enjoying himself now as he just grinned at that. 'Well, it's up to you mate isn't it? After all, it's your funeral.'

Turning down Charlie and Wibble? Yes I guess it would be. These guys had an absolute knack of making the sorts of offers that you really couldn't refuse.

'But if you don't, well I think I'd invest in some portable protection, if you know what I mean.'

'Oh, and watch out for bikes drawing up beside you at traffic lights,' chipped in the Irish guy helpfully.

They surprised me with that. 'A drive by? I didn't think that was your guys' style? I thought you were more a little something under the car of a morning?'

'You know your trouble don't you?' Bung asked, putting down his tea, the smile suddenly gone from his face as the level of tension in the room shot up in a heartbeat.

'No,' I replied. 'Go on then, surprise me. What's that then?'

'You believe too much of what you read in the papers.'

'You forget,' I said, putting my mug down on the table as well and speaking slowly and deliberately. There was no way I wanted him to misunderstand what I was getting at, as underneath one half of my mind was screaming at me, we had a deal, I'd disappear and they'd leave me alone; while the other half was frantically trying to work out what had changed to make Bung turn up now and drive a coach and horses through the arrangement.

'I used to write what you read in the papers.'

'Oh no we hadn't,' he replied, equally carefully.

*   *   *

'So how am I meant to see them?' I asked.

'What d'you mean?' he seemed puzzled at the question.

'I mean practically. They're both inside.'

'Yes, and that's where they want to see you.'

'So how do I get to see them?'

'Same way as you saw Damage of course,' he said. 'You visit.'

Oh that was just great. I'm the bod they could use as a negotiator since I'm the one who can't go to the cops since Wibble had set me up as number one suspect for the murder of a copper that he'd carried out, and now he and Charlie wanted me to go waltzing into prison to see them? What were they on, I wondered?

'Hang on a sodding minute, let me get this straight,' I demanded. 'You want me to act as a bloody go-between? To visit them and shuttle between two guys on the inside and negotiate a deal? While I'm still a wanted man? How the hell do you think I'm going to get away with doing that?'

'Easy,' he said pulling out an envelope from inside his leather vest and dropping it on the table in front of him, 'with these.'

'So what's that?' I asked. Although with a heavy heart, even as he'd produced the envelope I immediately worked out what it had to be.

'Fake ID,' he said as though it was the most obvious and normal thing in the world.

'But what excuse would I have for visiting them?' I asked in increasing desperation.

'Oh that's OK,' he said, 'it's all taken care of. You're going to be a guy from their solicitor's office.'

I shook my head in disbelief, even as I started to realize this was really going to happen to me and that I had absolutely sod all choice about it, 'You have got to be fucking kidding me.'

*　　*　　*

Of course they were inside, after the fight.

There had been a message in the Union Jack tabs that Wibble and his crew had adopted along with Stu and his lads. It was just that I'd been too dim to see it. The clue was in the names.

Union, the union of the two UK clubs, The Rebels and The Brethren.

Jack, as in jacking in the old allegiance to the Yanks.

Listening to Bung explain what had been happening, it was clear that Wibble, Stu and Charlie between them had teamed up to pull off an MBO. Only in this case it was a bit more of a management bust out.

'Hadn't the Yanks suspected something was up? Once you'd got together with The Rebels and all?'

There had been bad blood between The Brethren and The Rebels clubs in the States for longer than any of the current participants in the eternal bush war could ever remember. It had become almost a Hatfield and McCoy's thing, a hillbilly style blood feud stretching down through the generations years after the original reasons and offenders were long dead and forgotten.

So the two clubs' British arms joining up in an outbreak of, if not outlaw biker peace and love, then at least mutual respect and working arrangements, wasn't something that would have gone unnoticed on the other side of the Atlantic, by either mother club. God knows what they would then have thought about a formal cessation of hostilities such as had happened at The Brethren's August 2009 Toy Run, never mind that latest development.

'Sure they did,' Bung said, 'but what could they do? And anyway, by the time they did work it out, it was too late, we'd done it.'

And 'it' was what the patch on the back of his cut represented; the one I'd seen in the Press, on the websites and now grinning over the back of the chair as I'd walked into the room. The one with the Union Jack coloured skull in the centre, the words Great Britain underneath across the bottom rocker, and across the top rocker the new club name; one that had never been seen before, until this New Year's day when the two clubs finally came together to put on their new patches, and declare themselves a new club, one that answered to no one in the USA and which called itself The Rebel Brethren MC.

Strategically, for the clubs in the UK, I could see that the merger made perfect sense. It was Wibble it seemed, who else, who had named it Project Union Jack. Unite and jack it in, unify and declare UDI, combine the clubs together and take over the UK.

It was simple, it was brilliant, it was unprecedented, and it was impossible to say how very, very dangerous and challenging a step it was to the accepted international order of things.

In a club like either The Brethren or The Rebels it was a simple equation. You died, or, if you lived long enough and you were a member of sufficiently good standing, you might sometimes, with the club's permission retire, or you got chucked out in bad standing. Those were the only three ways you exited a club.

No one, but no one, just upped and left. Not as an individual, and certainly not as a club. Never had, never could, never would – until now.

It was, I knew, the reason for the fight at the airport, the logic of each side's position was inexorable. The Yanks wouldn't stand for it, and had come over to take care of business. It was just that when they landed, the club was waiting for them in arrivals, resulting in the stills from the CCTV images that I'd seen splashed across the paper, bodies grappling, weapons raised, casualties on the floor; and then right at the end, a strange and so far unexplained image.

It was a shot of two men, taken from a camera high up in the roof of the building, and facing towards the immigration doors by the looks of it, so it had only caught them from the back as they stood over one of the bodies. Both their faces were obscured by the camera angle but all the same I had known with a lurch in my gut who they were the instant I had seen the photo.

But what I didn't understand as I stared at the pixelated image, was why Wibble and Charlie had each come to a riot armed only with a medium sized stuffy bag.

*   *   *

As the split had come about over the last few months it had made me reassess everything I had seen so far in my dealings with Damage, Wibble and The Brethren, and made me question my understanding of what I had seen.

It was a moot point now I guessed, but it had made me wonder. The big mystery in my mind was still who had killed Damage and why. Knowing now about where the club politics had been heading I asked myself if it had actually been Thommo who'd moved against Damage in a bid to become national Prez?

I had always dismissed the thought before as it seemed to me that it would have been a very, very risky plan without some serious back up given Damage's position, contacts, and importance to the club's business.

But the present situation cast it all in a new light. What, I wondered to myself, if the roots of this went back further? What if Thommo had believed he actually did have back up? Serious back up? What if the Yanks had put him up to it? To stop Damage who had been planning the split that Wibble had then gone on to execute?

Did that also explain the decision about succession? That Thommo had tried to become Prez but had been held off by the Damage loyalists led by Wibble? If so, that could explain why it was so sudden, and why it had been a triumvirate, as a way of balancing, at least temporarily, the potentially warring factions.

It would also explain the beef between Wibble and Thommo which had always seemed to me to have had a real personal edge to it.

*   *   *

But back at the here and now, they had worked out the practicalities, I'd give them that.

When I'd got out last time it had been in a hurry and I'd had to make my own arrangements. 'We ain't no fucking travel agents,' Wibble had growled at me when I'd started to ask about where I should go. And to be honest, once I'd got my head around the fact I was still alive at all and started thinking straight, I realized of course that The Brethren were the last people in the world I wanted knowing about where I was intending to hole up.

This time it seemed was going to be different.
Bung and the striker were here to collect me, but I had time to pack some things.

'Oh don't worry too much, we won't be that long,' said Bung vaguely, when I asked how much to take. The plan was they would drive me back over the border and across to Belfast airport. Bung and I were to fly back, and he would sort me out with a hotel room once we got there, the striker got the balls ache of the ferry and then slogging it down from Stranraer to get the car back.

The striker wasn't saying a word, but then I didn't expect him to. Strikers very much lived a speak when spoken to sort of life. Training, Damage had called it. While a full patch was around, a striker would always defer to let them do the talking. The hierarchy and etiquette was ferociously strict. A striker had to give respect to a patch, not only of his own club, but of any other friendly club, since as the logic went, even as part of another club, the man had earned his patch, whereas the striker hadn't. A striker couldn't even call a club member 'brother'; he hadn't yet earned the right.

'So Bung's your sponsor huh?' I asked.

The guy stayed dumb until a shrug from Bung let him know he could respond, but even then he just nodded warily.

'You want to ask him what happened to the last guy.'

'I don't give a shit what happened to the last guy,' he said.

OK, so he had to hold his end up. I got that.

Frankly, after the crap talking to a striker had gotten me into last time, he was on his own. What the hell. If he'd chosen to get involved with this mob, it was his look out, not mine.

'So what am I supposed to use to pay for this trip of yours?' I asked turning back to Bung.

'You shouldn't need much cos you'll be with me.'

'And you're picking up the tab are you?'

'Not me mate, the club. Anyway, you can use what's in there,' he said, pushing across the envelope he'd put on the table, 'It's part of the deal.'

I opened it.

It was a complete package, a new identity. A new life almost. if I wanted it, but one supplied by, and therefore completely in the hands of, the club; so probably not.

There was a passport and a driver's licence, in the name of Michael Adams but each with my photo inside and a passable imitation of how I would write the name as a signature.

I was impressed. 'A bit of work's gone into these hasn't it?'

'Money, it gets shit done,' he shrugged dismissively, 'They're real, it just costs a bit to set up that's all. There's people who can organize getting it arranged for you if you need it.' It seemed it wasn't a big deal as far as he was concerned, just a service you bought when you needed it.

Apparently, I saw, I lived in Reading and worked at a solicitors' firm in town since I had a company photo ID tag on a lanyard as well.

'That's real as well,' he said as I held it up, 'and you're on their personnel records too. They're Wibble and Charlie's solicitors so that's your ticket inside.'

That was what was worrying me.

'As far as the screws are concerned there's going to be nothing to see. You're just going to be a bloke from their lawyers coming to see them about getting ready for the hearing. Nothing to it, no sweat.'

He seemed completely relaxed about it, but then he wasn't going to be the one trying to pull this off.

Then for access to dosh, there was also a debit card and PIN.

'Like I said, you're going to be with me so it's not like you'll need much but we'll keep an eye on it and make sure the account is kept topped up, so you'll have enough to pay for what you need to get around as and when, food, booze, that sort of shit. But not too much access, you know what I mean? So keep it budget eh?'

Sure enough, when I checked later at a machine, there was a balance of a grand to keep me going.

But the underlying message was clear, the club weren't trusting me to pick up my bags and go trotting back over the water just because they had called. Bung wasn't just here to invite me back, he was here to escort me as well. However much he didn't say it, we both knew he was a tour guard, not a tour guide.

*	*	*

We stayed overnight in Belfast and on Sunday we took the early afternoon flight out of the City airport down to Gatwick. Sitting shoved in together in row fourteen we ignored the stewardess doing her fixed grin, arm swinging synchronised exit signing and useless lifejacket training. We were just another anonymous pair of travellers in a hundred seater turboprop powered steel smarties tube with wings about to hurl itself into the air, I thought she looked a bit like Eamur.

But of course Eamur wasn't with us. No, she was going to stay behind. As insurance.

*Excerpted from *The Brethren Trilogy: Heavy Duty Trouble* by Iain Parke (2012), ISBN 9780956161567.

Iain Parke imports industrial quantities of Class A drugs, kills people and lies (a lot) for a living, being a British based crime fiction writer. He became obsessed with motorcycles at an early age, taking a six hundred mile cross-country tour to Cornwall as soon as he bought a moped at the tender age of sixteen. After working at a London dispatch job delivering parcels on a motorcycle, he built his first chopper in his bedroom at university, undeterred by the fact that the workshop was upstairs.

Armed with a MBA degree, Iain first worked in insolvency and business restructuring in the UK and Africa, where he began work on his first thriller *The Liquidator*. The success of that novel propelled him to write a 'biker lit' trilogy about the Brethren Motorcycle Club, which has recently been optioned as a series for television in the UK. Today Iain lives off the grid, high up on the North Pennines in Northumberland with his wife, dogs, and a garage full of motorcycle restoration projects. He is currently working on a number of book projects, including another biker-based trilogy.

Duke The Barbarian

By Gene Lewis

I'd lived in this old house in North Beach for a long time now. It was small and quite the dump but suited my basic needs. The landlord charged me cheap rent because he never had to fix anything on this wreck. I took care of it. Most importantly—it had a small garage with everything I needed to work on bikes—including my beer fridge. But there was no dependable power now to run the fridge and booze of any kind was hard to come by. I got what little I had by trading with the Guardians. I got used to drinking warm beer again. That was too reminiscent of Nam.

There was a large box in the corner of the garage where everyone would throw their empty beer cans. With all the bikers who spent time here tweaking on their machines I was able to throw a party every year with the money from the recycled cans. It became known as "JC's Annual Beer Can Recycling Party." Those were the good ole days that would never be seen again as long as I stayed in the City.

While I thought about my plans I started work on the Super Glide. First I checked the fluids and all the seals. I found some used but low mileage plugs in the garage that would work. Unlike the newer Harleys this ole girl had a kick start. That would be important as I knew the old battery wouldn't have any life in it. It would be too dangerous to try and take it outside to push start. These old glides would kick start even with a weak battery. But it would be better to have a good battery—if possible.

I had a biker babe calendar on the wall I bought myself for Christmas—just before the shit hit the fan here with the Regional Wars. I was marking off the days since then and it was mid April. Over five months in hell now! If I was going to try an escape I wanted to be on the road by sometime in May. That was still in the wet months along the coast so the nights would probably be cool and foggy. The fog could be good or bad news—depending on who was looking for who. I was also tracking the full moons on the calendar as best I could. Patrols were always different in a full moon.

I was working on the bike late at night when I heard someone moving outside the garage. I reached for my shotgun and closely watched the door. If it was the Guardians they were gonna want to know why I was working on the bike. Then I heard a familiar deep voice, "JC—you in there?"

"Who's there?" I asked wanting to be sure.

"Who do you think it is you long haired hippie biker freak—Captain Midnight? Do you want me to slide my decoder ring under the door?" It was Duke. I lowered the shotgun.

"Come on in you smelly old psychotic hunk of scooter trash."

Duke was my closest biker bro but I hadn't seen him in over a week. He'd been a Ranger in Nam in the seventies and was a really big boy. Well over six foot and 300 pounds. In the biker crowd he was known as Duke the Barbarian. He was famous for his short temper and lust for a good fight. I don't think he lost very many unless he was greatly outnumbered. Before I met him he'd been an outlaw but left the club to work on his own. Didn't like taking orders—from anyone.

We were a strange pair to be such good friends. Me being only five ten and about 180 pounds—in better times. We looked like Mutt and Jeff when we rode together. He was known for his rough ways and I preferred to be a lover rather than a fighter.

I first met him at a biker bar in the City called Stinky Dicks. I was playing a friendly game of pool with Big Jim and Nasty Pete—in what Stinky Dick liked to call his Ball Room—when Duke challenged the winner. He smelled like whiskey—matter of fact—he just smelled. I already knew his reputation but had never run into him. So when Jim and Pete quickly threw the game I had no option but to take him on. Even though he dwarfed me I never back down from anyone. Something Dad had taught me from his coal mining days in Morgantown. Maybe a touch of the Marine now to boot.

Dad was a small man but had the reputation for being one of the toughest fighters in the mines. He told me many times, "When you're the smallest guy everyone will pick on you. But if you fight back they'll eventually leave you alone cause the bullies don't want to get their asses kicked by someone smaller than them. It's bad for their reputation." Mom liked to call me her "bantam rooster" because I never backed away from a fight. But Duke the Barbarian was really big!

So we played our game of eight ball. Everyone thought I would just let him win to avoid the consequences of confronting the Barbarian. But that made me even more determined to whip his butt. When I was a young stud my uncle Zeke owned the little general store back in Mount Pisgah. He had an old pool table in the back room where the local boys met to shoot the shit and sip their moonshine. So I got to play a lot as a kid. Made some good side money in the Marines hustling pool with the newbies.

Duke was drunk and I was determined to beat his sorry ass at the game—even if it meant getting mine kicked. So when I sunk the eight ball the bar went silent. I guess not too many bikers had ever been foolish enough to beat the Duke. He came over and stared at me with his dark eyes that were sunk into a large head of long black hair and scraggly beard. "So the little man is feeling cocky today. Maybe I should just kick your fuckin' ass and teach you a lesson." I grabbed onto my pool stick tightly and prepared for the worst. I wasn't going to start the fight but intended to hold my own as long as I could against this big man.

He just stood there for a while and glared down at me—breathing these long whiskey saturated breaths. I stared back into his dark mysterious eyes. This was a really scary guy who I knew was capable of mayhem without a thought. He studied my vest and saw my faded Marine patch. He leaned over and surprised me when he asked, "You serve in Nam?"

"Yeah—in '69. So what?" I thought he was just playing with me waiting for the right time to throw the first punch.

We stood there for a while locked eye to eye. Everyone was waiting for the fight to start. And then Duke surprised the crowd—and most of all me—when he reached over—grabbed my vest—and said, "Then let's have a drink to remember the boys we served with in Nam!" And he pulled me toward the bar.

To this day I'm not sure why he changed his mind about taking me on. Maybe it was the determination he saw in my eyes? Maybe he was having his once a decade feeling of melancholy? I never asked. But we drank until we couldn't stand up and passed out together in the corner. That was after many toasts to the good men we left behind in the war. I had that hangover for a long day. Damn brown bottle flu. That was when Duke and I became regular riding bros.

"You almost got your head blown off," I teased him.

"You wouldn't shoot anyone—little man—you're too much of a fuckin' paac-i-fist." He kind of spit the words out as he always liked to make fun of my easy going ways. "Workin' on the bike. Good to see that. How's it comin'?"

We moved over to inspect the bike. "She's been sitting for a long time. Not sure yet if I can make it run."

"Hell yes you can! It's a Harley and you're the best damn mechanic I know. And besides—you got me to help you get the ole gal runnin'. Surely two mechanical geniuses like us can figure this out." Duke wasn't the world's greatest mechanic—he preferred wrecking them to fixing them—but he knew his way around a wrench.

"But first I have a present for you," he announced as he pulled out a big joint and a whiskey flask. "I borrowed this from a couple of Guardians. The fuckers didn't want to share so I had to persuade them. Hell—I didn't even break a sweat!" We both laughed because I knew what that meant. Somewhere in town there were a couple of Guardians who wished they hadn't said no to the Barbarian.

We sat on the floor and mellowed out. The weed smelled like pretty good stuff. Didn't take long before I felt good. It had been a while...

"Did you miss me?" Duke inquired in his deadpan way.

"Hell no—I figured you were dead. How could I miss your sorry ass?" We sat there in silence for a while enjoying the high.

Then he got my major interest with what he said next. "Well partner—I been thinkin' about your plan to get out of the City and head north along the coast to the New Society." Duke was the only one I had told about my plans. "Getting across the bridge is your biggest problem to start—so I figured out a way." Now he had my full attention. We sat there quiet as I waited to hear the rest.

"So—are you going to tell me or am I going to have to beat it out of you?" He thought that was funny.

As long as Duke and I had been riding together I'd never known him to care about any woman—except once. Not too long ago he'd fallen for a little biker chick we all called Barbie Doll. She looked just like a little Barbie Doll with big boobs and blonde hair. She was a tiny thing but she captured him completely. Kind of like watching Beauty and the Beast when they were together.

I didn't think he even had a gentle side but he would do anything for Barbie. The crew and I kept trying to figure out what she saw in him. At times it was like watching this really sexy bear trainer with this big hairy beast on a leash. But no one was going to tell Duke he was pussy whipped—at least not to his face.

Shortly after the Guardians took control several of them found Barbie in a biker bar waiting for Duke to show up after a drug run. They tried to rape her but not until she had taken one out with a derringer and kicked another in the nuts. She put up quite the fight but there were too many. They had their way with her and then slit her throat. When Duke found out he went crazy—way beyond anything I'd ever seen him do before!

Duke had fists like steel ingots and a kick like a Missouri mule. Me and several of the boys were at his house when he got the news about Barbie and he went berserk. He punched holes in the walls and took a door off with a kick. I lost track of what all he broke. When we finally cooled him down to a small roar we packed into his van and headed for the bar. It was a mess. Lots of blood. Duke picked up Barbie's small body in his arms and just drove away in the van. We didn't see him again for a while. I never brought up the fact later that I saw him crying as he carried her out.

Duke found out the names of the Guardians at the bar that day. He started a search to find each of them and take his revenge. He made sure that each died slowly—painfully—and that they knew why this angel of death had sought them out. There was still a few he was looking for but they were hiding out. The Guardians knew of his vendetta but considered it good drama. He knew many of them from his drug running days so they didn't interfere. I even heard they were taking odds on how long it would take him to find all the perpetrators. It became the sole focus of his existence.

"Barbie had a brother you never met," Duke finally continued. "He's a garbage man known as Gladman. He still makes runs for the Guardians taking crap out to the dump at Stinson Beach. He can get you across the bridge in the back of his garbage truck."

I looked at him carefully to see if he was pulling my leg but he was dead serious. "Are you shittin' me? That sounds pretty bizarre—even for you."

"Trust me bro. I know it'll work. I tried it out a few days ago. Both ways. Pretty fuckin' smelly but it worked." He took another drink and told me the story.

"Gladman hates the Guardians for what they did to Barbie so he wants to help. We rigged up a container at the bottom of the load and I went all the way out to Stinson Beach. I stayed there for two days and did some recon for you. Learned a lot about the Guardian patrols and where I think some of their outposts might be. We just hafta make the container bigger to hold the bike." He paused for a moment to let it all sink in. "So what you think about that little man?"

I was stunned. Of all the schemes I'd imagined I never thought about leaving in a garbage truck. I jokingly replied, "Doesn't sound like a very exciting start to my adventure."

"What do you care—if it works?" He was right about that.

"Why didn't you stay once you were across the bridge?" I remembered Duke had talked about heading north also.

"Well—let's just say I have unfinished business here in the City." I saw that familiar anger in his eyes. "When I go I plan on walking to the north and Gladman will be my way across the bridge when that time comes. As long as you two don't get caught." He looked at me intently and I understood. "Besides—what fun would it be to get to the New Society if you weren't there? So you get to go first."

As incredible as it sounded—I now had a hope I could at least get out of the City. "What else did you learn?"

"The Guardians mostly run their coast patrols on bikes. Normally two at a time on some hot lookin' rice grinders—possibly with turbos. They're well armed with M16s but they carry them on their backs so it would take a few seconds before they could get them to the ready. It ain't easy to fire an auto from a bike." That sounded like experience talking.

He continued, "They must not be expectin' too many insane enough to try Route 1 as they only make patrols about every four hours but with no regular schedule. They run them through the night too. Their first checkpoint after the bridge is along the ridge before you drop down to Stinson Beach. Some of them are stayin' at a ranch just on the other side of the hill."

"What about in Stinson Beach?"

"There aren't any there. They can't stand the smell from the dump. So Stinson Beach would be your place to stage once you're off the truck." I couldn't believe he had learned so much. It was pretty good recon info. But then—he'd been a Ranger. I was getting excited about the possibility of my plan working after all. At least the first part…

"How about checkpoints further north?" I asked wanting to know more.

"Nobody seemed to know much about that—just hunches. So we'll check your map and see where we'd put checkpoints if it was us. I have some ideas. Sure you do too. Some of the folks left in Stinson thought it might be as far north as Gualala—or Point Arena—to tie up with the New Society." He turned and stared at me with those black eyes. "You think the old jarhead is up to this?" That was a real good question from a friend.

"Don't think I have many options if I want my freedom again." That was easy to say but it was going to take a lot of determination and will power at my age. But there was no other choice I could see. I had to give it my best Marine try.

"There's one other thing you otta know. The Guardian who commands the coast road is a real nasty dude called Blackie. He's a killer the Guardians released from prison and he's supposed to be one mean son of a bitch. I saw him with a patrol when I was scoping the road from outside Stinson. He looks like a picture of Rasputin the Mad Monk I saw in a book once. Long black hair and dressed all in black. Rides a black bike. I hear he takes pleasure in catching people trying to get north and torturing them. He'll be a tough cookie if you run into him." These were serious words coming from Duke.

"Well—so much for the good news and the bad news," I responded to his somber advice. "As the Romans used to say before a battle—do you want to live forever?" and I took another swig.

We sat there for a while enjoying the high—and the whiskey—and remembering back on life before the Regional Wars. I knew Duke was thinking about Barbie Doll—though he never said a word.

"So JC—let's take a look at this ole hunk of HD metal and figure out what it's gonna take to make her run like a champ. Once we know what parts we need we can contact Rat if he's still alive. He can find anything.

He's the best scrounger in the business and he owes me a favor. Besides—he about shits his pants every time he sees me because he's such a timid little man. Kind of like you—you paac-i-fist!" Duke said laughingly as he put me in a head lock and squeezed. Damn that boy was strong!

After a few seconds he finally let go and said, "Let's get to work little man..."

*Excerpted from *A Run Up The Coast* by Gene Lewis (3rd Edition 2013), ISBN 9780978876197.

Gene Lewis has been riding - and writing - for over forty years. He attended his first Rider Rights Rally in San Francisco in 1975 and remained an activist with ABATE for over two decades promoting motorcyclist rights and rider education. In '75 he also experienced the unforgettable exhilaration of traveling solo around the country on a Triumph Trident witnessing America and freedom at its best. Over the years he has belonged to numerous motorcycle organizations and clubs including the American Motorcycle Association, HOG, the Platte River Valley Riders Club, the 40+ Motorcycle Club, the Motorcycle Touring Association, and the Mountain and Plains Riders Club.

Gene is a proud veteran (Air Force - '68 to '73) who holds in esteem all those who have served in peacetime or war. He wrote this story as a recognition for fellow veterans who often don't receive the gratitude they deserve in our country. His publishing record includes over 30 articles and several technology textbooks - although he enjoys writing motorcycle stories the best. He is a musician who likes playing drums with his surf band - *Vintage Winds* - whenever possible.

Kung-Fu

By Max Billington

Connor decided to spend the rest of that day within the safety of the Libertines compound. He sat inside the clubhouse nursing beers by himself and pondered what his next move was going to be. He knew that he was going to have to debrief the prospect on what had happened and find out whether or not he had spoken to the police. He began to grow impatient as he waited for the prospect's arrival. After another fifteen minutes, Scott finally came walking into the clubhouse and handed Connor a pack of cigarettes as Terry had requested for him to pick up. Connor stood up and greeted Scott and they both had a seat at the table.

"So," began Connor, "have you talked to anyone about last night?"

"No, I haven't really had a chance to. I went home last night and pretty much stared at the ceiling all night. I couldn't fall asleep. That fucker deserved what came to him, but I have to be honest, I am feeling pretty guilty about killing him."

"Well, that makes two of us, but we both have to get past that shit and be ready for what might be coming next. That fucker did get what he deserved and if I could kill him again I would. I have to know that your loyalty lies with us and that you are not going to be a fucking turn coat."

"You can be one hundred percent sure that I am with you, man. I will do whatever it takes to earn my patch. I hope that what I did with you last night will help to prove that point."

Connor responded, "That certainly helped your case, but it didn't exactly get it sewn on your back. Now, I need for you to go to my house. My wife shouldn't be there. I need you to go inside and go to my bedroom in the back of the house. You will see a cell phone charger sitting on my nightstand. Grab that and bring it back up here to the clubhouse. Here's my keys."

After Connor explained how to get to his house, Scott took his keys and left. Connor was once again alone inside the clubhouse and decided that he did not want to be without some form of company. He walked outside and Terry was sitting at the picnic table. He walked over to where Terry was sitting and sat on the other side. He reached into his pocket, rapidly packed the cigarettes against his wrist, tore off the top, took the first cigarette out of the pack and lit it.

Terry looked at Connor in amazement and said, "Man, I haven't seen you smoke in forever. When did this start?"

"I really don't know why I was craving them. It's probably nerves or something. After last night, I need something coursing through my veins to help calm me down, and the beer sure as shit isn't doing the trick."

Terry then changed the subject, "So, what's your plan tonight? You can't hide from your ol' lady forever you know."

"I know. I know. I'm still not going home tonight. I will probably end up just crashing here at the clubhouse and I will go home tomorrow. I'm thinking I need a night out at a different bar that I'm used to. You game for that?"

Terry replied, "Hell, I'm always game for a new place. There's a place that just opened toward the other side of town. I haven't heard much about it but I don't think it is too uppity. Maybe we should give that a try. What do you think?"

"Sounds like a plan. When the prospect gets back we can go grab some food and hit that place for a few beers."

Scott returned soon thereafter with Connor's cell phone charger and handed him the charger and his keys. Connor then told Scott to take his cell phone into the clubhouse and plug it in for him, but to leave the phone turned off, which Scott did.

Scott, Connor, and Terry bummed around the clubhouse for a bit that afternoon, playing some pool and telling jokes back and forth when it became evident that the trio was hungry and needed to fill their bellies with food before they consumed any more alcohol.

The three hopped on their bikes and stopped in at Bubba's, where they had some bar-be-cue sandwiches, on the house of course, and after a brief stay decided to head to the new bar in town to scope it out.

Historically in Clark, new bars didn't make it. The cops tended to harass people leaving bars, trying to arrest them for drunk driving, and whenever a new place would open, the cops would camp usually across the street or just down the street and wait for someone to leave, follow them, and pull them over. The entire police force in Clark was nothing more than a squad of dorks with little man syndrome as far as the club was concerned. Most of the time, the cops did not bother with the Libertines due to their reputation of not being afraid to go to jail.

When the three pulled up to the bar, they noticed a sign on the side of the building that said, "Clark Tavern" and joked to each other that the owner didn't really get too creative at giving the new place a descent name. The Clark Tavern was an older house that had been converted into an antique store and now bought out to open up a bar. The exterior of the building had been redone with updated materials to resemble a log cabin. There was no motorcycle only parking, which was not uncommon for the town, but the parking lot was freshly paved. The lot, which could accommodate approximately thirty vehicles, was almost to capacity, but there was a spot available fairly close to the door.

The trio walked into the tavern, and for a small place with a maximum capacity of fifty or so people, it was packed. The walls had been done in a false wood in hopes of trying to look rustic and expensive, but came off as cheap and gaudy. There were three flat screen televisions hanging over the bar, all tuned to the same cable sports network. The bar ran most of the length of one wall, with tall tables and stools at the far end.

The crowd there that night seemed to be mostly middle class folks, wearing polo shirts and khaki pants, and a few typical alcoholic older men bellied up to the bar sipping on whiskey and waters minding their own business. The men that were inside the bar were dressed in more expensive clothes than the women, and none of the men in the bar appeared that they had ever had dirt under their fingernails. The looks of the women were plain at best, not ugly but not pretty, which was usually what Terry sought in his female conquests.

Connor and Terry found their way to a table rather than sitting at the bar, and instead of sitting on the bar stools, they pushed them aside and leaned against the table. They waited on Scott to return from the bar with some beer and they watched as he did.

Terry looked at Connor and said, "So, you do realize that your prospect only has two futures. Either he will patch in or if he doesn't, we will have to kill him."

Connor thought for a moment and said, "That's one way to put it. I never thought about it that way, but you are right."

At that moment, Connor realized that those were in fact the only two possibilities of Scott's future. If he patched in, Connor would not have to worry about Scott giving him up in the murder, and patching him in was the only way to make sure that he kept his mouth shut, otherwise, he would have to die.

Scott returned to the table with the three. Since both Terry and Scott were single, they decided to make a casual glance around the room and take an inventory of possible women to hit on. Connor listened as the two commented to each other about the variety of women and the lack of any seemingly available woman that was out of their league. Terry and Scott finally decided that they would approach a couple of women sitting alone on the other side of the bar.

As they walked away, Connor wished them well. He sat alone at the table now, watching from a distance as the two single men were doing their best to impress a pair of ladies, all the while their goal being to get them into bed that night. It only took about two drinks worth of time until both women were full on flirting with Scott and Terry and by the time the third drink was finishing, the four were tabbing out.

The two newly made couples walked over to the table where Connor sat alone and said, "These nice young ladies would like to see what the inside of the clubhouse looks like. You ready to go?"

Connor replied, "Not quite yet, but I will be back at the clubhouse in a little while. I will see you when I get there."

"Suit yourself," replied Terry as the four found their way out of the bar.

Connor then found himself drinking alone again, at least alone at the table. He was surrounded on either side of him with people, who were doing their best to not be noticed. He drug a stool from beside the wall and sat down. He felt a slight nicotine withdrawal urge and reached into his pocket for his cigarettes.

Connor took one out, lit it up, and took a nice long drag. As he blew the smoke from his lungs, the smoke cloud made its way to the table beside him, where a man and a woman had been sitting there minding their own business.

As the smoke encircled the couple, the man stood up from his barstool, and in a very unassuming and polite manner looked at Connor and said, "Excuse me, but do you mind putting out that cigarette?"

Connor, who remained on his stool, looked at the man. He was probably a few inches shorter than him and Connor easily had the man outweighed by 30 or 40 pounds. He was dressed in a white dress shirt and black slacks with a fairly nice sport coat on. His hair was cut quite short, he lacked any trace of facial hair, and he wore a pair of thin wire framed glasses containing round lenses. Connor thought to himself, *this guy had quite a set of balls to make that request."*

Connor, in his slightly inebriated state, retorted in a very condescending tone as he held his cigarette in the air at the eye level of the man, "I will put the cigarette out. Sure. Give me about two or three minutes and when I am done, I will put it out."

He then smiled at the man and returned his focus back towards the bar as he continued to smoke. He knew that he was a Libertine, an outlaw biker, a bad ass, and someone that should not be fucked with. There was no way this dude was going to tell him what to do.

The man took a harmless step toward Connor's table and once again in a polite manner, said, "Sir, my wife doesn't really care for cigarette smoke, and to be quite honest, I do not either. I find it disrespectful that you cannot accept my request. Would you please reconsider?"

Connor then stood up from his stool and got within inches of the man's face and said, "Look, fellah, I will put my cigarette out when I am good and God damn ready."

After this statement, he stared into the man's eyes with a daunting glare figuring that his size, his tone of voice, and the patch on his back was enough to back the man down. The amount of eyeball visible from his face had now doubled as he was displaying his disdain for this conversation.

As the two remained locked in eye contact, the man spoke once more, and lacking any fear in his voice pleaded, "I do not appreciate the tone that you are taking with me. I am not looking for trouble. I simply want you to not smoke around us. It would be in your best interest to comply with that request."

"My best fucking interest, huh? It would be in your best fucking interest to leave this fucking place before you have to be carried out of here. You got me, you sawed off little bitch?"

Connor barley finished his last word when he hit the floor. In a whirlwind of a move, the man had hit him. Before he could regain his composure and focus, the man had pinned his arms down with his knees and hit him two more times with blows that struck him in the nose. The man then extinguished the cigarette with his foot, which had fallen to the ground, and looked down at his victim.

As Connor raised his head, the man said to him, "I suggest you lay there for a minute and decide whether or not the next words or actions out of you are wise."

Connor put his head back down on the ground, in utter pain. He had been hit before, this was nothing new, but he had never been hit this hard or this quick. Noticing that Connor did not seem to have any fight in him whatsoever, the man then reached down and took a hold of his hand and helped Connor to his feet, who was still in a bit of a daze.

The man then said, "Now, sir, have a seat at my table. Let me buy you a beer."

Connor blinked his eyes repeatedly; trying to reestablish his senses and without hesitation complied with the man's request and sat down.

The man's wife took a look at Connor and then her husband and looking back at Connor said, "I'm sorry that happened."

By this time, the manager had made it over to the table, and not wanting any more trouble, looked at the man and said, "Sir, I am going to have to ask you to leave."

Before the man could reply, Connor turned to the manager and said, "There is no need for that. This was just a misunderstanding and my fault. You have my word that there will not be any more trouble."

The manager stood and contemplated this situation, still in a bit of shock that the man had put a Libertine on the ground so quickly and the Libertine was not shooting or stabbing him. Reluctantly, the manager nodded his head and returned to his station behind the bar.

Connor then removed his head from his hands and looked at the man, and in a still confused manner, said, "What the fuck just happened?"

The man replied, "I hate resorting to violence, but sometimes it is a necessary evil to make a difficult point. I hope that you will think twice in the future before acting the way you just did. I know that you guys in your club don't want to be judged incorrectly, just as I do not either. Most people fear you because of that patch. However, I do not. This instance has been the first time that I have been shown disrespect by one of your members. Let's just have a beer and part as friends."

Connor, still confused, said, "Who the fuck are you? Batman?"

The man laughed and replied, "My name is Jeff. I'm just your average guy, but your average guy you just don't want to fuck with, if you know what I mean, and judging by the look on your face, I'm pretty sure you do."

"That ain't no shit, Jeff. Man, you whooped me up pretty good and pretty quick at that. Where did you learn that?"

"I didn't learn it overnight. I don't want to bore you, but let's just say I have a military background and used to also be a professional fighter."

"Damn!" exclaimed Connor, "I did pick the wrong guy to fuck with tonight."

"Yes. Yes you did. Now, let me go get you and me a beer."
Jeff walked up to the bar to fetch a couple of beers and Connor sat at the table with Jeff's wife. He looked at her and said, "I tell you what, I have met a lot of people in my life, but that husband of yours is one unique dude."

She replied, "Yes, he certainly is. He could tell you stories that would make your biker stuff seem as tame as a Sunday school class. He doesn't really talk about it much, though, since he doesn't really have any friends."

Connor inquired, "How can that guy not have any friends? Seems like a real nice guy."

"Oh, he is, he's sweet as candy. He just has a real tough time making friends. He doesn't do well in social situations and if it wasn't for his sister introducing us, he probably wouldn't be married."

"I got you. Sometimes you meet the nicest folks in the strangest of situations."

Jeff then returned to the table and handed Connor his beer. He raised his glass and toasted Jeff and they took a drink.

Connor then asked Jeff, "So, do you ride Jeff?"

"I have in the past. I haven't in a long time though. It is something that I would like to get back into but the opportunity has never presented itself at the right time."

Connor continued, "I know what you mean. I just got back into riding not that long ago. The right deal at the right time found me. Anyway, I'm really sorry about this shit. I've had a rough couple of days and I let my temper make a bad decision for me."

Jeff replied, "No big deal."

"Look, I want to invite you to our next party at the clubhouse. You will be my guest. Don't worry about not having a bike or anything. Just come and hang out. It's the least I can do."

Jeff answered, "That would be great."

He handed Connor one of his business cards, which Connor put into his wallet and the two men shook hands. Connor then walked outside the bar and hopped onto his bike and headed to the clubhouse.

The whole ride back to the clubhouse Connor was replaying the situation in his head and was still mystified by the whole experience. Even though he took a quick ass whooping, he knew that it was probably best that this happened while Terry and Scott were not with him, because it could have been much worse for all involved.

He continued toward the clubhouse and made his way to the gate of the compound. He keyed in the pass code and the electric gate opened up. He then parked his bike and looked up, noticing that much to his surprise, Julie's car was in the parking lot. When he got off his bike, he saw the door to the car open and Julie getting out. He cocked the handlebars of his bike to the left, pulled the key out of the bike, and hung his head.

Only one word entered his mind as Julie approached. *"Fuck!"*

*Excerpted from *The Libertines Motorcycle Club: Deception & Betrayal* by Max Billington (2012), ISBN 9781480177321.

Max L. Billington has worked in the insurance industry and as a consultant in the aerospace industry. He is an avid motorcycle enthusiast, has been riding motorcycles for more than 20 years, and is actively involved in community charitable functions and the organization of local motorcycle events. The writing bug bit him in 2011, after a good friend of his suggested that he should put his imagination to use by writing a book. Although his literary works are fiction, some of the subject matter is based on the biker culture of which Max is a part of on a daily basis.

Time For Revenge

By Vic Shurtz

Maggie sat her wine glass on the coffee table before she turned toward her front door.

"What do you think dog, should we put the chain on the door, or will you protect me."

Maggie started toward the door. She thought she heard footsteps on the gravel outside.

"Who would be out there at this time of night?" She said to herself as she reached for the door. She saw the doorknob start to turn. She grabbed for the chain, the door exploded open. The force of the door caught her full in the face. She staggered back. Out of the night, a man rushed in slamming the door behind him. The dirty hair, the ugly teeth and the smell told her who it was.

"Well, well, look what we have here."

He said as he grabbed her wrist.

"I've come to say good-by. I'm glad you dressed for the occasion." Maggie tried to pull her hand free. Her head still swam from the impact of the door.

"You're not going anywhere." He sneered.

"You're going to give me a little loving before I leave."

His fist crashed into her face shattering her lip.

"I want you to know what a real man could have given you. It'll be better then that trash you've been fuckin'." Her head rocked back on her shoulders when he backhanded her across the face leaving her ears ringing.

"Let's see what we have here." He sneered as he grabbed her shirt tearing it away, to expose her naked body. Maggie tried to knee him in the groin. His fist smashed her nose. Maggie could feel herself falling, but couldn't stop it. She collapsed on the floor.

"You don't want to hurt him." He said.

Staring down at her, he continued. "He's going to make you a real woman!"

Naked, Maggie struggled up on her hands and knees. Agony exploded inside her when his boot struck her ribs, she felt one snap. The side of her face crashed into the coffee table spilling her wine and tearing a gash across her cheek. He reached down and grabbed her by the legs. He rolled her over. Maggie knew she was losing consciousness when the darkness started to close in on her mind. He knelt between her thighs.

"This one is for the trash you run with." His fist collided with her face once again. He grabbed her legs and spread them wide. He unzipped his jeans. "And this one is for you." His hideous laughter filled the small room.

* * *

The ringing phone woke Preacher from a troubled sleep. He had gone to bed in a good mood. His dreams, however, were anything but good. His thoughts prior to retiring had been of a baseball team and a puppy. His dreams had been the sight of his puppy after the accident; the crushed body, the blood on the road, and the hideous laughter as the driver drove off.

He reached for the phone.

"What!" He answered.

"Ah, Preacher?"

"Yea."

"It's Hank, we have a problem. Maggie's been hurt."

Preacher bolted up to a sitting position.

"What!"

Hank paused.

"Maggie's been hurt."

Preacher swung his legs out of bed.

"Explain." He said.

Hank told him about the slamming door, he told him about the truck, he told him about finding Maggie on the floor.

"Preacher, she's hurt really bad. Tina is with her right now. I called the hospital and the helicopter is on its way. I should be here anytime now."

Preacher slowly stood up.

"Hank, I want you to listen very carefully. I will be there before the sun's up if I can. Do whatever you have to do to make sure she gets the best care the hospital can give her. Do NOT call the police! I will handle everything."

"Preacher, the hospital may want to call the police, a crime has been committed."

"Hank, do NOT call the police. I don't want them involved. I will handle everything."

"Whatever you say Preacher."

Preacher paused.

"I'll be there as soon as I can. Hank take care of her. I'll meet you at the hospital."

"Okay." Hank said. He hung up the phone.

He turned toward Roy.

"Preacher's on his way. He'll meet us at the hospital. He said to not call the police."

Roy stood in amazement

"He doesn't want us to call the police?" With concern in his voice he continued. "She's been beaten and raped, and he doesn't want us to call the police! What the hell is the matter with him!"

Hank shook his head and raised his hands. "Roy, settle down. He said he would handle everything."

He looked at Roy.

"And, if I know Preacher, he will."

Roy deflated. "Let's hope so." He responded.

Preacher immediately called Daymond. He got the answering machine.

"Daymond get ahold of the Kid. He's at Apache's. Tell him I had to leave for a few days. Tell him to get the slab poured. Have Apache help him. I'll be in touch when I can."

Within minutes, Preacher was dressed. He grabbed his saddlebags, his pack, and his leathers. While he secured his pack he talked to his black beauty. "Well old girl, I'm going to have to trust you to get me there and back. I know you're tired, and I will rebuild you this winter. Just get me there."

Having secured his pack, Preacher straddled his old girl. He hit the starter button. The old girl roared to life. One click down and he was gone.

* * *

The day security guard looked up when he heard the Harley pull into the parking lot. The man that crawled off the big black bike, stood next to it while he stretched out his back and legs. After looking around, he started toward the entrance. The guard stood up. The biker looked like trouble. The vest he wore over his black leather jacket sparkled in the morning sun. Pins and patches covered almost the entire front. His black chaps rustled as he walked up to the entrance.

"May I help you?" Asked the guard.

"No!" Was the biker's reply as he walked past the guard. He picked up his radio. The guard stepped through the entrance doors. He watched as the biker inquired at the front desk.

When he turned and started down the hallway, the guard hurried up to the desk.

"Who's he looking for?" He asked.

The Candy Striper looked down the hallway at the biker.

"The woman they assigned a guard to."

"Oh shit." The guard said as he raised his radio.

The nurse, at the station, noticed the guard at the woman's door when he stood up while talking on his radio. She turned and looked down the hall. A big man, dressed in black leather, marched purposefully down the hall. The guard folded his arms as he stepped in front of the patient's door. The biker's boots echoed in the hallway. As he passed the waiting area, the older man, who had been waiting, rushed out.

"Preacher, you're here!" He exclaimed.

"Where the hell did you expect me to be?" Preacher replied not breaking stride.

"Where's Maggie?"

Hank hurried to keep up.

"She's over there." Hank pointed. "The door with a guard." Preacher stopped.

"Why the guard Hank, I told you no cops!"

"I tried." Hank whined. "They called them before we got here."

Preacher looked at Hank through blood shot eyes.

"Is she awake?"

"Yup, Tina is with her now."

Preacher looked over at the guard. The guard stood up a little straighter.

Preacher chuckled.

"He better call some backup."

Preacher started toward the door.

"I'm sorry sir. Only authorized visitors." The guard said in a shaky voice.

"I'm authorized." Preacher said as he pushed past the guard.

Hank rushed forward. He stopped in front of the guard. "Just leave him alone. He won't hurt anybody, yet." Hank smiled.

The guard stared at Hank.

"He can't just walk in there like that. She's in protective custody."

Hank stood a little straighter.

"She is now. That's her husband."

"Oh." The guard said. He hitched up his belt, over his oversized belly.

"Then add his name to the list." The guard ordered.

Hank smiled.

"Yes, sir."

What Preacher saw stopped him in his tracks. Maggie's eyes were mere slits between the ugly red and black swelling around them. Here nose had a wide strip of tape holding it in place. Her lips were split and swollen. A gauze bandage covered her right cheek. The contrast between her red hair and her complexion, made her face look even paler. Tina sat at her side. She jumped up and rushed forward.

"Thank God you're here Preacher." She said.

"She's been waiting for you. They want her to press charges, but she won't talk to them. Preacher you've got to do something."

Preacher hadn't taken his eyes off Maggie. He noticed her try to smile. He nodded in recognition.

"I will." He looked down at Tina.

"Now leave us."

Tina stared up at him. She nodded, turned, and exited the room.

Preacher waited for the door to close behind him before he moved. When he ambled forward, Maggie noticed his bloodshot eyes. She patted the side of the bed. In a mere whisper, between swollen lips, she spoke.

"Thanks for coming."

Preacher sat on the side of the bed. He smiled. "This is a party I couldn't miss. Where's the band?"

Maggie winched when she tried to chuckle. Preacher placed his hand on her ribs. He could feel the binding that held them in place. Fire flashed across his eyes.

"Do you want to tell what happened?"

She nodded. "I ran into a door."

Preacher chuckled. "It must have been one hell of a door."

"It was." She said. "A big, ugly, sleazy one."

A tear escaped her swollen eye. Preacher wiped it away with his thumb when he placed his hand gently on her cheek.

"Take your time." He said as he caressed her cheek. "I'm not going anywhere at the moment."

Maggie reached up and took his hand. She told him everything that happened, at least as much as she could remember. As she told him the story, she watched his face change from concern to rage.

"The next thing I remember was waking up here, in the hospital." She noticed the concern return to his face.

Preacher sat still for a moment.

"Throughout your story, you only called this piece of shit he. Do you know who it was?"

Maggie nodded. "Yes."

"Preacher, I want you to beat this asshole within an inch of his life. I want him to know what it's like to be helpless and still be beaten some more." She squeezed his hand. "But I don't want you to go to prison. Don't kill him. Leave him scared for life, but don't kill him. I will heal. He's not worth your going to jail. Promise me baby."

Preacher took a deep breath.

"I don't know if I can live by that promise."

Maggie nodded. "I think you can. I want your word Preacher."

"I'll try." He kissed the back of her hand.

"That's all I can ask." She flinched when she tried to take a deep breath.

"It was Eddie?"

With tears spilling out of her swollen eyes, she continued.

"He raped me Preacher. I want him punished."

Lightning flashed across his eyes. He responded in an even voice.

"And he will be punished." Preacher paused. "An eye for an eye."

Tina looked up when Preacher exited the room.

"Well, did you talk some sense into her?"

Preacher's cold stare stopped Tina from any further conversation.

"There will be no charges filed." He turned toward Hank.

"My friend, I want you to take her home as soon as she can be released. She'll need some help for a few days. I'm counting on you Hank, to help her. I'll be back as soon as I can." He turned toward the exit. Tina grabbed his arm.

"Preacher, your wife-to-be is in there! Where the hell are you going!" She exclaimed.

Preacher looked down at Tina's hand. Tina jerked it away. He looked up at Hank.

"I'll see yah when I see yah."

Hank nodded. He stuck his hands in his pockets. "Where 'are' you going?" He asked.

Hank looked into eyes that were as black as coal.

"Hunting." Was all Preacher said.

He turned and started toward the exit. Everyone in the hall moved out of his way, as he marched down the hall toward the exit.

Hank watched the big leather clad warrior leave.

Tina still fuming asked.

"Hunting, what does he mean by that?"

Hank shook his head.

"Tina, I think somebody is going to die."

Tina thought for a moment. She nodded her head. " Good." She looked over at Hank. "I'm going to check on Maggie."

* * *

Eddie sat at the end of the bar. He nursed his whiskey while he watched the young whore work the bar. She seemed to have a clientele amongst the patrons. New customers got little attention. She noticed him once in a while, but she mostly stayed with regulars. Her name was Satin. He heard several people comment that she was as smooth as satin.

The night was still young. Eddie decided to give her more time to build up her bank; then he would ask for her time.

He noticed when the two bikers strolled into the bar. They scanned the room. Their eyes settled on him briefly, then continued moving. He smiled. Satin stood up from her booth and ambled up to the big one.

"Critter, what brings you out tonight?" she asked.

Critter smiled. "Satin, if I wasn't married, I'd take you out of here."

Satin laughed. "And I'd go." She paused as her eyes settled on Apache. "And who are you?" She asked. Apache stood a little taller.

"Somebody that will take you out after a while. Right now, I'd like a drink. Would you care to join us?"

Satin smiled a crooked smile.

"Sure, I'll have a drink. Why don't you two have a seat at my booth, and I'll get the drinks. What will it be?"

Critter grinned. "I'll have a whiskey and so will my friend. Get whatever you like." He handed her twenty dollars.

"Have a seat and I'll be right back." She turned and sashayed up to the bartender. Critter nodded at him. He nodded back.

Satin just sat down when the jukebox started blaring. Critter looked over at the bartender. He motioned for Critter.

"Excuse me Satin. I need to talk to Tom for a minute."

Satin smiled. "Don't be too long." She said.

Critter laughed. "Just keep my friend happy. I'll be right back. He strolled up the bar.

"Tom, what the hell. How are you doing?" He said as he placed his boot up on the rail at the bottom of the bar. Tom smiled.

"Just fine Critter. How's Ma?"

"She's doing good. How about you?"

Tom picked up a bar towel and began wiping the bar.

"I think the guy at the end of the bar is someone I don't want to know. What do you think?"

Critter nodded. "I think you're right. I think he's someone you might want to forget."

Tom grinned. "I can forget anybody if someone offers me the right reason."

Critter laughed. "I'll just bet you could. How long has he been hanging around?"

Tom shrugged.

"About three days. His name is Eddie." He says he's from up North. He also said he's headed for Arizona for the winter. He's staying down the road a ways in an old motel."

Critter nodded. "That'll work, thanks."

Tom nodded. "Not a problem."

Critter started to turn away. He stopped and looked back at Tom.

"Is the back door locked?"

Tom chuckled. "Yea, but you know how to unlock it, don't you?"

Critter laughed. "Yes I do." He said.

Tom nodded. "Then do what you need to do."

Critter nodded. "Thanks Tom."

Critter strolled back to the table.

Apache and Satin were laughing when Critter returned.

"What are you two laughing about?" He asked.

Satin looked up. "Apache was just telling me about a run they had a few weeks ago."

Critter smiled. "Good. I'll be right back."

Critter strolled toward the back of the bar. A sign over the hallway that led to the back door, read 'Restrooms'. Critter turned down the hall.

Critter stepped out the back door into the crisp evening air. He noticed the glow of a cigarette in one the trucks parked behind the bar. Smiling, he started toward his truck. Preacher stood next to it.

"Preacher, I think we have found your man. He's sitting at the end of the bar."

Preacher nodded. "Is he drunk?"

Critter shook his head. "I don't think so. He seems to be happy just sitting there watching."

"Good." Preacher answered. "I don't want him drunk. I want him to know what's happening."

Critter smiled. "Then why don't we walk back in the bar so you can meet him."

Preacher shook his head. "I don't think so. I'll just wait out here until he comes out. That way, when he doesn't come back, everybody will think he just went home, no witnesses."

Critter nodded. "That works, I think. It may be a while before he comes out."

Preacher looked over at Critter.

"Then I'll wait."

*Excerpted from *Preacher: Eye For An Eye* by Vic Shurtz (2007), ISBN 9781601451774.

Vic bought his first bike, a 1971 FLH, in 1977, and has traveled extensively throughout the western United States and Canada. The author of five books about the biker lifestyle, he is a ten year member of the United Bikers of Northern California, a 501C Organization, and the owner of motorcyclefiction dot com, the website for biker books.

Nowhere To Run

By Edward Winterhalder & James Richard Larson

Everyone was expected to attend church. Like a good Catholic or Protestant, the members took church seriously, yet instead of observing the sacraments and providing the worship due the blessed savior; the hardcore one percenters heard and obeyed the gospel according to the will of the Skuldmen motorcycle club.

Unseen and unknown by outsiders, with a meeting hall accrued as well as any medieval warlord's lair, even in this den of cunning, ruthless outlaws, Robert's rules held sway.

Before the meeting, Loner moved from man to man, group to group, judging the opinions of the brothers as to Beckman's sins, determining if and when he should speak in the prospect's defense.

During the formal meeting, after club business and the treasurer's report, the floor recognized Milwaukee Phil, the president.

"I think by now most of you know what's going on with the prospect, Beckman. But for those of you who may not know the details, I'm going to lay it out for you now. For one thing, the prospect disrespected the patch. Seems like he can't hold his liquor or his tongue. He's running his mouth. He's behind on dues and he owes us money.

"Now. In his defense, he lost his job. He might be having personal problems—from what I hear it's woman problems, for one thing." The Boss raised his head, looked down his nose at the room full of bikers and said, "Hell, that's a first."

A few members chuckled. When it was quiet, the Boss continued.

"So maybe his old lady ran off on him—maybe he lost his job—had a run of bad luck. We all have our own little problems, but we never, and I mean never disrespect the patch, or a patch holder. Loner here sponsored Beckman, but I was the one who pushed for it. No disrespect to Loner, but as of here and now I make the motion that we kick Beckman out."

One of the brothers raised his hand and said, "I'll second that."

"All in favor?" the Boss said.

Nearly every man in the room raised his hand.

"Opposed?"

Not a single man opposed the motion.

The Boss then said, "He has club property, including his bike. I want it back—all of it, including the money he owes. Anybody want the job? Otherwise I'll assign it."

In the front row, Loner stood. "I'll take care of it, Boss," he said.

Zipper raised his hand. Beside him, T-Bone did likewise. "Me and T will go along with Loner," Zipper said.

"Good enough," the Boss said. "One other thing. I want him left with a big reminder about what happens to assholes who disrespect the patch."

From the back of the room, the enforcer Snake Campbell said, "I can take care of that job, Boss."

Grinning, T-Bone Lopez turned in his chair and said, "If you don't mind, Snake, I already have that covered."

*   *   *

In the attic, Michael sat in the easy chair, the mirror reflecting the gold cups and coins laid out neatly on the floor and the tables. He had removed some of the Nazi treasure from the crates and a three by five foot Nazi flag now graced the ceiling. Armbands, posters and swastikas adorned the walls, with a portrait of Adolf Hitler framed and hanging on the entrance wall beside the door.

The mirror beckoned, pulling his eyes toward the shimmering surface.

I want to go in, but what if I can't get back for some reason? Tiffany never came back; neither did the shine. Where did they go? There's only one way to find out and that's to just do it. Am I a chickenshit? Am I scared to do it? I went in before— twice I went in and I came out all right. Then why am I so petrified?

The ringing phone downstairs pulled him from his reverie. Grunting, Michael got to his feet. When the ringing stopped, he hesitated on his way down the steps. Ten seconds later it started ringing again. When he got to the living room and reached for the phone, he picked up to the dial tone. He checked the caller ID display.

Lacy. Shit. I wonder what she wants?

Why should I give a shit what she wants?

About to go back upstairs, the first ring made him jump.

Lacy again. Might as well answer. Don't blow it. Be nice.

"Hello?"

"Michael is that you?"

"Yeah, it's me. Hi Lacy."

"What did you do to Tiffany you son of a bitch? I found out some things and I want to know what you did with my daughter! Where is she?"

"What are you talking about? I don't know where she is! Jesus Christ Lacy if you thought I knew something don't you think I'd tell you?"

"You lying son of a bitch! What did you do with them?"

"Them? What did I do with *them*? What the hell are you talking about?"

"*Tiffany and Maurice! Where are they? You know! Tell me!*"

"Look, Lacy. I know you're upset. Believe me so am I. But I honestly don't know where she is. So don't be thinking that way. And how am I supposed to know where her nappy headed boy is?"

"*You're gonna get yours, Michael Beckman. You just wait and see!*"

"I don't have to listen to this shit. Bye, Lacy."

Michael slammed the phone down on the receiver.

What does she know? The bitch is fishing. She doesn't know a damn thing.

* * *

When the doorbell rang, Michael lifted the mini-blind and looked out the opening. The unmarked car with the black-wall tires and no trim had police written all over it. Checking the blind on the door side, he saw the two bulls on the porch. He'd seen them before, Detectives Scheid and Anderson.

God dammit I knew I should have switched cars and parked the Chevy in the garage. Either way they know I'm here. Shit! I might as well answer it.

Michael opened the door and said, "Good evening, Detectives. What can I do for you?"

"Just a few questions, Mr. Beckman," Anderson said. "Damn, it's cold out here. Mind if we come inside?"

"Yeah, sure. Come on in. What's this about?"

"We'd like to know if you had any contact with Maurice Pitts. We have a witness that claims she saw the two of you together prior to his disappearance."

"Well, she's mistaken. I really don't even know what the guy looks like."

"So Mr. Pitts never got into your car in the parking lot of the Lakeshore Apartments?"

So that's it Michael thought. *Somebody saw me. I wonder how much they know? Did someone take down my license number? I doubt it. Why would they?*

"Sorry to burst your bubble, guys, but it wasn't me," Michael said. "I never heard of the Lakeshore Apartments. Must have been somebody else. There's lots of cars around like mine."

"Well, we just had to check, we have to follow up," Detective Scheid said.

They don't have the license number! Michael thought. *Asshole cops!*

"No problem, Detective. Uh . . . actually . . . I'm kind of busy. I'm on the Internet—job hunting, y'know? I got laid off from my last job. So if you guys are finished, I'd like to get back to it."

"Just one more question, and you can get back to your computer," Scheid said.

"Yeah, go ahead," Michael said.

Scheid gave a million dollar smile and said, "Is that your coat there, Mr. Beckman? Do you want to put it on? We'll wait."

"Huh? Is this some kind of joke? I told you guys. I don't know anything about Pitts. Nothing."

Anderson said, "Put your coat on, Beckman."

"Aw c'mon you guys. What are you taking me in for? I'm innocent. I didn't do anything."

"Look Beckman, it's cold outside, unless you want to go the way you are. I really don't give a shit," Scheid said. "You're under arrest."

"For what? I didn't do anything. Hey, listen now. I got no idea where Tiffany is. None. She took off and that's all I know. Same goes for her black boyfriend. How am I supposed to know where they went? Shit! When you find him you'll probably find her."

"Mr. Beckman, were you recently involved in an accident?"

"Accident?

"A car accident."

"I don't know what you're talking about."

"You were involved in a hit and run accident. You failed to remain at the scene of the accident and you failed to report it. You're also being charged with . . ."

"What? You gotta be shitting me!" Michael interrupted, "You're arresting me for leaving the scene of an accident? I don't believe this bullshit!"

"Vehicular manslaughter in the death of a Mr. Tyrone Cooley. Now get your coat on," Scheid continued

"I told you, goddammit, I don't know what you're talking about!"

Detective Anderson pulled Michael's arms behind his back and strapped the heavy vinyl loop over his wrists, cinching them extra tight.

"You have the right to remain silent," Scheid began, "Anything you say may be used against you in a court of law. You have the right to an attorney. If you cannot afford an attorney the court will appoint one. Do you understand these rights?"

"I'm not saying anything until I talk to a lawyer."

* * *

"Hey, you're walking better," Detective Anderson said when Detective Scheid entered the office.

"Yeah, it's going away, thank God," Scheid said. "I could really use a drink but I don't dare. It'll come right back."

"And here I was, going to ask you to stop for a couple over at Kelley's."

"Yeah, well, what the hell do we have to celebrate? We're right back where we started. I can't believe that Beckman made bail."

"He still has to go to trial," Anderson said.

"Yeah. There's that at least."

"I have something else. Maybe good news."

"Yeah?" Scheid said, pouring a coffee from the pot. "What might that be?"

"Judge Lebowitz must not have liked Beckman's attitude. Either way it doesn't matter. Because Beckman's car was involved in a fatal accident Judge Lebowitz ordered that the car be impounded. We should have it in the garage this afternoon. If we can put Maurice Pitts in Beckman's car…"

"It will corroborate Monica Whalen's testimony," Scheid said. "And it will prove Beckman's lying. I'd better give the lab a call."

"I did that already, John," Anderson said. "Soon as we get the car, they're on it."

Scheid raised his cup in salute. "Sounds like you've been busy, Harry."

"One other thing. I checked with the assistant D.A., just to make sure. While we're going over Beckman's car, if we do find any trace of Maurice Pitts the evidence is admissible."

"It'll be there."

"I know."

*   *   *

With the last blood and skin samples taken from the underside of the green '92 Chevrolet, the analysis was now complete. The DNA proved to be that of Tyrone Cooley. When his parents provided hair samples from Maurice Pitts, the DNA matched that of hair and spots of blood found on the front seat of Beckman's car. Intermingled with Pitt's blood were traces of C-H, known on the street as the date rape drug.

"We got it!" Scheid said, hanging up the phone. "We have Pitts in the car! It looks like Beckman might have drugged him. There was C-H in the blood sample. The judge signed the warrant to search Beckman's house! Let's do it!"

"We can't bring him in on that alone." Anderson said. "We can search the place but what if we come up empty?"

"Michael Beckman's not going anywhere; we still have him on the vehicular manslaughter charge."

*   *   *

"More coffee?" Zipper said.

"Yeah, thanks."

Cup in hand, Loner wandered to the front window. "Hey, here comes T. Looks like he brought one of the repo trucks instead."

"I thought he was going to bring the pick-up," Zipper said.

"This is better yet," Loner said. "Less work for us."

"Yeah. You want to let him in?"

"Sure."

Loner met him at the door. Ramon "T-Bone" Lopez gave him a quick hug and said, "Hey Bro. Kind of nippy out there. You got any more coffee?"

"Yeah, Zipper just made a pot. Come on in."

When they were seated at the kitchen table, Zipper said, "I can spice the coffee up for you if you like. The bar is open."

"Nah, I'll pass," T-Bone said. Loner shook his head.

"Suit yourself. So, how do you want to do this?" Zipper said. "We gotta get in the garage, get the bike, and get the rest of the club property from inside the house. I think with the three of us he'll cooperate—but what's the plan if he doesn't?"

"We'll promise him that we're just there to take back what belongs to the club," T-Bone said. "We'll tell him not to worry. After he hands everything over, then I'm going to stomp the living shit out of him. He's got that coming from me."

"What if he don't let us in?" Zipper said. "What if he calls the cops?"

"Let me talk to him alone first," Loner said. "He'll trust me, I think. Once he lets me in, you guys follow."

"And if he's armed?" Zipper said. "I got the feeling he's going to figure out what's coming down. He's no dummy."

"I'll stick my gun in his face," Loner said.

"You're giving him too much credit," T-Bone said. "Once we're inside I'll just knock his lights out. He's a pussy. He ain't gonna do shit."

"Either way, I'm bringing along bracelets and duct tape in case we have to restrain him," Zipper said. "You got a piece, T?"

T-Bone pulled his jacket aside, revealing a 40 caliber Glock in his shoulder holster.

"Then we're good to go," Zipper said. "Ready to rock and roll?"

"Let's do it."

* * *

Loner rode shotgun, with Zipper in the back of the crew cab. No one spoke as T-Bone drove through town, heading south.

T-Bone clutched and brought her up a gear. Checking the rear view mirror, he said, "Ah, dammit! Not now!"

"What is it, T?" Zipper said.

"There's a cop behind us. He just turned his lights on. Shit!"

The squad car closed in fast. The policeman inside hit the siren for a quick shot and then turned it off.

T-Bone pulled the repo rig to the curb. Expecting the cop to pull in behind him, everyone was surprised when the police car cruised by. Another black and white tailed the first police car, with an unmarked squad taking up the rear.

T-Bone grinned like the cat. "I don't believe it. Must be our lucky day."

"We got about a mile," Loner said. "Straight on."

When they came to the next stoplight, Loner said, "The screws stopped up ahead—a couple blocks up."

"I see 'em," T-Bone said. "How much further is Beckman's house?"

"I don't know—close" Loner said. "Shit, it's got to be right on top of where they're stopped. Look. There's another cop car coming from the other way."

"You want me to turn?" T-Bone said.

"No," Loner said. "Keep going straight. See what the hell is going on."

When they arrived at the stop sign on Beckman's street, Loner said, "Look there. East side of the street. That's Beckman's house. Right there."

"The one with the cops in front?"

"Yeah. They're at his house. Make a left turn. Now."

"What do you wanna do?" Zipper said.

"Slow down at the alley," Loner said. "Look! See 'em? There's cops in the back, too. Holy shit."

"Do you want to hang around and see if they arrest him?" T-Bone said. "I'll park it on the next block."

"No, let's get out of here. There's too many damn cops around," Zipper said. "We got connections at the precinct. When they book him, we'll know about it. We can take care of the rest of this shit later."

"That's good by me," T-Bone said. "Loner?"

"Yeah, let's go."

*Excerpted from *The Mirror: A Biker's Story* by Edward Winterhalder & James Richard Larson, published by Blockhead City (2010), ISBN 9780977174720.

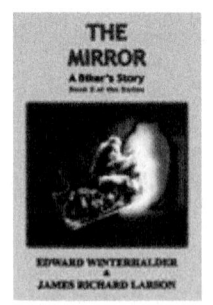

Edward Winterhalder is one of the world's leading authorities on motorcycle clubs and the Harley-Davidson biker lifestyle; his books are published in multiple languages and sold all over the world. He was a member, and/or an associate, of outlaw motorcycle clubs for almost thirty years. The creator and executive producer of the *PHASS MOB*, *Biker Chicz* and *Living On The Edge* television series, Winterhalder has appeared worldwide on television networks such as Bravo, Prime, CBC, Fox, National Geographic, History Channel, Global, AB Groupe and History Television. In addition to his literary endeavors, he is a consultant to the entertainment industry for TV, feature film and DVD projects that focus on the Harley-Davidson biker lifestyle.

James Richard Larson lives in Wisconsin and is a United States Navy veteran who served in the Vietnam War. An electrician and an avid Harley Davidson enthusiast for his entire life, he is the author of multiple books that feature the Viking lifestyle and Nordic mythology.

I Know A Man Who Can

By Iain Parke

'Shit! Shit! Shit! Sod this,' I shouted out loud as I thumped the steering wheel. Outside the hazard lights strobed the world black and orange, syncing with the metronomic tick from the dashboard.

The engine was dead.

The road ahead was pitch black.

I was stuck in the middle of nowhere, ten miles or so from home. And with the car's dying momentum I hadn't even made it to the lay-by, the curb of which lay tantalizingly just at the edge of the dulled headlights' beam.

'Shit!' I said again, switching to the sidelights to save the battery and reaching down to pop the bonnet release. There didn't seem to be anything for it but to get out and have a look. To be honest, with no torch in the car, and no real idea what the hell to look for, or what I would do if I found it, I suspected that all I would achieve was a broken nail. But it just felt as though I had to do something.

I knew nothing about cars. This was my first one ever. A three year-old 1984 Ford Fiesta XR2 Dad had helped me to find and buy.

'Make a good little run around,' he'd said.

Really I had needed to get a car because, having finished my PGCE, I had got my first job at a little village primary school in Yarrow Wood. I had Year 2, thirty six-year-olds, which took some getting used to, but I'd been loving the job. I'd found myself a small place to rent in Innerleithen, and so for the past month I had been commuting daily through the unfamiliar and stunningly beautiful countryside, with its narrow roads winding through the Kirkhouse Forest between dry stone walls enclosing fields dotted with grazing sheep.

I'd been feeling all grown up.

Now, I suddenly felt all alone and vulnerable, scared even, with no one at hand to rescue me.

I peered into the blackness of the engine well and shivered at the cold despite my cardigan pulled around me, I wasn't exactly dressed for this, and other than feeling welcome waves of heat coming off the radiator, I was still none the wiser.

A low continuous rumble made me move out from under the bonnet to where I could see back past the car an aurora of approaching headlights glowing above the tree line, probably about a mile or so back along the twisting country lane, but closing rapidly on where my car sat just after the last curve.

Terror jumped my pulse to double time.

I slammed down the bonnet and dived back into the car, desperately jamming the key in the ignition in a last-ditch attempt to inch the car away from the bend and towards the potential sanctuary of the lay-by, before whoever it was came tearing round the corner and straight into the back of me. I slapped my palm against the steering wheel and turned the key again.

'Come on, come on.'

Nothing happened.

The noise was much louder now, a gut-churning roar. I flicked my eyes up to the mirror, I could see the blaze of the looming lights streaming around the bend. They were almost upon me and then, BANG!

I winced as the blazing lights swept around the corner and flared directly into my mirror as well as lighting up the road to my side. I heard the screeching brakes, the roar of engines changing down. I could only hope that the warning flash of my hazards had given enough time for avoiding action.

I closed my eyes.

And then to my relief the lights were passing me, and I remembered to breathe as I dared to open my eyes and caught sight of the infamous patches on the back of the column of a dozen bikers or so racing around my car, before the sight of the brightly menacing brake lights following the lead bike into the lay-by brought my panic roaring back.

Oh Shit! I fumbled for the central locking and at least heard the comforting click of the doors, although I didn't think locks would actually protect me for long.

Christ, just how much worse could this get?

I still had spots floating before my eyes from the beams in my mirror, but even so I could make out several figures hurrying towards me from where the bikes were parked up. Silhouetted black bodies blocked my view of the bikes' tail-lights as they got nearer. I sat frozen, my knuckles whitening as I clung to the steering wheel with some kind of death grip. Was this it? They'd almost run into my car. Besides which, you heard all these stories…

And then they were past me. Three or four were round the back of the car and I wondered what they were going to do. A tap, tap of a knock at the window made me start.

It was as though time had stopped in my little world. Slowly, as if in a dream, I turned to my right and looked out, straight into the eyes and face of a bearded man leaning down to stare in at me from the darkness. He mouthed at me as though underwater and made a circling movement with his hand; the internationally recognized code for 'Can you wind the window down?'

Unthinking, I reached out for the switch, and with my heart in my mouth and the quiet whirr of the motor, the glass slid down, letting the cold night air in against my skin.

'D'you want to take the handbrake off and stick it in neutral, thanks love, and we'll get you into the lay-by,' he said pleasantly. I just nodded, reached down and did as he asked.

'Great,' he said, 'you just steer.'

'OK lads,' he shouted behind him, reaching into the car with one hand and putting his shoulder against the window frame. 'Now push!' I felt the car move and we rolled steadily towards the sanctuary of the blue P sign at the side of the road.

'OK,' he said, as we reached it. 'Now just swing in, that's it, and… handbrake on. Great.'

I caught my breath at the familiar ratchet noise as it engaged and, out of habit, slipped the gears into first. With their help, I was off the road and parked up, well clear of the bikes, which I realized had been deliberately pulled up at the other end of the gap so as to leave room for more. At least my car was safe.

'Pop the lid, love,' he said, looking in again. 'We'll have a look at what's wrong.'

He stood up as I sprung the catch again with a clunk, but stayed next to the door.

There was a huddle of bodies around the engine. Somebody produced a torch. A working one. Now why didn't I remember to carry one?

There was some discussion outside.

'Try turning it,' he said, leaning back down to me.

I tried the key. The dashboard lights were on, there seemed to be life in the battery as I heard the click and clatter of the starter motor trying to engage, but in terms of life from the engine there was nothing doing. Dead as a dodo.

'Again?'

I tried again, but there was still nothing as the weird orange light from the hazards clicked on and off, one and off.

Well at least I was off the road, so I didn't really need them anymore. I turned them off thinking I might as well try and save the battery.

There was a bit more of a huddle and the sound of a laugh and a comment directed at the bloke still stood by my open window.

'Are you sure, Dobbo?' he said, to a figure who joined him at my window and dropped down to look in at me with piercing blue eyes.

'I think you've seized it, love,' Dobbo said with a rueful smile. 'I just checked the dipstick and traditionally the engine's supposed to have some oil in it. When was the last time you checked it?'

I just shook my head. This was all my own fault.

'Well this car ain't going anywhere on its own,' he spoke gently. 'have you called recovery?'

I nodded this time. 'They said they'd be on their way soon,' I said in a small voice.

'OK then,' he replied.

'Well we can't just leave you here like this,' said the first man, who seemed to be in charge.

My eyes widened with panic. This was what I'd feared when they first pulled over. I was alone in the middle of nowhere, completely at their mercy. Abduction. Rape, Murder. Anything could happen. Absolutely anything.

'Fuck knows who might come along,' he continued, echoing my thoughts exactly.

'So the tryouts'll stick around till they get here. Make sure you're OK,' he announced. No one's going to mess with you with any of our lads around.'

I was dumbstruck. I didn't know what to say, but then there wasn't really anything to say because he was gone, walking back towards the parked bikes, the rest of the group falling in around him, pulling on their helmets, throwing away the ends of cigarettes and swinging their idling bikes upright.

The car was full of the thrumming noise of the engines revving as they got ready, formed themselves up, then with a growing roar, staggered pairs of red tail-lights rose up and out onto the road, and disappeared off into the darkness, the noise slowly dying away behind them.

Leaving just me.

And the bloke called Dobbo, who had now stood up and was pulling out a packet of cigarettes.

As my eyes adjusted to the dark again, I realized that I wasn't alone here with just Dobbo. There were two bikes still parked up ahead of me, and I could just make out a standing figure lurking beside them.

'Um… Dobbo?'

He turned to look at me. 'What's up? Do you want a fag?' he asked, offering me the open packet.

'Err, no thanks,' I've given up.

'Good job,' he said, as he tugged one out and stuck it in his mouth. 'I ought to,' he continued as he cupped his hands around his mouth, and I head the click and saw the flash of a lighter. 'Costs a fucking packet these days.'

'No, I mean, thanks but no. What I wanted to ask was, who's he?'

'Who?'

'Him,' I said pointing towards the bikes.

'Oh him,' Dobbo said, blowing coiling smoke into the air. 'Don't you worry about him. That's Stu, he's another tryout, so as far as the guys are concerned, we don't really count.'

*   *   *

Dobbo leant one forearm on the car roof as we talked.

I hadn't unlocked the doors or made any move to get out, and he'd not made any suggestion about me doing so or about him getting inside, even though he'd been standing out in the chill air for a good quarter of an hour.

He explained how Stu and he were serving their apprenticeships to become members of the club, and how their jobs included guarding the bikes and suchlike whenever they stopped, which was why Stu hadn't approached the car.

'Look, you know you really don't have to wait,' I said. 'I'm off the road now and I'm sure it'll be fine.'

'Oh, don't worry about it, love. It's no problem. Besides which Mal...'

'Mal?'

'The bloke you were talking to. He's our P, so he's in charge. What he says goes. If I goofed off before your tow truck arrived, I'd catch all sorts of shit, let alone what'd happen if I did and then something happened to you. No, we'll hang on here. Like I said, it's no problem.'

'Oh, well, OK then, if you're really sure…'

*   *   *

The only thing was, it was a bit of a problem.

And now I couldn't work out what to do about it.

So I was stuck.

Because the truth was, there wasn't a recovery truck coming. I hadn't called one. How could I? I'd just said I had, out of panic.

I'd thought it might help, make me safe I mean, help make the bikers think there were people on the way, people who would arrive at any moment, who might see them if they did anything. The bikers clearly didn't know the nearest phone box was a couple of miles back. Even if I made the walk, I had no one to call. Dad had told me to join the AA or RAC or whoever, but like a complete dib, not only had I not put oil in the car, I'd never got around to sorting out breakdown cover.

The truth was, there was no one coming.

So now what the hell was I going to do?

OK, despite my fears and their reputation, they'd actually been fine, helpful, friendly even. But now, how on earth could I get out of this without telling Dobbo that I'd lied to his P and kept him and Stu waiting out in the cold for a tow truck that was never going to arrive.

And the thing was, the longer I sat there trying to work out what to say or do about it, the worse it was getting as minute after minute ticked away in the night air.

* * *

'You might get away with it,' he was saying, stamping his feet to keep warm. 'It just depends how badly it's seized and what damage has been done.'

'Do you know about engines?'

'Yeah, I'm a mechanic by trade.'

'In a garage?'

'Well, not a dealership or anything. I've got my own business, self-employed. Servicing and all that sort of thing. Do a bit of dealing as well. Buying 'em up and moving 'em on.'

'So it may be OK after all?'

'Yeah, could well be. I'd guess you weren't thrashing it, so once it's cooled down you could try putting some oil in and see if it's freed itself again.'

'Well that would be a relief. I had visions of needing to replace it.'

'Your recovery guys are being a while, aren't they?' he observed, looking back down the empty road. It had been about forty-five minutes now and not a soul had come by all the time we'd been waiting.

'You did tell them you were on your own, didn't you? I thought they usually gave stranded women priority.'

I really didn't have an answer to that.

* * *

I thought about it every which way but there was no way of getting out of this. I was just going to have to face up to it.

'Um Dobbo?' I began.

'Yeah?'

'Err.. well... I've got something I need to tell you...'

'Yeah? So what's that then?'

I took a deep breath. I was committed now.

'Well you know we've been waiting for the recovery...?'

He nodded.

'Well... the truth is, err...I've got a bit of a confession to make...'

'Which is?' And then a flash of comprehension crossed his face.

'Oh just wait a fucking minute!' he exclaimed, staring straight at me in amazement.

'Well, it was all so fast and he just asked, and I thought...'

'So, we've been freezing our arses out here for an hour for no good reason, is that it?'

'Yes, yes, I'm sorry.' I felt myself starting to go to pieces again. 'It's just, well... really, I didn't know what to say.'

I glanced up at him, my hand poised on the window winder button, as though having that whirr up would keep me safe, only to be taken completely by surprise when he flung his head back and roared with laughter.

'Jesus Christ,' he said after a moment. He calmed down to a guttural chuckle and squatted down beside the car to be at eye level with me again. 'What kind of monsters do you think we are?'

'I don't know,' I pleaded, shamefacedly. 'Look, I'm really, really sorry.'

'Ah well, Mal is going to love this one!' And he was off again, his head shaking as he tried and failed to suppress a chortle.

'Well then,' he said eventually. 'We can't wait around here all night, can we?'

He whistled to Stu's black figure, a clear signal for him to join us. 'Come on, out you get,' he instructed me.

It didn't seem as if I had any choice in the matter, so I just nodded, unlocked the door and got out of the car.

'How far away do you live?' he asked, as I folded my arms in front of me against the cold.

'Just down in Innerleithen,' I said, nodding in that direction.

'Do you need this tomorrow?' he said, indicating my poor little car.

Well, it was a Saturday tomorrow, so I didn't need it for getting to work I supposed. I shook my head.

'Right then, let's get you home first. We can sort this out in the morning.'

* * *

And so, a few minutes later, I found myself drowning in the stiff, oversized weight of Stu's thick biker jacket, while Dobbo's hands were under my chin as he fastened the strap of a helmet on my head.

'How's that?' he asked. 'Not too tight?'

Experimentally, I moved my head from side to side and then nodded, feeling the unfamiliar heaviness of a helmet. 'I think it seems OK.'

'Good. Ever been on a bike before?'

'No.'

'Don't worry about it, you'll be fine.'

With a huge jump on the kick start the bike barked into life. Straddling it, he pulled the machine upright, and then nodded to me to get on. Thank God I'd worn trousers, I thought.

He talked me through where to put my feet and waited until I'd settled myself.

'Should I hold on to you?' I asked.

'Sure, why not?' he grinned 'And just relax, it'll be great. You'll enjoy it.'

I wasn't so sure.

'Ready?' he asked.

I nodded.

'OK then, I'll take it easy,' he said, as the bike began to move under me and I instinctively tightened my grip around his waist, hugging myself into his back and sheltering down behind his broad shoulders against the chill of the night wind.

It was an unfamiliar sensation. The powerful engine vibrated through every part of my body. I was frozen rigidly in place to start with, hunched up against him, but as he swept gently through the first couple of bends, I began to relax. The bike lifted itself out of the corners like a spinning top that always swings back to upright even if you tip it over. Slackening my death grip around his waist to a softer cinch, my body automatically moved with his as he gently but firmly swayed the bike into the next set of curves.

I felt weightless on the back of the huge iron bike, effortlessly flying me home through the dark of the night. The harsh rumble of the exhaust and the rushing sound of the wind enveloped me.

OK, I wasn't dressed for it, I couldn't believe the way the cold of the night air bit against my bare face and hands, and I knew I would be freezing by the time I got home, but...

Soon there was the flash of yellow street lights, and road signs appeared. We passed a petrol station and the first of the out of town supermarkets. Houses, railings, and gardens, all the familiar outskirts of the town smeared by as the unfamiliar blast of cold air brought tears streaming to my eyes. We were getting close.

He knew roughly where I lived from the description I'd given him, so it was just a matter of tapping him on the shoulder and craning round to talk in his ear to give him final directions. With a last bark of the engine and a mechanical clatter as it died, we pulled up outside my front door. 'No need to wake the neighbours,' he joked.

His shoulders tensed under my hand as he braced the bike while I stood up on the pegs and semi-hopped, semi-slid off my perch behind him.

Dobbo kicked out a side stand and let the bike settle, the handlebars swinging round as he did so. He swung his leg over the pillion with an easy, practised motion, and dismounted. He stripped off his riding gloves and unclipped his helmet before reaching out to do the same for me.

'OK,' he said, lifting off my helmet. 'How was that?'

'Amazing,' I said, smiling at him. I shook my head to settle my hair, and gave an involuntary shiver. 'Bloody cold, but great.'

Dobbo gave a wry smile. 'Yeah, there's nothing like it.'

'Well then,' I said, wondering what to do next. I glanced at my front door. My fingers were about to drop off, I should go inside, but I didn't want to leave him.

He just looked at me. Waiting for me to decide, I think.

'So what do you think about my car?' I asked.

'Oh, I wouldn't worry about that. Stu can look after it.'

We'd left him sitting inside it. Well after all, he had lent me his jacket for the ride home so I could hardly leave him out in the cold.

I looked into Dobbo's amused eyes reflecting the street light and made up my mind. 'So do you fancy a coffee? To get warm I mean.' I gestured towards my door.

'Yeah, that'd be great, if you don't mind.'

'How about Stu?'

'Oh, don't worry about him,' he waved his hand dismissively as he did something with the bike's keys. 'Like I said, he's a tryout. He can wait as long as it takes.'

*   *   *

The next morning we rode across to a garage to get some oil, and then to a bike shop tucked away off a road beside the river. I found a helmet that fitted. Fifty pounds for a plastic hat and some gloves. It must be love. And then we went back to wake Stu with a lukewarm bacon butty and the fresh smell of coffee out of a thermos, and to sort out my car.

*   *   *

And as for Dobbo, well later, reader, I married him.

*Excerpted from *Operation Bourbon* by Iain Parke (2013), ISBN 9780956161581.

Iain Parke imports industrial quantities of Class A drugs, kills people and lies (a lot) for a living, being a British based crime fiction writer. He became obsessed with motorcycles at an early age, taking a six hundred mile cross-country tour to Cornwall as soon as he bought a moped at the tender age of sixteen. After working at a London dispatch job delivering parcels on a motorcycle, he built his first chopper in his bedroom at university, undeterred by the fact that the workshop was upstairs.

Armed with a MBA degree, Iain first worked in insolvency and business restructuring in the UK and Africa, where he began work on his first thriller *The Liquidator*. The success of that novel propelled him to write a 'biker lit' trilogy about the Brethren Motorcycle Club, which has recently been optioned as a series for television in the UK. Today Iain lives off the grid, high up on the North Pennines in Northumberland with his wife, dogs, and a garage full of motorcycle restoration projects. He is currently working on a number of book projects, including another biker-based trilogy.

ABOUT THE AUTHORS

EDWARD WINTERHALDER

Edward Winterhalder is an American author and screenwriter who has written eleven books and five screenplays about motorcycle clubs and the outlaw biker culture; a television producer that has produced programs about motorcycle clubs and the outlaw biker lifestyle for networks and broadcasters worldwide; and a singer, songwriter, musician, and record producer. His eleven books about the culture are sold internationally, and one, *The Assimilation: Rock Machine Become Bandidos*, has been published in multiple languages.

He has produced episodes, pilots and documentaries for television such as *Outlaw Bikers*, *One Percenters*, *Gang World*, *Iron Horses*, *Marked*, *Biker Chicz*, *Living On The Edge: Riding With The Vietnam Vets MC* and *Gangland*, and is the creator/executive producer of *Steel Horse Cowboys: Leather, Chrome & Thunder*, *Real American Bikers: War Dogs MC* and *Biker Chicz*.

Winterhalder was associated with motorcycle clubs and outlaw bikers for almost thirty years, and has been seen on Fox News (the O'Reilly Factor with Bill O'Reilly & America's Newsroom), CNN, Bravo, Al Jazeera, BBC, ABC Nightline, MSNBC News Nation, Good Morning America, History Channel, Global, National Geographic, History Television, AB Groupe, and CBC.

Winterhalder's screenplays include *Bloodline Redemption*, *Twin Roads To Revenge*, *Vindication*, *Das Portal* and *Biker Daddy*, and his books include *The Blue And Silver Shark: A Biker's Story* (co-author Marc Teatum - December 2015); *Biker Chicz: The Attraction Of Women To Motorcycles And Outlaw Bikers* (co-author Wil De Clercq - July 2014); *The Ultimate Biker Anthology: An Introduction To Books About Motorcycle Clubs And Outlaw Bikers* (co-editor Iain Parke - November 2013); *The Moon Upstairs: A Biker's Story* (co-author Marc Teatum - December 2012); *One Light Coming: A Biker's Story* (co-author Marc Teatum - October 2011); *Biker Chicz of North America* (co-author Wil

De Clercq - December 2010); *Die Ubernahme: Von Der Rock Machine Zu Den Bandidos - Der Bikerkrieg In Kanada* (co-author Wil De Clercq - March 2010); *The Mirror: A Biker's Story* (co-author James Richard Larson - January 2010); *L'Assimilation: Rock Machine & Bandidos Contre Hells Angels* (co-author Wil De Clercq - June 2009); *Biker Chicks: The Magnetic Attraction of Women to Bad Boys and Motorbikes* (co-author Arthur Veno with Wil De Clercq - May 2009); *All Roads Lead To Sturgis: A Biker's Story* (co-author James Richard Larson - February 2009); *The Assimilation: Rock Machine Become Bandidos - Bikers United Against The Hells Angels* (co-author Wil De Clercq - June 2008); and *Out In Bad Standings: Inside The Bandidos Motorcycle Club - The Making Of A Worldwide Dynasty* (November 2005).

IAIN PARKE

Iain Parke imports industrial quantities of Class A drugs, kills people and lies (a lot) for a living, being a British based crime fiction writer. He became obsessed with motorcycles at an early age, taking a six hundred mile cross-country tour to Cornwall as soon as he bought a moped at the tender age of sixteen. After working at a London dispatch job delivering parcels on a motorcycle, he built his first chopper in his bedroom at university, undeterred by the fact that the workshop was upstairs.

Armed with a MBA degree, Iain first worked in insolvency and business restructuring in the UK and Africa, where he began work on his first thriller The Liquidator. The success of that novel propelled him to write a biker lit trilogy about the Brethren Motorcycle Club, which has recently been optioned as a series for television in the UK. Today Iain lives off the grid, high up on the North Pennines in Northumberland with his wife, dogs, and a garage full of motorcycle restoration projects. He is currently working on a number of book projects, including another biker-based trilogy.

Printed in Great Britain
by Amazon